UNCONDITIONAL SURRENDER

U.S. Grant and the Civil War

ALBERT MARRIN

ATHENEUM   1994   NEW YORK

Maxwell Macmillan Canada TORONTO   Maxwell Macmillan International NEW YORK OXFORD SINGAPORE SYDNEY

Illustration Credits

Anne S. K. Brown Military Collection, Brown University 167, 184; Chicago Historical Society 23, Aquelle print by L. Prang, after a painting by Thur de Thulstrup (1888) 63; *Frank Leslie's Illustrated Newspaper* (1861) 46; Library of Congress 17, 28, 31, 32, 34, 48, 63, 64, 67, 73, 80, 83, 91, 95, 101, 107, 122, 138, 145, 179; Massachusetts Commandery, Military Order of the Loyal Legion and the U.S. Army Military History Institute 76, 185; *McClure's* (May 1894) 7; Frederick H. Meserve Collection 187; National Archives i, 37, 53, 81, 103, 111, 115, 120, 142, 147, 148, 150, 151, 157, 161, 162, 165, 171, 182; National Portrait Gallery, Smithsonian Institution 20; White House Historical Association 167, 184

Atheneum
Macmillan Publishing Company
866 Third Avenue
New York, NY 10022

Maxwell Macmillan Canada, Inc.
1200 Eglinton Avenue East
Suite 200
Don Mills, Ontario M3C 3N1

Macmillan Publishing Company is part of the Maxwell Communication Group of Companies.

First edition
Printed in the United States of America
10 9 8 7 6 5 4 3 2 1
The text of this book is set in 10.5 Century Schoolbook.
Book design by Kimberly M. Adlerman

Library of Congress Cataloging-in-Publication Data

Marrin, Albert.
Unconditional surrender : U.S. Grant and the Civil War / by Albert Marrin.—1st ed.
p.   cm.
Summary: An account of Grant's life and his role in the Civil War.
ISBN 0-689-31837-5
1. Grant, Ulysses S. (Ulysses Simpson), 1822–1885—Military leadership—Juvenile literature. 2. Appomattox Campaign, 1865—Juvenile literature. 3. United States—History—Civil War, 1861–1865—Campaigns—Juvenile literature. [1. Grant, Ulysses S. (Ulysses Simpson), 1822–1885. 2. Presidents. 3. Generals. 4. United States—History—Civil War, 1861–1865.] I. Title.
E672.M3   1994

973.7'3'0092—dc20   *93-20041*

CONTENTS

To my wife, Yvette,
who always finds the right words

Now, I have carefully searched the military records of both ancient and modern history, and have never found Grant's superior as a general. I doubt if his superior can be found in all history.

—Robert E. Lee

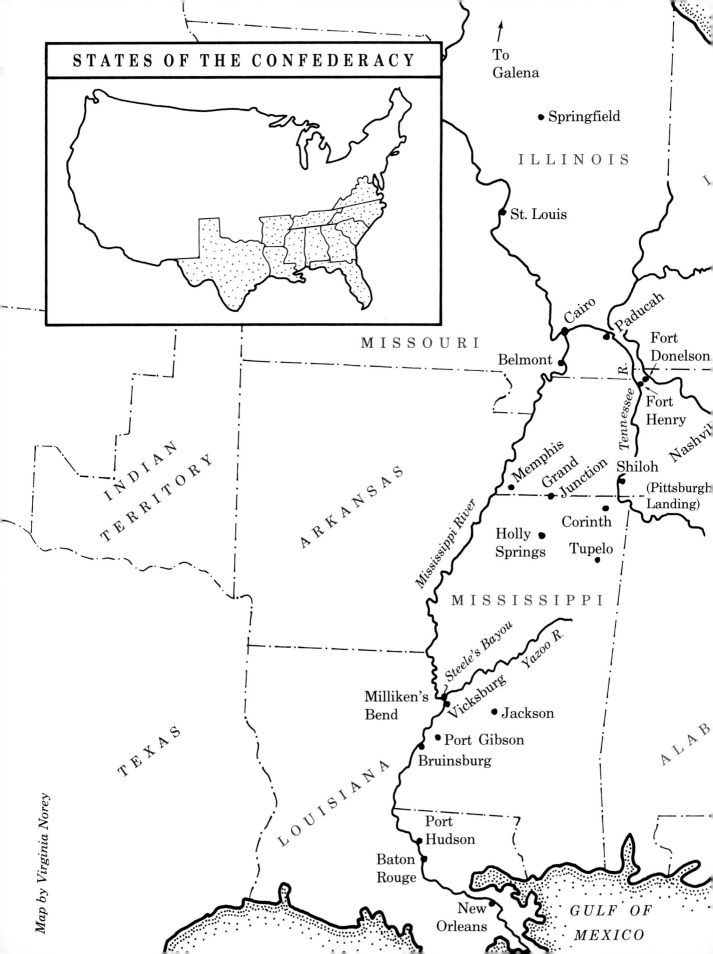

STATES OF THE CONFEDERACY

To
Galena

ILLINOIS

• Springfield

• St. Louis

MISSOURI

Cairo

Paducah

Fort
Donelson

Belmont

Tennessee R.

Fort
Henry

Nashvil

INDIAN

TERRITORY

ARKANSAS

Memphis

Grand
Junction

Shiloh

(Pittsburgh
Landing)

Corinth

Holly
Springs

Tupelo

MISSISSIPPI

Mississippi River

Steele's Bayou

Yazoo R.

Milliken's
Bend

Vicksburg

Jackson

TEXAS

Port Gibson

Bruinsburg

LOUISIANA

ALAB

Port
Hudson

Baton
Rouge

New
Orleans

GULF OF
MEXICO

Map by Virginia Norey

THE
✧ CIVIL WAR ✧

0   100   200

SCALE OF MILES

PROLOGUE ✦ WILLARD'S HOTEL

The town looks like a large straggling village reared in a drained swamp.

—George Combe, *Notes,*

1842

Washington, D.C., Tuesday, March 8, 1864. A dreary day with gray skies and icy winds blowing off the Potomac River. Rain the night before had left puddles in the unpaved streets, and pedestrians moved gingerly to avoid being splattered by speeding carriages.

At 5:30 P.M., a cab pulled up in front of Willard's Hotel at Pennsylvania Avenue and Fourteenth Street. Willard's was the finest hotel in town; it had any convenience you could imagine, including that marvel of modernity, running water in every room. After paying his fare, the passenger stepped onto the sidewalk. His boots were scuffed, and he wore a rumpled blue uniform with two stars on each shoulder, indicating a major general in the United States Army. Carrying a carpetbag in one hand and holding a thirteen-year-old boy by the other, he walked into the lobby.

Willard's was bustling with the usual crowd of politicians, businessmen, and army officers going to their next assignment. No one paid attention to the newcomers as they waited their turn at the registration desk. Generals often stopped at Willard's, but their coming was always heralded by aides who fussed over the accommodations. Only when they were satisfied did their chief appear in all his finery, surrounded by his staff.

This general was no picture-book soldier; actually, he looked quite seedy. He was in his early forties, stood five feet eight, weighed 135 pounds, and walked stoop shouldered. He had light brown hair, a short beard of the same color, blue-gray eyes, and a wart on his right cheek. He had no military escort. He seemed like a nobody, compared to the other folks who gathered at Willard's.

That was what the desk clerk thought. Asked what was available, the young snob frowned and offered a small room on the top floor. The general shrugged, signed the register, and headed for the stairs. Just then, the clerk turned the book around to enter the room number next to the name. His eyes bulged when he read the entry: "U. S. Grant & Son, Galena, Ill." It was General Ulysses S. Grant and his eldest son, Fred.

Instantly, the clerk became all smiles and politeness. There was a mistake about the room, he stammered. Of course he had a better room; an entire suite, in fact. Willard's would be proud— no, *honored*—if General Grant took Parlor Six. President and Mrs. Lincoln had stayed in Parlor Six almost three years ago to the day. From there, "Honest Abe" had left for his inauguration on Capitol Hill.

Grant had, in fact, come on direct orders from the White House. He had recently been named commander of all the armies of the United States and was in the capital to receive his commission from Lincoln in person.

Grant wanted to clean up, rest, and have a quiet dinner before going to the White House. But when he and Fred went down to the dining room, they found five hundred guests waiting for them. Word of his arrival had spread through the hotel, and everyone wanted to see this famous man. The moment he appeared, ladies and gentlemen leaped to their feet, cheering and waving handkerchiefs. He bowed, shook hands with those closest to him, and sat down. But it was hopeless. No matter how he tried to eat, well-wishers would not leave him alone. Finally, he threw down his napkin, took Fred by the hand, and went upstairs.

That evening Grant walked alone to the White House. There was a full moon, and he could see the city's landmarks outlined against the sky. To his left stood the Capitol, with its uncompleted dome; to his right rose a huge white slab, the unfinished Washington Monument. Washington was as dirty and smelly as any city he could remember. Pigs ran about the streets leading into Pennsylvania Avenue, its main thoroughfare. Stables gave off an odor of sweat, manure, and stale straw. The smells that came from the drainage ditches reminded one visitor of "twenty thousand drowned cats."

The White House was ablaze with lights when he arrived. The president stood in the reception room, or Blue Room, surrounded by cabinet members. At six feet four, Lincoln towered above everyone, was thin as a rail, and wore a collar a size too large and a broad necktie carelessly knotted.

"Why, here is General Grant!" said Lincoln, seeing him over the heads of the other guests. "Well, this is a pleasure, I assure you!" They had never met before, but he knew all about the general. He had followed Grant's career closely, admired him, and defended him against critics.

Word that Grant had arrived caused a mob scene. Guests crowded around, eager to see him and hear his voice. "There's Grant! Grant! Grant! Grant! Grant!" they cried.[1] People became so rowdy that Secretary of State William H. Seward asked him to stand on a sofa to give everyone a look. It was an hour before they let him down, his hand aching from being shaken so often.

Lincoln had need of such a man. For nearly three years, war had been raging across the land. Although no one could have known it then, the Civil War would cost more American lives than all the nation's other conflicts put together; even World War II (292,100 dead) and Vietnam (58,000 dead) pale by comparison. Before it ended, over 623,000 men, Union and Confederate, would lose their lives. There would be 10,455 military actions, including 76 major battles, some of which took more lives than the fiercest actions of World War II. The total cost to the federal government alone would be $11.6 billion, a lot of money even by twentieth-century standards.

There seemed to be no way out—early in 1864. Although the North was wealthier and had far more men, it seemed unable to defeat the rebellious South. The problem was one of leadership. Lincoln had not been able to find a commander to bring the ordeal to an end. No sooner did he name a commander than the man came down with a disease the president called "the slows." He would move too slowly, refusing to risk battle without more reinforcements. This allowed the Confederates to recover from defeats, reorganize, and counterattack.

The burden of the war fell on Lincoln's shoulders. Not only did he have to make important military decisions, he had to deal with personal tragedies. His eleven-year-old son, Willie, took sick and died. His wife, Mary, was so depressed that at times he feared for her sanity. Even when things went well, he could never quite relax. There was always a part of him, deep inside, that could not be soothed. "Nothing touches the tired spot," he'd say sadly.[2]

At last Lincoln had his man. People used to speak of the "miracle" of Ulysses S. Grant. Even in a land of opportunity, his story seems miraculous. At the start of the war, he was an unknown shop clerk, a failure at whatever he tried. Then everything changed. This terrible war gave him his chance, and he grabbed it with both hands. Within three years, he commanded the armies of the United States. Four years after that, he became the eighteenth president of the United States.

The key to Grant's success lay in something Lincoln saw in him from the first: grit and determination. At their first meeting, in the Blue Room, they shook hands and chatted for a few minutes. Grant tugged at his lapel and lowered his eyes, blushing with shyness. But when he met the president's eyes, his gaze was steady, his jaw set. He might be shy, but he was no weakling. A brother officer said it best: "He habitually wears an expression as if he had determined to drive his head through a brick wall, and was about to do it."[3] Grant was tough. And stubborn. Once he set his mind to something, he went for it with every ounce of his energy. He never turned back, never stopped trying.

This book is not a history of the Civil War, but the story of one man who played a large part in it. Grant's Civil War is an American epic. Like the epics of antiquity, it is filled with pageantry and tragedy. Larger-than-life heroes perform daring deeds against terrible odds. By the time this war ended, the United States was more than a group of loosely connected states. For better or worse, it was a united nation; or, as a Confederate soldier put it: "The American continent has no north, no south, no east, no west."[4] The war also answered a question that had bothered patriots and statesmen since the beginning of the United States of America: If, as the Declaration of Independence proclaims, all people are created equal, how could slavery be justified? It could not. In this respect, however, the war left some unfinished business. Though it ended slavery, it did not abolish racism, the idea that the color of their skin makes some people better than others.

Without Ulysses S. Grant, there is no telling how the Civil War would have ended. By 1864, the struggle was his to win or lose. He won. And for that reason, Americans will remember his name so long as they fight wars.

I ✧ DOWN-AND-OUT

Ulysses Grant was born April 27, 1822, in Mount Pleasant, Ohio, a village on the Ohio River. This was beautiful country, a land of blue waters, virgin forests, and rich farmland. In the days before railroads, the Ohio was the nation's gateway to the West. Each year hundreds of steamboats, their twin smokestacks belching black smoke, came south with the produce of the American heartland: grain, timber, furs, horses, cattle. They sailed down the Ohio until it joined the Mississippi at Cairo, Illinois, then on to New Orleans, Louisiana, and the world beyond. In addition, thousands of flatboats—huge log rafts—were floated downstream laden with cargo. Steamers made the voyage from Cairo to New Orleans in about five days; flatboats did it in two weeks.

Grant was always proud of his family. "My family," he wrote in the last year of his life, "is American, and has been for generations, in all its branches."[1] His ancestors, Matthew and Priscilla Grant, arrived in Boston Harbor aboard the *Mary and John* in 1630. Industrious people, they settled in Connecticut as farmers. Their descendants followed in their footsteps, cultivating the land, marrying, and raising families. Eventually, some drifted westward in search of a better life. Among them was a great-grandson, Noah, who settled in Ohio after the Revolutionary War. Little is known about Noah, except that his wife died, leaving him to care for their eight children by himself. Since there were too many mouths to feed, the youngsters were sent to live with families in the neighborhood. This was not unusual at the time; labor was scarce on the frontier, and people gladly took in orphans who could work for their keep.

One of the boys, Jesse, went to live with a family to learn the tanner's trade. Turning animal skins into leather was a good business; Ohio was growing, and settlers needed plenty of boots, belts, saddles, and harness. After learning the basics, Jesse moved in with Owen Brown at his tannery. Brown was an abolitionist, one who wanted slavery abolished. Though he argued his case calmly, it was different with his fifteen-year-old son, John, who also happened to be Jesse's roommate. The youngster wanted slaveholders sent straight to hell, preferably with their throats cut. We shall hear more of John Brown later.

Jesse became a skilled tanner, and in 1821 opened his own business at Point Pleasant. Shrewd, ambitious, and quarrelsome, he did not make friends easily. Having a conversation with Jesse was more like a fight than an exchange of ideas. He knew he was right, insisting that anyone who disagreed was a fool or a liar—most likely both.

That same year Jesse turned twenty-seven and decided to settle down. He married Hannah Simpson, twenty-two, the daughter of a local farmer. Gossip had it that she was old before her time; in fact, "born old." As a girl, she never played with other children or shared their interests. No matter what happened, her face always had a peaceful expression. Deeply religious, she believed God took care of everything, so there was no point getting excited; all would be well in the end. No one remembered ever hearing her laugh, let alone cry or raise her voice. She was a solid, decent person who got along with everyone.

After the arrival of their firstborn,[2] a family conference was held to choose a name. Grandfather Simpson favored "Hiram," because it sounded "manly"; Grandmother Simpson preferred "Ulysses," a famous hero of Greek mythology. Jesse decided to call his son Hiram Ulysses. It was an unusual name in a frontier community and was seldom used. Nearly everyone knew him as Lysses or Lyss.

Lyss was a year old when the family moved to Georgetown, Ohio, twenty-five miles to the east. The hillsides around Georgetown were covered with oak forests. Oak bark supplied tannic acid, which cured the raw hides and gave the tanning business its name. Georgetown would be the boy's home for the next sixteen years.

Lyss took after his mother in that he was exceptionally calm and self-controlled. Jesse was proud of him, though he showed it in odd ways. One day, for example, he carried the baby to a gathering in the village square. A fellow with a new pistol wondered what Lyss would do if it went off next to his head. Jesse bet he would do nothing. To prove his point, he had the child's fingers wrapped around the trigger while an adult squeezed. *Crack!* The shot was so loud that passersby, taken unawares, jumped. Not Lyss. He lay in Papa's arms as relaxed as in his own bed.

Hannah never fussed over Lyss. If he got sick, she refused to nurse him. Trusting in the Lord, she would dose him with castor oil, put him to bed, and go on with her chores. By the age of three, Lyss was exploring the world by himself. Neighbors would rush to tell Hannah that the little fellow was crawling between the feet of wagon teams standing outside the tannery gate. The horses were stamping their feet and flicking their tails at the flies that buzzed around their heads; one false move and they would have kicked the child into the next world. Lyss would swing on horses' tails, laughing so hard that tears rolled down his cheeks. Hannah listened patiently, then answered, "Horses seem to understand Ulysses."

Hannah and Jesse Root Grant about the year 1866. By then, their son was a national hero and on his way to becoming president of the United States. From a picture in the May 1884 issue of McClure's *magazine*

Actually, Ulysses understood horses. He was a natural, or, as they said in Ohio, had "a way" with "the critters." He would go up to strange horses, sit down in front of them, and gaze lovingly into their eyes. He was a master rider almost from the time he could walk. If it had hair and four legs, townspeople observed, Grant's boy could ride it.

Jesse let him water the workhorses at the creek when he turned five. If being alone with them was a joy, riding them was heaven. Lyss would return, standing barefoot on the back of a galloping animal, balancing himself with the reins. By age nine, he was breaking and training horses for money. Farmers would bring their animals to him, and people stopped what they were doing to watch him in the village square. If a horse bucked, he put his arms around its neck, dug his bare feet in behind its shoulders, and hung on until it realized who was master.

Like other boys, Lyss enjoyed fishing and swimming in summer, ice skating and sledding in winter. However, he had certain quirks that set him apart. For one, he was very modest, refusing to swim in the nude, as was the custom. Years later, as a general, he would bathe in his tent with the flaps tightly closed, while other generals stood naked in front of their tents as aides doused them with buckets of water. Nor did he swear; his strongest expressions were "by jinks" and "by lightning." Being tone deaf, he could not stand the sound of music. It hurt his ears, so that he would go miles out of his way rather than listen to a band. He knew only two songs, he said: "One was 'Yankee Doodle,' and the other wasn't."

Lyss went to school when and where he could. Since there were no public schools on the frontier, parents would band together to hire a teacher, whom they paid in cash or with room and board. Pity the poor frontier teacher! He or she could have forty pupils, aged from three to twenty-three, crowded into a one-room schoolhouse. Pupils learned the three R's—Reading, 'Riting, 'Rithmetic—and little else. Lessons were memorized and recited without thought to their meaning. Lyss recalled being taught that "a noun is the name of a thing" so many times that "I finally believed it." His best subject was "mental arithmetic," solving math problems in his head. His worst subject was public speaking; he was so shy that he would rather pay a six-cent fine than speak before the group.

Lyss was not afraid of work, however. Anything that could be done with horses was just fine with him. At ten, he'd borrow Jesse's horses and wagon to haul freight to the steamboat landings near Georgetown. Those trips earned him as much as a dollar a day, a lot of money for a youngster. Sometimes he took loads to distant places like Cincinnati, Ohio, and Louisville, Kentucky. He had no qualms about driving lonely roads or staying in hotels alone. The only thing he would not do was backtrack. If he took a wrong turn, he would do anything—zigzag, circle, take strange roads—to avoid retracing his steps.

Lyss dreaded the tannery. Preparing hides for tanning required a strong stomach and a weak sense of smell. Wherever you looked, or stepped, there were piles of bloody cowhides to be scraped clean of hair, meat, and fat. The buildings where hides were stretched swarmed with flies and stank of rotting flesh. Lyss got nauseous whenever he went near them. These experiences gave him a life-long dislike for red meat. "If blood appeared in any meat which came on the table," a friend recalled, "the sight of it seemed entirely to destroy his appetite."[3] He would only eat meat broiled dry and black around the edges. He was also uneasy about hunting. He enjoyed target shooting with a pistol, but never fired at an animal.

He had just turned sixteen when Jesse asked him to help in the tannery. "Father," he burst out, "tanning is not the kind of work I like. I'll work at it, though, if you wish me to, until I am twenty-one; but you may depend upon it, I'll not work a day longer at it after that."

Jesse Grant was a hard man, but not a cruel man. "My son," he said, "I don't want you to work at it now if you don't like it and don't mean to stick to it. . . . Now, what do you think you would like?"

Lyss said he would like to be a farmer or a "down-the-river trader."[4]

That was not good enough for Jesse. Although he had gone to school for less than a month in his entire life, he respected learning. Self-taught, he constantly wrote letters to newspapers, wrote poetry (mostly awful), and enjoyed reading. At a time when few people went to college, he valued a sound education. But college cost money, and he was a miser.

One college, however, was free: the United States Military Academy at West Point, New York. A neighbor's son had recently flunked out, making his parents so ashamed that they forbade him to come home. Upon hearing the story, Jesse knew that his problem was solved. He wrote his congressman, who owed him a favor, and asked that the vacancy be given to Lyss. Months passed, but the congressman finally sent good news.

On a cold winter's day in 1838, Lyss saw his father open a letter and read it. "Ulysses," he said, smiling, "I believe you are going to receive the appointment."

"What appointment?" the boy asked, puzzled.

"To West Point. I have applied for it."

"But I won't go," Lyss insisted.

Jesse disagreed.

"He said he thought I would, *and I thought so too, if he did,*" Lyss recalled.[5]

*   *   *

Lyss arrived at West Point in May 1839, only to find that his name was not on the list of new students. There was an Elihu Grant from New York and a Ulysses S. Grant from Ohio. The congressman had forgotten the boy's full name. Knowing that he was called Ulysses, and that his mother's maiden name was Simpson, he inserted the *S* on the appointment papers. Lyss explained that he was the Ohio Grant, asking to have the error corrected. Impossible, said the registrar; only the War Department in Washington could change a name, and that took years. Rather than battle army red tape, Lyss decided to keep the new name. From then on, he would be U. S. Grant.

Many young men who were to earn fame as soldiers attended West Point in the late 1830s. Among them was William Tecumseh Sherman, who said Lyss's initials stood for "Uncle Sam." Shortened to Sam, it became his nickname among army old-timers. Lyss became friends with James "Pete" Longstreet, a gentle giant from South Carolina, at their first meeting. There was also Simon Bolivar Buckner, a proud Kentuckian; George H. Thomas, quiet, solid, dependable; and Richard S. Ewell, a daredevil horseman. Remember these names; we shall meet them again in less peaceful surroundings.

West Point operated on the belief that he who would command must first learn to obey. Obedience—prompt, precise, unquestioning—was drilled into cadets. The first lesson, and by far the most important, concerned the soldier's relation to the civilian government in a democracy. A soldier's chief loyalty is not to the army, but to the nation it serves. The army is an instrument of the law, not a law unto itself; to have it otherwise would mean a military dictatorship. As Grant explained it: "So long as I hold a commission in the army I have no views of my own to carry out. Whatever may be the orders of my superiors and the law, I will execute. . . . When Congress enacts anything too odious for me to execute, I will resign."[6]

The school day began at sunrise. At the first drumroll, cadets sprang out of bed. Moving quickly, they dressed and did their morning chores. After a small breakfast, they returned to "police" the barracks for inspection. On Saturdays, they went down on their knees to scrub the floors. There were no luxuries such as running water; to take a bath, you had to pump your own water and carry it up several flights of stairs in wooden buckets. Classes consisted of regular college courses, plus specialized military subjects like engineering and tactics. Between classes, cadets had lunch, studied, and practiced with various weapons. The drums sounded "lights out" at 10 P.M. Sunday was a day of rest, except that everyone was required to attend church.

Cadets were rated on conduct as well as classwork. Breaking even the most trivial rule brought demerits, or "black marks," against your name. You could get demerits for such things as failing to brush your clothes, not having your coat buttoned, or lateness at roll call; lying, cheating, and stealing brought instant expulsion. Demerits reduced your class standing, which hurt your chances of getting a good assignment upon graduation.

Learning the routines was a drudgery; and when Cadet Grant did learn them, he had trouble following them. A heavy sleeper, he earned demerits for being late to roll call. He was always being marked down for his messy appearance; once he got eight demerits for missing church. The honor system, by which cadets reported one another for breaking the rules, could also be a problem. He was embarrassed to report a classmate for calling another "a damned shit ass."[7]

Unless there was a family tragedy, cadets were forbidden to leave the academy during the first two years. That was too much for Grant. Saying good-bye to Hannah had been painful; we don't know how he felt about leaving Jesse. He wrote to her often, pouring out his loneliness in long letters. "I seem alone in the world without my mother," he said during his freshman year. "There have been so many ways in which you have advised me . . . that I cannot tell you how much I miss you. I was so often alone with you, and you so frequently spoke to me in private, that the solitude of my situation here . . . in my lonely room, is all the more striking. It reminds me more forcibly of home, and most of all, dear mother, of you."[8]

The loneliness gradually passed. Grant was liked by his classmates, who admired his horsemanship. Even the half-wild York, demon of the stables, calmly went through his paces with Grant in the saddle. Moreover, Grant could stand up for himself. Jack Lindsay, a colonel's son and the faculty's pet, was the school bully. A big, strapping fellow, he thought it great fun to shove Grant, half his size, out of the drill line. Grant asked him to stop, but that only encouraged him. Then he shoved once too often. Grant spun around and, in a flurry of fists, knocked him down. The other cadets stood at attention, chins in, chests out, grinning from ear to ear. No one, of course, knew what had happened to poor Lindsay, and he was too ashamed to tell.

Grant's classwork left room for improvement. Although he excelled in mathematics, in other subjects he studied only enough to pass. He took no interest in military affairs. He read none of the military classics and knew little more of history's great soldiers than their names. Napoleon, for all he cared, could have been the inventor of a cream-filled pastry. The French emperor's campaigns, which others studied in minute detail, were a mystery to the tanner's son. His favorite reading was novels borrowed from the academy library or purchased by mail order from New York City.

He stuck it out at the academy because Jesse wanted him to, and because he saw a payoff at the end. Half of West Point's graduates never made the army a career. After serving the required four years, they resigned and took civilian jobs. Grant wanted to do the same. Upon graduation, he hoped to become a mathematics instructor at the academy, then find a position in a small college. Becoming a general, let alone fighting battles, was the furthest thing from his mind. "A military life had no charms for me," he recalled, "and I had not the faintest idea of staying in the army even if I should be graduated, which I did not expect."[9]

Yet he *did* graduate, in 1843. He graduated twenty-first out of thirty-nine, almost exactly in the middle of the class. He had hoped to be assigned to the cavalry, but his class standing was too low. Instead, he was appointed as a second lieutenant in the 4th Infantry.

Before reporting to the regiment, he visited his parents at their new home in Bethel, Ohio. Hannah was thrilled—in her quiet way—to see him looking so fit. Jesse, loud as ever, boasted of his son's achievements. Ulysses was proud, too. Wearing his dress uniform, a sword flapping at his side, he went to Cincinnati to impress former schoolmates, particularly the girls. He rode tall in the saddle, imagining that everyone was admiring him. Suddenly a barefoot boy, his face crusted with dirt, ended his daydream. "Soldier, will you work?" the boy jeered. "No sir-ee; I'll sell my shirt first!" Returning home, he was greeted by a drunken stable hand wearing blue pants—the color of his uniform—with a strip of white cloth sewn down each side. The drunk flailed his arms and sang rowdy songs, just like a drunken soldier out for a night on the town. Bystanders thought it a joke, "but I did not appreciate it so highly," he recalled.[10] These incidents made him dislike uniforms. From then on, he avoided wearing a full uniform and sword.

The 4th Infantry was stationed at Jefferson Barracks, Missouri, on the outskirts of St. Louis. Jefferson Barracks was the largest army base in the country, and Lieutenant Grant had plenty to do. Beside his duties, he studied mathematics at night. The mathematics professor at West Point wanted him as an assistant, but said he must wait until a position opened. It never did, at least not for U. S. Grant.

During his last year at the academy, Grant's roommate had been Frederick Dent, Jr. Before joining his regiment on the Great Plains, Fred invited him to visit his family at White Haven, its farm near St. Louis. That invitation turned out to be the nicest thing anyone had ever given him.

Grant was received with open arms. Colonel Dent,[11] the family head, was a prosperous farmer and slave owner. Any friend of young Fred was a friend of his—so long as he didn't argue about slavery. Fred's mother thought Grant a genius, because he explained politics in language she could understand. Emmy, their eight-year-old daughter, could not take her eyes off him. "He's as pretty as a doll," she kept saying to herself.

Grant made White Haven his home away from home, dropping in whenever he had time to spare. During one visit he met Julia, the Dents' other daughter, just back from boarding school in another city. Julia, age seventeen, was daddy's little princess. He denied her nothing; she even had a personal slave named Black Julia. Lyss thought her "as dainty a little creature as one would care to see, plump, neither tall nor short, with beautifully rounded arms, brown hair and brown eyes, and blonde and rosy complexion. She had a beautiful figure."[12] One of her eyes was crossed, but he seems not to have noticed, or cared, about it. He had never known such a warm, cheerful person. She always found the right words, always knew how to put him at ease. It was love at first sight.

There is no telling how long Lyss would have taken to "pop the question." He was a cautious fellow, not given to impulsive behavior. Moreover, he knew that Colonel Dent was not keen on "Yankees," as he called anyone from a nonslave state. And Ohio was definitely a free state. Had it not been for the army, Lyss might have waited a long time to propose. But during the spring of 1844, troops were being sent to the Texas border in case of trouble with Mexico, and his unit was among those ordered south. He had to act immediately, or risk losing Julia during his absence.

A few days before leaving, he drove her to a neighborhood wedding. It had rained heavily the night before, and they had to cross a rickety bridge over a swollen stream.

Julia was frightened, or at least *said* she was frightened. Her lieutenant played the strong, silent soldier. She must not worry, he said, firmly; he would protect her come what may. Still she was frightened. As the buggy rolled onto the bridge, she grabbed his arm with both hands, promising to cling to him come what may.

"Well, I clung to you, didn't I, Ulysses?" she said when they reached the other side. "You certainly did," he replied. Then he looked into her eyes and asked: "How would you like to cling to me for the rest of your life?"[13] She would like that very much indeed. But instead of marrying at once, they agreed to wait until he finished his tour of duty. Little did they know that the Mexican War would force them to wait four years.

Texas was originally a province of Mexico. In the 1820s, the Mexican government invited Americans to settle in this vast open land of scattered ranches and nomadic Indians. Life was good in Texas, and, within a decade, thirty-five thousand settlers were living there. Outnumbered ten to one, Mexicans came to feel like strangers in their own country. Worse, they distrusted the newcomers' intentions. Settlers had pledged their loyalty to Mexico, but deep down they were still Americans; in fact, they spoke of breaking away and bringing Texas into the Union. Early in 1836, they rebelled and defeated the Mexican dictator, General Santa Anna, in the Battle of San Jacinto. In exchange for his life, he recognized Texas's independence.

Santa Anna fell from power soon after returning to Mexico City. The new government argued that his promise had been made under the threat of death and was therefore not binding. Texas was not independent. Mexican troops could go wherever they pleased in Mexican territory. In the years that followed, they launched repeated raids into the Lone Star Republic.

Matters came to a head when Texas applied for statehood. The United States was not interested in Texas alone, but in California and the Southwest. Gaining these territories was part of its Manifest Destiny, its God-given "right" to own everything between the Atlantic and Pacific oceans. President James K. Polk wanted to take over peacefully, perhaps by purchase. But if the Mexicans refused, these were prizes worth taking by force.

Not that Americans would fire the first shot, for that was aggression. The Mexicans must be goaded into making the first move. The excuse would be a dispute over the border. Mexico claimed the Nueces River as its border with Texas. The Texans said it was the Rio Grande, 150 miles to the south. Since few people lived in the area, it was impossible to tell who had the better claim.

The 4th Infantry joined an Army of Observation in Louisiana. Officially, the army's mission was to prevent smuggling across the Texas-Louisiana border. Nobody believed that for a moment. Nick-named the "Army of Provocation," its aim was clear: prod the Mexicans into war, then smash them in "self-defense."

Everything went according to plan. When Texas became the twenty-eighth state on December 29, 1845, the army advanced to the Rio Grande and built a fort on its northern bank, near the present city of Brownsville. The Mexicans opened fire. Congress promptly declared war, and American forces invaded Mexico.

The Mexican War (1846–1848) was our first foreign conflict. That was a strange thing for Americans, and many opposed it loudly. An Illinois politician, Abraham Lincoln, called it a bully's war. Those were fighting words, and a rival challenged him to a duel, which Lincoln accepted, provided he selected the weapons. He chose "cow-dung at five paces."[14] Everyone laughed, forcing the man to drop his challenge.

Grant also denounced the Mexican War. To the end of his days, he said it was unjust and should never have been fought. He called it a "wicked war," an "unholy war," and "one of the most unjust [wars] ever waged by a stronger against a weaker nation." As a soldier, this troubled his conscience. By staying in the army, he would be fighting in a war he knew to be wrong. On the other hand, he had accepted a free education from his government and had sworn to serve his country. To resign just when he was needed seemed dishonorable. Grant was above all an American patriot, and, as he put it, "my supreme duty was to my flag."[15] Thus, he was bound to serve his country, be it right or wrong.

On May 8, 1846, the opposing armies met at Palo Alto. They glared fiercely at each other, waiting for the signal to charge. Meantime, cannonballs came bouncing through the tall grass. They traveled so slowly that you could easily see them and jump out of the way. Some men, however, were not fast enough. Grant saw a single cannonball behead a soldier and go on to hit a captain in the face. The captain, he wrote a friend, lay with his lower jaw "gone to the windpipe, and the tongue hanging down upon the throat. He never will be able to speak or eat." Yet Grant remained calm. "You want to know what my feelings were," he continued, "I do not know that I felt any peculiar sensation."[16] Calmness in the midst of confusion and horror: that was a quality he had never seen in himself. It would serve him well in the years ahead.

The Americans' next objective was the city of Monterrey. By then, Grant had become regimental quartermaster, its chief supply officer. As quartermaster, he was to stay with the supply wagons while the regiment went into action. Nevertheless, once the battle began, he grew restless. His duty, he felt, was not to wagons and mules, but to his comrades. As soon as they went forward, he joined the charge.

Monterrey showed Grant that he could think clearly in the face of almost certain death. The Mexicans were putting up a fierce fight when American ammunition began to run low. Fresh supplies had to be brought from the rear at once. Unfortunately, Mexican guns covered every street crossing, exposing any messenger to a hail of bullets. Nevertheless, Grant thought he could get through by riding Indian-style. He set out at top speed, enemy bullets popping overhead. If they came too close, he "vanished," that is, dropped over the side of the horse, with one foot hooked over the saddle and one arm around the animal's head. Moments after he arrived at headquarters, ammunition wagons were speeding to the front.

After Monterrey, Grant was transferred to the force that captured Veracruz on the Gulf of Mexico. This area is steeped in history—violent history. In 1519 Hernán Cortés set out from there to conquer the Aztec empire with a tiny Spanish army. Now the Americans, led by General Winfield Scott, "Old Fuss and Feathers," were following in the footsteps of the conquistadors.

To reach Mexico City, they had to cross a twelve-thousand-foot pass between the twin volcanoes of Popocatepetl, "Smoking Mountain," and Ixtacihuatl, "White Lady." The Americans were awed by the beautiful scenery, as they advanced against weak opposition. Upon reaching the top of the pass, they saw the Valley of Mexico spread out below like a map fifty miles across. The boy from Ohio had never imagined that such places could exist. For him, Mexico was adventure and beauty, mystery and romance all rolled into one. In the midst of another, greater war, he would sit by a campfire, talking about that marvelous place far into the night.

As the army approached Mexico City, his colonel sent him on an errand to General Scott. He had just stepped into Scott's headquarters tent when a colonel, noticing his messy uniform, politely turned him away. The general, he said in a soft Virginia drawl, expected visitors to be neat; Grant would have to spruce up and

Ulysses S. Grant at Mexico City. During the battle he had a light cannon brought to a church steeple overlooking one of the city's main gates. Thanks to his initiative, the defenders were driven away, allowing the Americans to break through.

return later. This colonel already was regarded as the best soldier in the army, sure to rise to the top. One day former Colonel Robert E. Lee and former Lieutenant Ulysses S. Grant would meet as equals.

The army reached Mexico City in May 1847. In the battle that followed, Grant helped turn the tide at a key point. A fight had broken out at one of the city's gates. Each time the Americans charged, they were driven back with heavy losses. Grant noticed that the belfry of a church overlooked the Mexican position. Nearby stood a small cannon known as a howitzer. Belfry and howitzer: they were the perfect combination. He helped the crew lift the gun into the belfry, then turned it on the gate, driving the defenders away. Mexico City fell soon after, ending the war with an American victory.

It was a seasoned veteran, slim, tanned, and confident, who reined in his horse at White Haven during the summer of 1848. Julia and her beau had waited long for this reunion—*too* long. After four years apart, they would not postpone their marriage any longer. True, Ulysses's salary of $480 a year was not much. But they were young, and in love, and would learn to make ends meet.

The wedding—"a sweet old-fashioned wedding," Emmy Dent recalled—took place on August 22, 1848. Several of Ulysses's brother officers were present, including Pete Longstreet, a distant cousin of the bride as well as the groom's friend. The only disappointment was the absence of the groom's parents. Jesse and Hannah had been invited, but refused to come to St. Louis. Not that they opposed the marriage, or disliked Julia in any way. Rather, they wanted nothing to do with Julia's slave-owning parents.

If ever there was a "perfect" marriage, this was it. Julia was Ulysses's true love; apart from their children, he never cared for any human being as much as he did for her. She was his "Dearest Julia"; he was her "Ulyss" and "Dudy." Lover, friend, companion, nurse: Julia was all of these at once. If he felt low, she cheered him up. If things went wrong, she encouraged him. If he fell ill, Julia cared for him in a way Hannah never had. She constantly looked in on him, asked how he felt, and did whatever she could to soothe him. She was especially good at treating his headaches. Grant suffered from migraine, pounding headaches that came on suddenly and lasted for days. She made him rest in a darkened room and bathed his feet in hot water mixed with powdered mustard seed. He trusted her completely.

The newlyweds spent three and a half years in army camps at Sackets Harbor, New York, and Detroit, Michigan. These were happy years, made still happier by the birth of their first child, a son, in May 1850. The child was named Fred, after Julia's brother, who had brought them together. Ulysses had forgotten about becoming a teacher and was content to be a career soldier in a peacetime army. He had Julia and Fred. He had his work. All in all, life had been good to him.

Then things turned sour. Ahead lay years of failure and hardship.

Much of the blame lay with the Mexican War. A peace treaty had forced Mexico to accept the Rio Grande border and give up California, New Mexico, and Arizona. Grant's schoolmate William Tecumseh Sherman was stationed in California at this time. Soon after the treaty was signed, he left for Washington with startling news. Rumor had it that gold had been discovered near San Francisco. Sherman brought proof that the rumor was a fact. Overnight, Americans were bitten by the "gold bug," the urge to strike it rich. "California or bust" was their motto, and they flooded into the gold fields by the tens of thousands. The War Department had to send reinforcements to the West Coast to keep the peace.

The 4th Infantry received its orders in the summer of 1852. Today, a fully equipped regiment can fly across the continent in six hours. Back then, the journey was a dangerous operation lasting months. The regiment had to travel southward by ship from New York City, cross the Isthmus of Panama to the Pacific coast, then board another ship for the northern leg of the voyage. Many soldiers brought their families along. Grant would have done the same, but since Julia was pregnant again, they decided that the family would join him later. It was a wise decision, as Grant soon discovered.

The journey began smoothly enough. The sea was calm, and they reached Panama in eleven days. Summer, however, was the worst time to cross the isthmus. Cloudbursts turned jungle trails into swift, muddy streams. The moment the rain stopped, the sun beat down without mercy. The hot humidity was smothering, like trying to breathe with a wet towel over your face. The ground, a tangle of rotting vegetation, gave off the odor of wet garbage. An epidemic of cholera, a disease brought on by polluted water, killed 140 men, women, and children in less than two weeks. It killed swiftly and painfully. "My God, I've got the cholera!" said a major, grasping his belly with both hands. "No, Major, you've only eaten something that doesn't agree with you," said Grant.[17] The major died before sundown.

Quartermaster Grant met the challenge head-on. He hired porters to carry the sick in hammocks and bought mules to haul the regiment's heavy gear. Often he had to pay four times the regular price, yet he paid gladly, since lives were at stake. The money came from the regimental fund, which had been left in his care. A fellow officer remembered him as "a man of iron . . . seldom sleeping, and then only two or three hours at a time. . . . He was like a ministering angel to us all."[18] Those weeks on the Isthmus

Lieutenant Ulysses S. Grant in 1848, soon after his return from the Mexican War

of Panama taught him an invaluable lesson: be prepared. In years to come, Grant's troops never lacked supplies. They could always count on the old quartermaster for everything from beans to bullets.

Grant was assigned to Fort Vancouver in the Oregon Territory, near the present city of Portland. After a few months, he was promoted to captain and transferred to Humboldt Bay, California, 240 miles north of San Francisco. These were dreary outposts, with little to hold his interest. He cared nothing for the amusements of his comrades: hunting, gambling, chasing after American Indian women. Occasionally, when he had a few days' leave, he toured the countryside. He did not like what he saw. The mining camps were wild, lawless places, where men killed for a handful of gold nuggets. Most of all, he sympathized with the Indians. They were in bad shape, thanks to the whites. The Indian, he wrote a friend, "is fast wasting away before those blessings of 'civilization,' whiskey and small pox. . . . Those about here are the most harmless people you ever saw. It is really my opinion that the whole race would be harmless and peaceable if they were not put upon by the whites."[19]

Grant's own life was becoming unbearable. Prices were high, even the simplest item costing five times what it did back home. Clearly, his army pay would not allow him to support a family on the West Coast. He tried to raise extra money in any way he could. He planted potatoes, only to lose the crop in a flood. He raised chickens, but they died when he put them aboard a ship to San Francisco. He simply did not have a knack for making money.

God, how he missed his family! Julia's letters took months to get to him. Yet news from home only deepened his loneliness and sense of isolation. Whenever a letter arrived, he would sit alone for hours, reading it over and over again. One letter contained the inky print of a baby's hand. It was that of his second son, Ulysses, Jr., born a week after he sailed for Panama. He showed it to a sergeant, his lips quivering, tears in his eyes.

After eleven years in the army, resignation seemed out of the question. Thoughts of quitting filled him with fear. He wrote Julia on March 6, 1853: "I sometimes get so anxious to see you, and our little boys, that I am almost tempted to resign and trust to Providence and my own exertions for a living where I can have you and them with me. . . . Whenever I get to thinking about the subject, however, *poverty, poverty,* begins to stare me in the face and then I think what would I do if you and our little ones should want for the necessaries of life. . . ."[20]

He began to drink—a lot. Not that he was an alcoholic, one addicted to alcohol. Far from it. He got drunk when he was bored or lonely. But when Julia was around, he never touched a drop of whiskey. Nor, so far as we know, did whiskey ever prevent him from doing his duty.

His commanding officer, Colonel Robert C. Buchanan, had not liked him since their first meeting at Jefferson Barracks. After one drinking bout, Buchanan made Grant write a resignation, promising to send it to the War Department if he ever got drunk again. He did. The colonel kept his promise, and Grant left the army in the spring of 1854.

Grant was so poor that army friends in San Francisco took up a collection for his passage to New York City. Arriving there with scarcely a penny to his name, he rented a room in a cheap hotel by the waterfront. Desperate, he looked up a former classmate, Simon Bolivar Buckner, who paid his bills until his father sent a check from Ohio. Jesse was not pleased at this turn of events. "I think after spending . . . so many years in the [service] he will be poorly qualified for the pursuits of private life," he said.[21]

He was right.

Meantime, Ulysses had what he wanted most in the world. He was reunited with his wife and children. Never again would he be separated from them for long. His task now was to feed them and put a roof over their heads.

Julia's father had given her a wedding present of sixty acres of undeveloped land near St. Louis. Ulysses tried to turn that land into a farm. While his family lived at White Haven, he cleared a tract and planted wheat. From the trees he felled, he built a house called "Hardscrabble," a sly dig at the fancy names of other homes in the area. Until the crop came in, he cut firewood, which he hauled by wagon for sale in the streets of St. Louis. Years later, when he was president, there were still those who remembered him well. They described a figure with a scraggly beard in a faded army coat and mud-spattered pants tucked into frayed boots. Now and then he met army friends, who scarcely recognized him. "Great God, Grant, what are you doing?" an officer asked. "I am solving the problem of poverty," he replied.[22] But he wasn't.

After months of work in the fields, his efforts came to nothing. His first crop was harvested just as the Panic of 1857 struck. Banks closed across the nation. Unemployment soared. Farm prices tumbled, making crops nearly worthless. The next year brought more bad luck: a spring cold snap ruined Grant's crops. To make matters worse, he came down with ague, high fevers that left him dazed and unable to work for six months. Those who saw him in this weakened condition jumped to conclusions. The reason for his leaving the army was well known; clearly, they said, he was drinking again. Meantime, Julia had two more children: Nellie in 1855, Jesse in 1858.

Having failed at farming, Grant traded Hardscrabble for a rundown house in St. Louis and went into the real estate business with a cousin of Julia. Yet real estate was not for him; indeed, he seemed unfit for any occupation. After a few months of trying to sell property and collect rents, he quit. Neighbors whispered about poor Mrs. Grant, stuck with that no-account husband. Ulysses! No, they sneered, that could not be his real name. It must be "Useless." He was down-and-out, a man with no job, no money, no hope.

Ulysses swallowed his pride and went to his father in May 1860. Jesse had recently opened a leather shop at Galena, Illinois. The business, run by his younger sons, Orvil and Simpson, was doing so well that it needed another employee. The former army captain was hired as a bookkeeper and salesman at a salary of six hundred dollars a year. It wasn't much of a salary, but beggars can't be choosers. At least it paid the rent on a small house next to the town cemetery and put food on the table.

A poor salesman, Grant kept to the back room, writing bills and tending to the ledgers. Still, his troubles did not make him bitter. As always, he found happiness at home. Home was a place of calm, his retreat from a harsh world. He might have a bad day at the shop, but his mood changed the moment he opened the front door. Little Jesse would always be waiting with a challenge: "Mister, do you want to fight?" And Papa, who knew about fighting, would reply: "I'm a man of peace, but I'll not be hectored by a person of your size." Then they wrestled until Ulysses begged for

The Grant & Perkins leather store in Galena, Illinois, as seen in a photograph taken about the year 1865. When Ulysses's fortunes were at their lowest, his father hired him as a clerk.

mercy and his son cheered at having defeated the "best battler in the world."[23]

A man of peace. Grant knew his heart; he did hate war.

The best battler in the world. Time would show that he was that, too.

It would not be long. Eleven months after the Grants settled in Galena, the winds of war swept across the land. Nothing would ever be the same for them, for their country, and, most of all, for U. S. Grant.

II ✧ A HOUSE DIVIDED

Grant's down-and-out years saw his country drifting toward civil war. Although the war had several causes, these were all linked to slavery in one way or another. Slavery runs through the history of Grant's America like a scarlet thread, always present, always visible, always menacing.

Slavery had existed in North America ever since a Dutch ship brought its human cargo to Jamestown, Virginia, in August 1619, a year before the *Mayflower* brought the Pilgrims to the New World. For over two centuries thereafter, slavery was legal in the British colonies, then continued to be so in the United States.

The Founding Fathers had a bad conscience about slavery. Thomas Jefferson began the Declaration of Independence with a ringing defense of human rights: "We hold these truths to be self-evident, that all men are created equal, that they are endowed by their Creator with certain unalienable rights, that among these are life, liberty and the pursuit of happiness." "All men," however, applied only to free white men. The Founding Fathers belonged to their time, as we belong to ours. In their time, slavery had existed for thousands of years in all parts of the world. Jefferson himself owned slaves, though he believed slavery wrong and expected it to disappear gradually. So did his fellow Virginian George

Washington, who inherited slaves from his father but refused to buy any of his own.

Slavery did, indeed, seem doomed. In the early 1800s, slavery was outlawed in the Northern and Midwestern states, areas of small farms and factories that had no need of forced labor. Congress ended the African slave trade in 1807. Southerners, too, felt that slavery had outlived its usefulness. As an "enlightened" people, many thought it only a matter of time before they buried this relic of barbarism.

Until 1793, tobacco and rice were the chief crops produced by slave labor. Cotton counted for very little, then. It simply didn't pay, since it took ten hours to separate a pound of cotton fiber from its seeds by hand. But in that year Eli Whitney invented the cotton gin, a machine able to separate a thousand pounds a day. Cotton was the ideal fiber—inexpensive, lightweight, and easily cleaned. World demand soared, and with it the need for more field hands. Thus, without intending to, Whitney gave slavery a new lease on life and set the stage for the Civil War.

By 1860, there were four million slaves in the South worth about $2 billion. Slavery seemed justified because it was both profitable and "natural." Racism, the belief that certain races are naturally inferior to others, was as widespread then as it is today. This idea was expressed in language that robbed blacks of their humanity, turning them into things to be exploited for the benefit of others. Blacks were not people, but "niggers," "coons," "darkies," and "Sambos."[1] A black man was a "boy," a black woman a "girl," a black child a "pickaninny." Considered lazy, dirty, and violent, blacks supposedly neither deserved nor needed the rights enjoyed by whites. Dark skin, it was said, meant that God intended them to work long hours in the sun. Slavery, some claimed, was a blessing in disguise. It forced blacks into regular habits, taught them cleanliness, and gave them steady work.

Each state had its own slave laws. Though differing in details, these held that a black person had no rights a white person need respect. Slaves could be bought, sold, and traded at will. Slaves could not legally marry, and families could be separated at any time; children belonged not to their parents but to their owner. Women slaves could be sexually abused by their masters; in the 1850s, there were 348,874 mulattos, people of mixed race, in the South. Slaves could not own property, testify against whites in court, or gain an education. Teaching slaves to read and write was a crime in every Southern state.

A slave could be punished for any reason, or for no reason at all. Whipping was the most common punishment. Some masters were ingenious when it came to inflicting pain. Robert Burns, a former slave, recalled such a man in the 1930s. "My moster would put slaves in a calaboose [or locked shed] at night to be whipped de next morning. He always limited de lashes to five hundred. After whipping dem, he would rub pepper and salt on deir backs, where whipped, and lay dem before de fire until blistered, and den take a cat, and hold de cat, and make him claw de blisters, to burst dem."[2]

Masters, however, were not always cruel. A slave told how his owner "fed us reg'lar on good 'stantial food, just like you'd tend to you hoss, if you had a real good one."[3] It was to the owner's advantage to care for his property, animal and human, as best he could. He was in business to make money, which required healthy workers; it made no sense to harm them deliberately. Good workers were rewarded with better food and housing. An especially loyal slave went up to the "big house," where he or she cooked the owner's meals, cared for his children, and did the chores. Sometimes masters and slaves became close, even regarded each other as family.

Meantime, up North, the Industrial Revolution was in full swing. Towns became cities. Factories expanded. Railroads joined cities and factories with ribbons of steel. Northerners wanted economic growth, that is, cheap raw materials and consumers to buy their manufactured goods. Though often racists, they resented slavery deeply. It wasn't that they wanted to interfere with the South's "peculiar institution." To many, slavery was fine in Dixie, a backward area compared to the North. But, they said, it destroyed people's ambition; a good portion of southerners considered many jobs "nigger work," unfit for whites. For the nation to prosper, slavery must be barred from its western territories and only free states admitted to the Union. That terrified slaveholders. Growing cotton wore out the soil quickly, which meant that slavery had to expand to survive. Limiting its expansion, therefore, threatened the southern way of life.

Abolitionists, however, ignored such issues. Profits, prosperity, ways of life: these meant nothing to them. The country could go broke, for all they cared. What mattered was doing the right thing. To them, blacks were fellow human beings. Enslaving them was a sin against God, in Whose image we are created. Whatever the cost, slavery must be abolished. As for the slaveholders, paying them for their lost property would be like rewarding them for sin. They should not receive a penny.

William Lloyd Garrison, a leading abolitionist, went further in his newspaper, the *Liberator*. Garrison noted that it was hypocrisy for the Constitution to preach freedom while at the same time protecting slavery. "No Union with slaveholders," he declared. "The United States Constitution is a covenant with death, and an agreement with hell."[4] To underscore his point, Garrison publicly burned a copy of the Constitution on the Fourth of July, 1854. Better for the free states to secede, breaking up the United States, than be identified with slaveholders.

Slaveholders talked secession, too, but for a different reason. If slavery as an institution was threatened, they vowed to set up a country of their own.

John Brown in 1856. A failure in every business venture he ever attempted, Brown convinced himself that God had appointed him as the liberator of the slaves.

Meantime, Jesse Grant's old roommate, John Brown, convinced himself that God had chosen him for a special mission. When he read his Bible, he did not find the Lord of Hope and Charity. His God was the Lord of Hosts, a Man of War whose sword thirsted for blood. His favorite quotation was Hebrews 9:22: "Without the shedding of blood [there] is no remission of sins." This told him that blood, and blood alone, would cleanse this land of the sin of slavery. And he, John Brown, would lead the holy crusade.

On October 16, 1859, Brown led seventeen men on a daring raid. Armed with rifles, they surprised and captured the federal arsenal at Harpers Ferry, Virginia. Brown planned to carry the weapons seized at the arsenal into the Blue Ridge Mountains. There he would rally the slaves and lead them to freedom over the bodies of their oppressors. That night, however, his "army" was overrun by a detachment of the U.S. marines under Colonel Robert E. Lee. Brown was later convicted of treason and hung. Not one slave had joined his crusade.

Brown's execution was seen as a tragedy by many in the North. Church bells tolled in mourning and flags flew at half-staff in his memory. People gathered to pray for his soul. Abolitionist writers compared his death to the crucifixion of Jesus Christ. And a new song was heard: "John Brown's Body." It was a war song, a promise of things to come:

John Brown's body lies a-mould'ring in the grave,
John Brown's body lies a-mould'ring in the grave,
John Brown's body lies a-mould'ring in the grave,
His soul goes marching on.

Glory! Glory Hallelujah!
Glory! Glory Hallelujah!
Glory! Glory Hallelujah!
His soul goes marching on.

Southerners saw John Brown as a terrorist. For him to be glorified like this was outrageous. Worse, they became convinced that abolitionists had taken over the North and, like Brown, hoped to drown the South in blood. It was as if Southerners' worst dreams were becoming reality. The truth, of course, was quite different, but frightened people do not analyze things coolly. They imagined hordes of black "savages," armed to the teeth, lurking in the shadows. As the panic spread, volunteer military companies were formed to protect white people. Those companies were the seeds of the Confederate army.

Things grew worse as the presidential election of 1860 drew near. The Democrats, a largely proslavery party, were opposed by the Republicans, led by Abraham Lincoln. Although Lincoln despised slavery, he was no abolitionist. Abolitionists, to his mind, were too hasty, too fanatical. Slavery, he felt, was a state concern that Congress could not disturb where it already existed. Yet Congress did have the right to bar slavery from the territories. If Congress used that right, as he hoped it would, slavery would die a slow, lingering death. In the end, however, it would be as dead as any abolitionist could wish.

Lincoln's hatred of slavery did not mean that he loved black people. Slavery was wrong, he insisted, because it was inhuman and made a mockery of American ideals. Nevertheless, he shared his countrymen's racist beliefs. He thought blacks inferior to whites and objected to their being American citizens. When the time came, he wanted free blacks to return to Africa or settle on some Caribbean island. He made this clear in a speech at Charleston, Illinois, on September 18, 1858:

I will say . . . that I am not, nor ever have been in favor of bringing about in any way the social and political equality of the white and black races, . . . that I am not nor ever have been in favor of making voters or jurors of Negroes, nor of qualifying them to hold office, nor to intermarry with white people; and I will say in addition to this that there is a physical difference between the white and black races which I believe will for ever forbid the two races living together on terms of social and political equality. And inasmuch as . . . there must be the position of superior and inferior . . . I as much as any other man am in favor of having the superior position assigned to the white race.[5]

Small wonder that black leaders resented Lincoln at this time. Frederick Douglass, an escaped slave and a respected abolitionist, called him "a genuine representative of American prejudice and Negro hatred."[6]

The election of Lincoln was the last straw for Southerners. It showed that John Brown was very much alive. His spirit *was* marching on—straight to the White House. On December 20, 1860, South Carolina seceded from the Union, followed by Mississippi, Florida, Alabama, Georgia, Louisiana, and Texas. They formed the Confederate States of America, selecting Jefferson Davis, a senator from Mississippi and a former secretary of war, as president.

Confederate leaders left no doubt that their country stood for racism and slavery. "Our Confederacy," declared Vice President Alexander Stephens of Georgia, "is founded upon . . . the great truth that the negro is not equal to the white man. That slavery—subordination to the superior race, is his natural and normal condition. This, our new Government, is the first, in the history of the world, based upon this great physical and moral truth."[7]

The Confederacy was equally serious about independence. An army and navy were quickly formed. Federal property, including shipyards and arsenals, was seized. On April 12, 1861, Confederate artillery under General P. G. T. Beauregard fired on Fort Sumter in the harbor of Charleston, South Carolina, forcing its surrender. That victory brought four more states—Virginia, Arkansas, North Carolina, Tennessee—into the Confederacy. The Civil War had begun.

Lincoln asked for volunteers to put down the rebellion. His first call was for 75,000 men, soon followed by a call for another 300,000. The United States desperately needed these men. There was no draft (as yet), and the Regular Army was not organized

for rapid expansion. Its 16,000 men were scattered among dozens of small outposts, mainly in the West, to keep tabs on the Indians. Of its 1,090 officers, 313 resigned to fight for the Confederacy. Several of Grant's friends—Longstreet, Ewell, Buckner—became Confederate generals overnight.

News of Fort Sumter sent Northerners flocking to army recruiting offices. Men enlisted because that seemed the right thing to do. Traitors had attacked their country and insulted their flag. More, the very existence of the United States was at stake. The American Revolution was still a vivid memory. People remembered their grandfathers' stories of that awful struggle, and what it took to build what one volunteer called "the best and noblest government on earth."[8] To them, the cause of the Union was greater than the Union itself. It was the cause of liberty throughout the world. If that cause failed, human progress would be set back a thousand years.

Slavery was the chief cause of the Civil War, but few Billy Yanks—Northern soldiers—were abolitionists. Billy Yank, like his president, might believe that slavery was wrong, yet he did not consider blacks his equal, and freeing them was certainly not

The bombardment of Fort Sumter began on April 12, 1861, and lasted two days. In this drawing, the Union guns have returned fire, killing a Confederate soldier. In fact, no one died on either side.

Johnny Reb. A photograph of Confederate volunteers taken early in the war, when hope was high and they still had no experience of the realities of battle

worth a war. His Civil War was the war for the Union; nothing more and nothing less. He agreed with Lincoln's war aims, which he explained in a public letter. "My paramount object in this struggle is to save the Union, and is not either to save or to destroy slavery. If I could save the Union without freeing any slave, I would do it; and if I could save it by freeing all the slaves, I would do it; and if I could do it by freeing some and leaving others alone, I would also do that."[9]

Johnny Reb—the Southern soldier —did not fight *for* slavery any more than Billy Yank fought *against* it. Only one-third of Southern white families owned slaves, and nearly half of these had fewer than five slaves. Most slaves belonged to a minority of wealthy landowners who controlled the Confederate government.

Southerners enlisted because they felt trapped. Conquering the North, they knew, was out of the question. The North was too powerful and had too many people (18,901,917 whites in the North to 8,099,674 in the South) for that. However, to save the Union, Northern armies would have to conquer the South. This meant invading the Confederacy, defeating its armies, and destroying its government. Obviously, if an invader comes into your country, and you resist, that is self-defense. Johnny Reb, quite simply, fought to protect his home from the "damn Yankees." A soldier song said it best:

> I'se gwine to jine the Rebel band,
> A fighting for my home,
> Cheer, boys, cheer, we are marching on to battle!
> Cheer, boys, cheer, for our sweethearts and our wives![10]

Johnny Reb and Billy Yank did share one common goal. They enlisted not only for high ideals, but out of high spirits and a thirst for adventure. They were young; the average age was twenty-five. Their worlds were small; most had never traveled more than a few miles from their birthplace. Going off to war was a way of escaping the humdrum of everyday life. They called it "seeing the elephant."

Elephants were rare beasts, seen only in traveling circuses. Those lucky enough to have a circus come to town had the thrill of their lives. Battle, however, promised to be the ultimate thrill. This was nonsense, as time would tell. But the boys of 1861 were ignorant of war. Their notions of what happened on a battlefield were basically romantic fairy tales. Battle meant waving flags, brass bands, and masses of men charging under a canopy of gleaming bayonets. It meant comradeship and heroic stories to tell their grandchildren. Death, if it came, was swift, clean, and painless. The dead lay in heroic poses, without bloodshed, among admiring comrades. The Mexican War had been small and far away; only 1,733 Americans had died in battle. Civil War recruits could not imagine that their war would be any different.

No one expected the war to last very long. The Southerner who said "We can whip the Yankees with popguns" was expressing a popular view. So were the Northerners who expected to "clean up" the rebellion in three months. A youngster had to be quick if he wanted to be part of the great adventure. Those under eighteen, the minimum enlistment age, found a clever way to bend the rule. They scribbled the number eighteen on a slip of paper, put it in a shoe, and stepped up to the recruiting officer. Asked their age, they could truthfully say, "I am *over* eighteen."

It was clear sailing from then on. A doctor asked if you were healthy, tapped your chest once or twice, and pronounced you fit for service. A sergeant then administered the oath, and you were in the army.

When a unit was complete, it assembled in the town square. Flags flew, bands played, and politicians gave rousing speeches about patriotism and sacrifice. As the unit marched to the railroad station, townspeople gave it a glorious send-off. Youngsters had roses thrust into the barrels of their guns. And the girls; well, they were wonderful—and free with their kisses.

America went to war as to a picnic.

Slavery concerned U. S. Grant personally. Colonel Dent had given him a man named William Jones. Julia had six slaves, including Black Julia, who worked about the house and helped on the farm. Grant seems not to have held any strong views on the

A romantic view of war. In the early days of the Civil War, people imagined that battle was neat and clean, and that men received easy-to-treat wounds. This soldier's return is all the more appreciated because he bravely wore a "red badge of courage."

subject of slavery. "I never was an abolitionist, not even what could be called anti-slavery," he told a friend.[11] Nor can we say how he felt about being a slave owner. All that is certain is that on March 29, 1859, he freed his slave at no small cost to himself. He was broke at the time, and Jones could easily have brought a thousand dollars at auction. But he let him go without explaining why. Because Illinois was a free state, he returned Julia's slaves to her father before moving to Galena.

Despite his troubles, Grant took a keen interest in current affairs. Customers at the leather store complained that he spent more time behind the counter, his nose buried in a newspaper, than attending to their needs. Yet the more he read, the more anxious he became. He thought John Brown a "fanatic or madman," just like those Northerners who compared him to Christ. Talk of secession became unbearable. "It made my blood run cold to hear friends of mine . . . deliberately discuss the dissolution of the Union. . . . I could not endure it. The very thought of it was pain."[12]

The election of 1860 gave further cause for concern. Grant favored Lincoln, but could not vote since he had not lived long enough in Illinois. Republicans celebrated when news of Lincoln's victory reached Galena. That night, happy crowds paraded through the streets, singing, cheering, and lighting their way with torches. Customers gathered in the Grant shop, where Orvil served oysters and whiskey; Ulysses would not take a drop. He was grim as he told them not to be too happy. Lincoln's victory was not the last word, but the first in an unfolding tragedy, he said. "The South will fight."

One day, as he was tidying the shelves, a man ran into the shop waving a newspaper. The South had seceded, he shouted. It had formed a separate nation and chosen Jefferson Davis president. The news struck Grant like a slap in the face. He turned, stared at the man for a moment, and spat out these words: "Davis and the whole gang of them ought to be hung!"[13] From that day forward, Grant spoke of his military education and how much he owed his country. Deep down, probably without being aware of it yet, he was preparing to rejoin the army.

The firing on Fort Sumter brought Galenians into the streets once again. This time there were no cheers, only cries for revenge. The Stars and Stripes had been insulted! Very well, they would honor it as never before. The flag was run up on every pole and hung from every window in town.

Drums beat, announcing a mass meeting at the courthouse. Grant attended the meeting and heard the speeches. They were patriotic speeches, speeches from men who loved their country as he did. "It is simply country or no country," said John Rawlins, a popular lawyer. "We stand by the flag of our country, and we appeal to the God of battles!"[14]

The flag of our country! The phrase went straight to Grant's heart. After the meeting, he and Orvil left together. It was a lovely night, with stars glittering against the black sky. They walked silently, deep in thought. "I think I ought to go into the service," Ulysses said at last. "I think so, too," Orvil replied. "I'll stay home and attend to the store."[15]

Like his countrymen, Grant expected the war to be over within three months. His main concern, he told Jesse, was not the Confederates; they would be broken easily. The blacks, however, were another matter. With their masters defeated, they might try to finish John Brown's work. If that happened, the army's main job would be to restore order in the South. In any case, slavery was doomed, since no Yankee would fight to return traitors' property.

President Lincoln had asked each state to send volunteers in proportion to its population. Illinois was to provide 4,725 men, a hundred of them from the Galena area. Men rushed to enlist, and soon a company, the Jo Daviess County Guards, was formed.

That was fine, except that no one knew what to do next. No one, that is, except U. S. Grant. As the only West Pointer in town, he automatically became its expert on military affairs. Women who wanted to sew uniforms asked him to select the cloth and sketch the patterns. Men wanting military training came to him for guidance. Each day he put them through their paces in a field outside town. He had them form ranks and, with sticks over their shoulders, taught them the basics of rifle drill. He did well, but when asked to become their captain, he refused. Having been a captain in the Regular Army, he saw the command of a volunteer company as a demotion. At the very least, he expected to be the colonel of a regiment.

Early in May, the company was ordered to a camp at Springfield, the capital, to be mustered into one of the state regiments. Galena gave it a merry send-off. The volunteers looked soldierly in their blue uniforms. The older men cheered. The boys shouted. And the ladies all turned out, waving handkerchiefs and blowing kisses.

Grant came at the tail end of the column, a lone figure in civilian clothes. Although not officially a soldier, he was going along to help the troops settle in. Besides, Springfield was the best place to go after that colonel's commission. We will leave him at the railroad station for a while.

The summer of 1861 saw scores of training camps spring up across the country. It was there that the armies assembled and recruits had their first taste of soldiering.

Armies on both sides were alike in their organization. Each army was built up from smaller units gathered into larger and larger formations. The *company,* 100 men led by a captain, was the basic fighting unit. Ten companies, 1,000 men, were grouped into a *regiment,* commanded by a colonel. Four regiments, 4,000 men under a brigadier general, formed a *brigade.* A *division* consisted of three brigades, 12,000 men under a brigadier or major general. A *corps* was composed of nine divisions, 36,000 men under a major general. Finally, two or three corps formed an *army,* 72,000–108,000 men. Union armies took their names from rivers, as with the Army of the Potomac. Southern armies were named by area, such as the Army of Northern Virginia. A major general led a Union army; a lieutenant general or a full general commanded a Confederate army.

An army had several "combat arms," or specialties. Since the infantry did most of the fighting, it was the most numerous. Foot soldiers were supported in turn by the big guns of the artillery. Both, however, looked to the cavalry for information and protection. The cavalry was the army's "eyes." Its duty was to report enemy movements and screen the

Billy Yank, an unnamed private in the 4th Michigan Volunteers. He is wearing a checkered shirt, not part of the regulation uniform, and has a bowie knife in his belt.

movements of its own army from enemy patrols. Cavalry seldom fought infantry, which usually had the advantage in numbers and firepower; most of their fighting was in clashes with enemy cavalry or in raids on supply lines. A cavalryman was armed with a sword; a six-shot pistol; and a carbine, a lightweight musket.

Recruits earned their pay. A Union private received thirteen dollars a month; by comparison, a master could easily rent out a slave for thirty dollars a month. Uncle Sam owned a soldier's every waking moment. At 5 A.M., rain or shine, buglers raised their horns and blew reveille. A piercing wail shattered the stillness; men swore that it sounded like "the devil-is-loose, the devil-is-loose, the devil-is-loose in the morning."

Tumbling from their blankets, they dressed as fast as they could. That took some getting used to. Many a farm boy had never worn underwear and was puzzled by those funny white pants cut off at the knees. Uniforms were of heavy, scratchy wool; wearing them down South in summer was pure agony. Nevertheless, many boasted about having the best suit of clothes in their lives.

Except for eating and sleeping, every minute of the day was devoted to drill. This was quite a letdown after all those heroic speeches and parades at home. Men joined up expecting excitement and glory. Instead, they were put through dull, boring exercises that had to be done correctly. A Pennsylvania volunteer explained the routine to his folks: "The first thing in the morning is drill, then drill, then drill again. Then drill, drill, and a little more drill. Then drill, and lastly drill. Between drills, we drill and sometimes stop to eat a little and have a roll-call."[16]

There were different drills for different purposes. Marching was absolutely necessary. Recruits marched across fields, through forests, and over hills. They slogged through sticky mud and under the broiling sun. Marching made you feel part of the group. You were no longer an individual with your own thoughts, but part of a fighting team. Marching also tightened your muscles, building stamina for the tough times ahead.

Farm boys might not know their right foot from their left. To teach them, the drill instructor attached a piece of hay to each one's left boot and a piece of straw to the right. Then, as they began to march, they would look down at their feet and follow his orders: "Hay-foot, straw-foot, hay-foot, straw-foot." They took up the cry, chanting:

March! March! March old soldier march!
Hayfoot, strawfoot,
Belly-full of bean soup—
March old soldier march!

Just carrying the gear required strength. Besides lugging a musket over his shoulder, a soldier had a bayonet, canteen, and cartridge box with "forty dead men" (forty bullets) attached to his belt. On his back he carried a knapsack slung from straps. It contained extra rations, a woolen blanket rolled in a rubber groundsheet, half a pup tent, spare clothes, overcoat, shaving supplies, mess kit, and toothbrush. In addition to his regular gear, a soldier carried personal items like tobacco (for chewing or smoking), books, writing equipment, letters, and pictures of loved ones. The pack weighed from forty to fifty pounds. Carrying this load made a person tolerant of dumb beasts. "I can appreciate the feelings of an animal in harness now" was how one soldier put it.[17]

Marching was more than getting from one place to another. Turning, about-facing, and quick-stepping in columns were essential maneuvers. Units normally moved in a column four abreast. A division, for example, occupied a space roughly eight feet wide by a mile long. This arrangement made for speed; a good outfit on a good road could do three miles an hour in cool, dry weather.

A marching formation, however, was not a fighting formation.

Upon reaching the battlefield, a column had to face the enemy in line of battle. This meant changing the column's shape so that it formed several lines standing side by side, or one behind another, each line perhaps a mile wide by two ranks deep. Only by long hours of drill could large bodies of men move about quickly and form up for battle; it also took practice to learn how to advance or retreat in an orderly fashion. Carrying out these maneuvers correctly could make the difference between victory and disaster.

Weapons drill involved skills of a different sort. The musket was the infantryman's basic weapon. The old-style musket was a smoothbore; that is, the inside of its barrel, or bore, was smooth, allowing it to fire a lead ball. Deadly at ranges up to one hundred yards, beyond that the smoothbore was useless. Grant said that an enemy might shoot at you all day from a distance of a few hundred yards "without your finding it out."[18]

This held true for more than two centuries. After the Mexican War, however, the smoothbore was replaced by the rifle-musket. Although it looked like the smoothbore, it was entirely different. It had rifling, spiral grooves cut on the inside of the barrel. Rifling made it necessary to change the shape of the bullet. This new bullet, or "minié ball," was an inch long, made of soft lead, and cone-shaped rather than round. The rifling in the barrel made the bullet spin, enabling it to travel as far as a thousand yards.

The rifle-musket was forty inches long, weighed nine pounds, and had an eighteen-inch bayonet. To load, the soldier took out one of his forty dead men. The cartridge was a paper tube containing a minié ball and gunpowder. Standing upright—he couldn't lie down since the weapon had to be loaded from the muzzle—he bit the tube open, poured the powder down the barrel, crumpled the paper into a wad, and packed everything tightly with a ramrod. Next he drew back the hammer at the rear and placed a firing cap on the iron "nipple" at the trigger end of the barrel. He then raised the musket to his shoulder and squeezed the trigger. The hammer struck the firing cap, which sent a jet of flame into the barrel. The result was a sharp *bang* and a puff of smoke the size of a cow.

A skilled infantryman could fire two shots a minute. Still, his weapon was so inaccurate that most shots missed. Soldiers believed that it took a man's weight in lead to kill one enemy; federal experts said five or six hundred bullets were needed to kill each Confederate soldier. Hence the line-of-battle formation. Since no single bullet was sure to hit its target, only massed firing could overcome the musket's inaccuracy. With lots of men firing lots of bullets in the same direction at once, some were bound to find their mark. The only problem was that the line of battle was itself a perfect target.

Handling cannon was work for experts. Each step had to be done right, or the cannon could misfire or, worse, explode, killing its crew and anyone who happened to be standing nearby. Cannon were loaded and fired like muskets, only their cartridges were larger and made of cloth. After firing, special care was taken to remove the smoking pieces of cloth that stuck to the inside of the barrel. This was done with a wet "sponge," a mop at the end of a long pole. Awful things happened when a fresh cartridge was rammed down a poorly cleaned barrel.

Artillerymen used different kinds of shot for different purposes. Round shot was a twelve-pound iron ball that could travel a mile and punch through an earthen wall a yard thick. A ball that hit the ground would bounce for hundreds of feet, killing or maiming everyone in its path. Cannon also fired shells, cone-shaped iron tubes filled with gunpowder and set off by a fuse. Impact fuses exploded shells when they hit a solid object. Time fuses exploded shells overhead, spraying pieces of metal in a wide circle. Small or large, these sped through the air, tumbling and twisting and cutting men to shreds.

Deadly as shells were, they were tame alongside canister and grapeshot. Canister was a tin can filled with hundreds of musket balls; grape was a container with nine lead slugs the size of golf balls. Both were "antipersonnel" weapons, that is, designed for use against troops in the open. The moment a gun was fired, the container burst, spreading its contents like pellets from a huge shotgun.

Nevertheless, the soldier's worst enemy was not gunfire. Just being in the army was deadlier than the most hard-fought battle. Until the medical advances of the twentieth century, disease was the greatest killer of soldiers. In the Napoleonic Wars (1799–1815), eight men died of disease for each combat victim. The numbers were six to one in the Mexican War (1846–1848), an improvement but still nothing to brag about. The Civil War was even better, with approximately two soldiers dying of disease for each battle death. Union army deaths totaled 360,222. Of these, 110,000 died in action or of wounds afterward; twice as many, 250,222, died of disease. Roughly 258,000 Confederates died in the war, of which three-quarters, or 193,500, fell to disease.

Disease struck in two waves. The first wave consisted of childhood diseases: mumps, chicken pox, whooping cough. Because most recruits were from isolated farm areas, they had not much contact with strangers. When they gathered in camps, joining city boys, the diseases struck hard. Although seldom fatal, they laid up entire units for weeks at a time. Measles was the exception; it killed 5,177 Union soldiers. "Though we enlisted to fight, bleed and die," wrote a Maine volunteer, "nothing happened to us so serious as the measles."[19]

The second wave were diseases related to dirt. Here men turned out to be their own worst enemies. Soldiers preferred convenience to cleanliness. It was easier to throw garbage into camp streets than bury it in a dump. Besides, old habits were hard to break. Farm boys were used to relieving themselves wherever they pleased, rather than going to the latrines, particularly at night. As a result, human wastes were everywhere, and you had to be careful about where you slept. "On rolling up my bed this morning," a soldier wrote in his diary, "I found I had been lying in—I wont say what—something . . . that didn't smell like milk and peaches."[20] Disgusting smells were a regular part of army life. Men referred to them as "the patriotic odor."

Army regulations called for the washing of hands and face every day and baths at least once a week. However, since hot water was scarce, men might go weeks without bathing. A popular story concerned a soldier who lost his socks. He searched everywhere, but to no avail. Then he washed his feet. Lo and behold, he found that he had been wearing them all along, buried under layers of filth. Another time, a colonel ordered his men to take haircuts, only to discover that "the pile of dirt disclosed beneath the earlocks of some must have been accumulating all winter and . . . would grow a hill of corn."[21]

Everyone had lice. Known as "graybacks" and "tigers," these tiny insects resembled hairy crabs. Totally democratic, they attacked privates and officers with equal appetite. Entire regiments could be seen scratching and squirming as they marched. During rest periods, clothes were singed over campfires or thrown into boiling water to kill the lice and their eggs, called "nits." It made no difference; lice were hardy and soon returned in greater numbers than ever. Desperate men prayed for relief:

> *Now I lay me down to sleep*
> *While graybacks o'er my body creep;*
> *If I should die before I wake,*
> *I pray the Lord their jaws to break.*[22]

Lice carried typhus, a disease that brought high fever often leading to death. Mosquitoes, for which the South was famous, carried malaria and yellow fever. Dirt in general brought dysentery, a type of diarrhea. Known as "the runs" and "the quickstep," loose bowels was the Civil War's chief killer. Records show that 1,739,135 Union soldiers suffered from diarrhea, of whom 44,558 died. Small wonder that troops passing each other on the road called out, "How're yer bowels?" It was not meant as a joke.

Army surgeons did the best they could, but had little to work with. The medicines they prescribed could as easily kill as cure. Corn whiskey was the most widely used "drug." Taken straight or mixed with such ingredients as red pepper, it was used to treat a wide variety of illnesses. A standard measles treatment, for example, was a swig of whiskey straight from the bottle. Calomel ran a close second to whiskey as a medicine. Made of mercury, a poison, it was prescribed for stomach complaints! Another drug was "blue mass," a mixture of mercury and chalk.

Food also sent soldiers to early graves. To prevent spoiling, beef and pork came in barrels filled with a strong saltwater solution. Men called pickled beef "salt horse," and, they said, horseshoes could be found at the bottom of the barrels. Pickled pork was "salt junk"; junk was slang for old rope and referred to meat kept in salt so long that it became a mass of ropelike fibers. A Yankee described his meat ration as a slimy, smelly, bluish mass: "one can throw a piece up against a tree and it will stick there and quiver and twitch for all the world like one of those blue-bellied lizards at home will do when you knock him off a fence rail with a stick."[23] This stuff was fried in hog grease, causing what doctors called "death from the frying pan."

Instead of bread, Union soldiers ate hardtack, a cracker three inches square and a half-inch thick, made of flour and water. Hardtack was so hard that it was nicknamed "teeth dullers," or "sheet-iron crackers." It was also called "worm castles" because it often *was* home to an assortment of wriggling creatures. Before eating hardtack, it was wise to tap it on a stone to shake out the larger worms and weevils; one soldier found thirty-seven worms in a single cracker. Men ate wormy crackers with their eyes closed, some finding, they said, the "fresh meat" tastier than the regular issue. All meals were washed down with mugs of coffee served "hot as hell and black as sin."

Confederates ate corn bread rather than hardtack. Moldy, filled with corncobs and sawdust, the best way to eat it was mixed with water and salt and fried in grease. "My share gave me such a pain in my stomach that I could hardly walk," complained one Johnny Reb. Another likened the corn bread to "a pile of cow dung baked in the sun."[24]

Given such living conditions, it is a miracle that so many men lived to reach the battlefield. They must have been very tough indeed.

Springfield was a busy place in the spring of 1861. Before coming under federal control, volunteer regiments had to be organized and their commanders appointed. Military ability had nothing to do with obtaining a command. Given the lack of experienced officers, and the fact that so many regiments were forming, every small-town politician saw himself as the American Napoleon. Day in and day out, they hounded Governor Richard Yates for commissions. The most influential became colonels, a rank that a Regular Army officer was lucky to reach after twenty years of service.

U. S. Grant was no politician. At first, the governor's aides could find nothing for him to do. After a few days, however, he was given odd jobs at headquarters. While the men from Galena settled in, he did everything from filling out forms to mustering units into the federal service. Still, he could not get a command of his own. He wrote the War Department in Washington, without receiving an answer; the letter was found in the War Department files a century later, still unopened. He asked army friends for help, but they had no ideas. Finally, Yates appointed him colonel of the 21st Illinois Volunteers, a job nobody else wanted.

The 21st Illinois was a rowdy bunch, and their first sight of Grant gave them no reason to reform. He was not much to look at, with his stooped shoulders and rumpled civilian clothes. "What a colonel!" one fellow jeered. "Look at the little 'un! Damn such a colonel!" shouted another. Two men shadowboxed behind him, "accidentally" hitting him on the back and sending his hat flying. That was a mistake, for this colonel was nobody's punching bag. Grant turned on them, saying nothing. Words were unnecessary; his eyes said it all. His gaze, cold as ice, cut through them and made them shudder. They stammered an apology and meekly hurried to their tents.

Grant showed the regiment who was boss. Obedience was rewarded with a salute and a "well done, soldier!" Disobedience, he said, was treated "by the application of a little regular army punishment."[25] That was an understatement. The army gave officers plenty of leeway in matters of discipline. Ordinary rule-breakers could be marched around camp balancing a log over one shoulder. Those who talked back were bucked and gagged, as painful a punishment as one can have without shedding blood. A bayonet was forced sideways into the offender's mouth and held in place by a string tied around his ears. He was then seated on the ground with his knees pulled up almost to his chest. A stick was placed under his knees and his arms tied in front. He could be kept this way for hours. Few needed a second dose of this medicine.

A month of drill and discipline turned the 21st Illinois into a first-class outfit. In July it went to Missouri with orders to attack a Confederate camp near the village of Florida. As it advanced, Grant felt as if his heart were rising into his throat, and "I would have given anything . . . to be back in Illinois." Not that he feared for his own safety; he had often risked his life in Mexico. But that was different. In Mexico he took orders; here he gave them. The responsibility for success or failure was his alone. What if things went wrong? What if lives were lost needlessly? These questions scared him more than Confederate bullets.

Grant needn't have worried, because the camp was deserted. The Rebels, hearing of his approach, had cleared out hours before. He was so relieved, he recalled, that "my heart resumed its place." Better yet, he realized that the enemy "had been as much afraid of me as I had been of him."[26] That is as valuable a lesson as a commander can learn. Fear is part of being human; but he who can make an enemy more frightened than he is himself has already won a victory. From that day on, Grant refused to be upset by talk of enemy power. He was more concerned about what he could do to the enemy, rather than what the enemy might do to him. It was because he could learn such lessons quickly, not because he was a genius, that he became a great leader.

Early in August, an aide rushed into Grant's tent with a newspaper. "Colonel," he cried, "I have some news here that will interest you." Glancing at the front page, Grant could hardly believe his eyes. The army, it said, needed another three dozen brigadier generals, and President Lincoln had asked Illinois's congressmen for the names of four qualified officers from their state. The representative from Galena recommended Grant, whose name now appeared on the list.

General Grant was ordered to Cairo, Illinois, to command the troops in southern Illinois and southeastern Missouri. Cairo was a hellhole. Swarms of mosquitoes made its citizens miserable; rats were so abundant that thousands were crushed each time a train came down the tracks. Yet Grant could not have been in a better place in 1861. The Ohio River, you recall, joins the Mississippi at Cairo. Across the Ohio lay Kentucky, a slave state but not a member of the Confederacy. Kentuckians were evenly divided, half wanting to secede, half wanting to stay loyal to the Union. Divisions were so deep that families split, their menfolk leaving home to join the opposing armies. The state government, however, hoped to stay neutral. Both the Union and the Confederacy kept their troops out of Kentucky, not as an act of kindness, but out of necessity. Neither wanted to make the first move for fear of driving the state into its enemy's arms.

Kentucky's position on the Ohio, however, made neutrality impossible. A glance at the map will show that two large rivers flow into the Ohio. Rising in the mountains of eastern Tennessee, the Tennessee and Cumberland rivers flow northward until they join the Ohio near Paducah, Kentucky. Confederate planners knew that river traffic can move both ways. Confederate gunboats, followed by troopships, could descend the two rivers and cut off the Ohio, the Union's lifeline from the Midwest. But by the same token, Yankee forces could sail upstream, stabbing into the heart of Tennessee, even capturing Nashville, its capital. Tennessee was the Confederacy's largest producer of iron, Nashville's arsenals and warehouses its chief supply dump in the West. More, Tennessee guarded the Lower South from invasion. Allowing the two rivers to come under Yankee control meant placing Mississippi, Louisiana, Georgia, and Alabama in serious danger.

The Rebels built two forts—Henry on the Tennessee and Donelson on the Cumberland—just south of the Kentucky border. As extra insurance, they decided to seize Paducah, thereby securing the mouths of both rivers. A large force was on its way when Grant beat them to the punch.

Grant arrived at Cairo on September 14. Learning that the Rebels were on the move, he wired St. Louis, headquarters of Union forces in the West. His message was brief: unless told otherwise, he would start for Paducah immediately. Receiving no reply, he loaded two regiments on steamers and ordered two gunboats to escort them to Paducah forty miles to the east. Two days later, he occupied the town without firing a shot. In one swift, bloodless move, he had kicked open the door to the Lower South.

Before passing through that door, however, Grant fought his

only battle of 1861. The Rebels had built a fort overlooking the Mississippi at Columbus, Kentucky. To strengthen their position, they occupied Belmont, Missouri, on the opposite shore.

Early in November, Grant received orders to move against Belmont. He put 2,700 men on transports and steamed down the Mississippi. The Confederates, taken by surprise, broke and ran. The inexperienced Yankees then acted as if they had won the war singlehanded. They went through the abandoned camp, taking souvenirs, shouting, and drinking "liberated" corn whiskey until the ground swayed beneath their feet. Crowds gathered to hear officers make flowery speeches about their glorious cause.

No one bothered to keep tabs on the Rebels, who had rallied at the riverbank. Meantime, two steamers left Columbus with reinforcements. The moment they landed, their Confederate comrades began to work their way between the Union transports and Grant's men. Grant saw them coming, but could not make his men leave the camp; they were having too much fun and refused to believe they were in danger. At last he sent officers to burn the camp and form line of battle.

It was too late. Instead of attacking, the Yankees panicked at the first shots. "We are surrounded and will have to surrender!" a hysterical officer shouted. "I guess not," Grant replied. "If we are surrounded we must cut our way out just as we cut our way in."[27]

That is exactly what happened. Following their chief's example, the troops headed for the transports. Bullets snapped overhead, and once some Rebels came within fifty feet of Grant. He turned his horse and moved away slowly, trying to make himself inconspicuous. At that moment he thought of his family and what might happen to them if he should be killed. But the question was pushed aside by the crackle of gunfire. Once at the riverbank, he waited until everyone was safely aboard, then boarded himself. The men cheered. His determination had saved their skins, and they knew it. Left behind were 120 dead and 487 prisoners. Rebel losses were about the same.

Back in Galena, Julia had just finished her housework. She was going upstairs to rest when a vision passed before her eyes. She saw Ulysses on horseback, staring at her with a sad expression on his face. When next they met, they found that her vision had come at the exact moment he was thinking about their family. Both felt that his concern for his loved ones was so great that it sent his image into their house hundreds of miles away.

Grant spent the weeks after Belmont studying his maps. And the more he studied, the more convinced he became that he could take the Rebel forts. The navy agreed. Flag Officer Andrew H. Foote, commander of the Mississippi River squadron, had several ironclads based at Cairo. These were a new type of warship: 175 feet long, 51 feet abeam (wide), with slanted sides covered by two-and-a-half-inch iron plates and carrying thirteen heavy guns. Infantrymen called them "turtles," but sailors saw them as fire-spitting dragons.

In January 1862, Grant took his plan to Major General Henry W. Halleck, chief of Union forces in the West. Nicknamed "Old Brains," Halleck was the nation's leading student of war. Unfortunately, most of what he knew about the subject came from books, having seen little action himself. Cranky and short-tempered, he resented anyone who had a good idea he could not claim as his own. So, when Grant came to headquarters, he gave him a cold

General Henry W. Halleck. Known as "Old Brains," Halleck was a brilliant writer on military subjects but a poor field commander.

reception. After a ten-minute interview, he cut him short as if his plan were childish. Grant returned to Cairo "very much crestfallen."[28]

Halleck soon changed his mind. Early in February, he gave Grant the go-ahead. The attack order landed like a bombshell in Cairo. Grant's aides were elated. They whooped and hollered, kicked over chairs, and pounded the walls with their fists. Their chief smiled, noting that they shouldn't make such a rumpus, as it could be heard all the way to Fort Henry.

The Confederate forts were earthworks, artillery positions protected by earthen walls surrounded by ditches. Fort Henry, Grant's first objective, was built close to the bank of the Tennessee River—*too* close. On February 6, he landed fifteen thousand troops a few miles downstream. It had rained heavily, causing the river to rise and break through the walls of the fort before they could even attack. In addition to this, four of the turtles steamed up to the fort and let go a storm of shot and shell. The Rebel commander decided to call it quits. After transferring the garrison to Fort Donelson twelve miles to the east, he surrendered. Thrilled by his success, Grant wired Halleck: "Fort Henry is ours. I shall take and destroy Fort Donelson . . . and return to Fort Henry."[29]

Grant marched his troops overland while the turtles steamed back down the Tennessee and then up the Cumberland to rejoin the army. Fort Donelson, however, was no pushover. Built on a high bluff, it overlooked the river with twelve of the largest guns in the West. Grant's friend Simon Bolivar Buckner was one of its three commanding generals.

On February 14, Yankee troops closed in by land while sailors prepared for action on the water. The Confederates were ready.

As the turtles drew near, they opened fire. The roar of cannon echoed off the hillsides, sending flocks of birds screeching into the air. Civilians came to watch the spectacle from a safe distance. What they saw was awesome. The fort and the turtles were enveloped in clouds of smoke. Again and again, tongues of flame darted from the gray clouds. Geysers of water erupted near the ships, shooting fifty feet into the air.

The Rebels fired straight and often. Solid shot struck iron plates, making deep dents before bouncing into the water. Shells burst overhead, pelting the decks with chunks of hot iron. The *Carondelet,* known as an unlucky ship, had two cannonballs come through her gunports at once, decapitating three men. The vessel's captain had never seen such an awful mess. Bleeding men, he later reported, "were borne past me, three with their heads off. The sight almost sickened me and I turned my head away."[30] One by one the Yankee ships were damaged and forced to steam out of range. Foote, wounded by flying splinters, finally broke off the fight. High on the bluff, Rebel gunners cheered and tossed their caps into the air.

Next morning, February 15, Grant boarded Foote's flagship for a conference. Foote had just given him a cigar when they heard firing in the distance. Rebel infantry had launched an attack on the Yankees' right flank. With reckless courage the Rebels pushed ahead, forcing Grant's men to give ground steadily. But just as they were about to break through, bugles sounded, calling them back to their positions. They were close to exhaustion, and their commanders wanted them to rest and regroup before continuing the attack.

Stopping while they were ahead was a mistake. The Confederate commanders had not reckoned on U. S. Grant. As he came ashore, he heard the latest reports and rushed to the front. He found his men confused and discouraged. The enemy had everything in its favor, they cried.

Everything? Grant asked what that meant. Rebel prisoners, a soldier explained, had three days' rations in their knapsacks.

Grant knew that soldiers defending a fort do not carry three days' rations, especially when they charge. Clearly, the Rebels were trying to escape and had pulled back only because they were weakening. There was no time to lose. "The one who attacks now," he said, "will be victorious, and the enemy will have to be in a hurry if he gets ahead of me."[31]

He galloped from regiment to regiment, shouting that the Rebels were in trouble. Every man must refill his cartridge box and fall into line of battle at once.

That was all the troops needed to hear. They re-formed their lines and surged forward. They would have captured the fort, had

Buckner not taken charge at the critical point. Buckner saved the day, though Fort Donelson was already doomed.

Riding back to camp at dusk, Grant passed a Yankee lieutenant and a Rebel private. Both were badly wounded and lay side by side. The lieutenant was trying to give the private a drink from his canteen but was too weak to lift it. Grant stopped and asked an aide to give them some whiskey. "Thank you, General," the Rebel groaned, while the lieutenant tried to salute. Stretcher bearers picked up the officer, but made no move toward the private.

Grant would have none of that. "Take this Confederate, too," he snapped. "Take them both together; the war is over between them."

That is how it was with U. S. Grant. While the battle raged, he fought with all his heart. But there was nothing personal in his fighting, no anger, no hatred, no spirit of revenge. He fought the enemy's cause, not the enemy himself. Rebels, he believed, were misguided people. Yet they were still people and must be treated humanely once they quit the fight. As he rode toward camp, an officer heard him whisper to himself:

> *Man's inhumanity to man*
> *Makes countless thousands mourn.*[32]

Grant was still a soldier who hated war.

That night the senior Rebel commanders—Generals John B. Floyd and Gideon J. Pillow—escaped aboard a steamboat, leaving Buckner to arrange the surrender. On the morning of February 16, Buckner wrote to ask about surrender terms. Grant fired off a reply: "No terms except an unconditional surrender can be accepted."[33]

Grant proved to be more generous than the Rebels expected. Unconditional surrender did not mean harsh treatment. His seventeen thousand captives were released; it was easier to do that than send them to distant prisoner-of-war camps. Besides, he thought (correctly) that most had had a bellyful of war and would go home rather than return for duty. Enemy officers were allowed to keep their pistols and personal servants, that is, their slaves. Only black construction workers at the fort, horses, and military equipment were seized as enemy property. The workmen were not freed, but kept with the army as paid laborers. Legally, however, they were still slaves.

After signing the surrender papers, the two generals renewed their friendship as if nothing had happened. They talked about West Point, Mexico, and how they got snow blind while climbing Popocatepetl volcano. Grant recalled Buckner's generosity eight years earlier. He took him aside, so as not to embarrass him before others, and offered him everything in his wallet. Thanks, but no thanks, was Buckner's reply; he had plenty of money. They remained friends for the rest of their lives.

The capture of Fort Donelson was the Union's first important victory of the Civil War. In the days that followed, Union gunboats steamed up the Cumberland, forcing the Rebels to abandon Nashville. Slaves greeted the blue-clad troops with cries of "massa done gone souf."

Grant's call for unconditional surrender electrified the North. Suddenly everyone knew the meaning of his initials; U. S. Grant was actually "Unconditional Surrender" Grant. Church bells rang out the nation's thanks. Parades were held and men got drunk in his honor. A Chicago newspaper announced that "any person found sober after nine o'clock in the evening would be arrested as a secessionist." In Cincinnati, citizens were "shaking hands with everybody else, and bewhiskered men embraced each other as if they were lovers."[34] And in Galena, folks wondered if Unconditional Surrender Grant was *their* Grant. Informed that he was, one fellow said he would never again doubt the existence of miracles.

Fame also brought Grant a material reward. During the battle, a reporter saw him with the stub of a cigar in his mouth, the same one Foote had given him aboard his flagship. Thinking the general liked cigars, he mentioned it in his article as an interesting fact. The public took the hint, and soon thousands of boxes of cigars were arriving at headquarters from every corner of the Union.

Grant gave up his pipe and became a cigar smoker. Actually, he was addicted. Each day, every day, he smoked at least two dozen cigars. Whenever battle was near, he had the habit of sitting under a tree while smoking a cigar and whittling on a stick. Passing soldiers knew this meant that hard fighting lay ahead.

U. S. Grant would smoke many a cigar and whittle many a stick in the months after Fort Donelson.

III ✧ Shiloh: Seeing the Elephant

Congress promoted U. S. Grant to major general for a job well done. Everyone was proud of him; everyone, that is, except Old Brains Halleck. Instead of offering congratulations, Halleck accused him of not reporting on the condition of his troops. In fact, Grant had sent reports; they never arrived because the telegrapher, a Rebel sympathizer, ran off with them. Rather than hear Grant's explanation, Halleck relieved him of command, hinting that he had "resumed his former bad habits." That was unfair; there is nothing to indicate that Grant was drinking at this time.

President Lincoln came to the rescue. Learning of Halleck's action, he insisted that justice be done, and done swiftly, for the good of the army. If Grant had disobeyed orders, Halleck must arrest him and have him tried at a court-martial. The president, in effect, had told the general to put up or shut up. Halleck shut up. Apologizing for the unfortunate "error," he told Grant to rejoin his army in Tennessee.

Grant found it encamped at Pittsburg Landing, a steamboat docking site on the west bank of the Tennessee River. Confederate forces held Corinth, Mississippi, eighteen miles to the south. After their recent defeats, they had retreated to Corinth, the junction of two key railways in the Mississippi Valley. Halleck planned to take Corinth as the first step in conquering this vital region.

Grant's army, numbering thirty-seven thousand, was to be joined at Pittsburg Landing by twenty thousand troops under Major General Don Carlos Buell, due to arrive any day from Nashville. Except for some veterans of Fort Donelson, both armies consisted of "greenhorns," soldiers fresh from boot camp. Many of Buell's men had yet to learn how to load a musket.

To counter the threat, Jefferson Davis sent reinforcements to Corinth, increasing the Rebel army to forty thousand. These troops, like their opponents, were greenhorns. Young and inexperienced, few had ever heard a shot fired in anger, let alone seen a person killed.

General Albert Sidney Johnston commanded at Corinth. Johnston, fifty-nine, was the Confederacy's highest-ranking field officer. Six feet tall, with blue-gray eyes and a large mustache, he had been a senior general in the U. S. Army. His deputy was P. G. T. Beauregard, the victor of Fort Sumter. Known as the Confederate Napoleon, Beauregard admired the Frenchman, taking him as his model. Each was brilliant in his own right, and Johnston and Beauregard made a first-rate fighting team.

Both men realized that Grant meant to draw them into an all-out fight for Corinth. Instead of waiting to be attacked by a larger force, they planned to strike before Buell arrived. Grant, surprised at Pittsburg Landing, would be defeated, making Buell an easy target. This was a battle they had to win. If Corinth's railroads were lost, Union forces could go on to control the entire length of the Mississippi River. And that would be the beginning of the end for the Confederacy.

When Grant's army first came to Pittsburg Landing, it found only a rickety dock and some warehouses at the foot of a steep bluff. The place was ideal for unloading supplies, but not for thousands of troops. Two miles inland, however, lay thick woods broken by fields and small farms. In one field, located midway between two creeks, stood a one-room church built of logs. It was called Shiloh, a biblical name meaning "place of peace." Before long, vast encampments surrounded the church. The Battle of Shiloh takes its name from this simple house of prayer.

Victory lay within the Rebels' grasp. All they had to do was make fewer mistakes than the enemy had already made. Victorious in Tennessee, the Yankees thought themselves invincible.

General Albert Sidney Johnston hurled his Confederate forces against Grant's unsuspecting army at Shiloh. While directing frontline operations, Johnston was shot in the leg and bled to death.

Even Grant, who should have known better, deceived himself. Convinced that the Rebels were demoralized, he believed they would sit still and wait to be destroyed. He had made a basic error of generalship: he assumed that the enemy would do what he wanted it to do.

Grant did not help matters by making his headquarters at Savannah, nine miles downstream and on the opposite side of the river from his army. He was there to meet Buell and because it was hard for him to get around. Recently, Grant's horse had stumbled; he was thrown and sprained his ankle. It was as if the army's brain was separated from its body. If anything went wrong, he would be the last to know. Fortunately, the Shiloh camps were commanded by William Tecumseh Sherman, a talented officer.

On April 3, 1862, the Rebels set out from Corinth. Johnston's plan called for a rapid march, followed by an attack next morning. But instead of taking a day, the march lasted three days. It was misery every step of the way. On the first day, torrential rains turned the roads into swamps. Guns bogged down in mud, requiring a hundred men to pull each one free. Overloaded wagons tipped over, spilling their contents. Regiments, blinded by the rain, lost their way.

On the third day, they halted two miles from the Yankee lines. Although ordered to be quiet, the men did as they pleased. They beat drums, blew bugles, and lit fires. Soldiers shouted to one another and fired their muskets to see if they would go off after the rain. Nevertheless, luck was with them. Yankee pickets, hearing the racket, thought it came from their own camps. Besides, everyone knew the Rebels were at Corinth, so there was nothing to worry about at Shiloh. Nothing much!

That night, Rebel commanders held a war council. Beauregard was troubled. A logical man, he tried to put himself in Grant's boots. With all the noise being made, he reasoned, any chance of surprise was gone. Grant's failure to act was itself a dangerous sign, he thought. No doubt the Yankees were "entrenched to the eyes," waiting for them to come into the open. Better to retreat with the army intact than rush into a trap.

Johnston, however, was determined to fight. "Gentlemen," he said firmly, "we shall attack at daylight tomorrow." Turning away, he told an aide: "I would fight them if they were a million."[1]

His plan called for three lines of battle, one behind the other, to roll forward like human tidal waves. By sheer weight of numbers, they would break the enemy line and pour through the gaps.

Any units that stood their ground would be "flanked"; that is, Rebels would move around their sides to attack from behind. Those who did not surrender would be killed where they stood.

The Yankees ignored warning signs even as it became clear that the enemy was nearby. On April 4, after pickets shot at Rebels in a clearing near his camp, Sherman dismissed them as a scouting party from Corinth. On the morning of April 5, as Rebel forces arrived in strength, hundreds of deer bounded from the woods and ran through the Union camps. No one, apparently, knew what to make of these strange doings. Later, when a colonel reported an enemy buildup in the woods, Sherman did not investigate. Instead, he threw a temper tantrum for the colonel: "Take your damned regiment back to Ohio. There is no enemy nearer than Corinth."[2] His chief was no better. That evening, as Johnston issued his final orders, Grant telegraphed Halleck: "I have scarcely the faintest idea of an attack . . . being made upon us but will be prepared should such a thing take place."[3]

The Yankees slept soundly that night. It was a lovely night, clear and mild, a full moon lighting the sky. Already the peach trees were ablaze with pink blossoms. Tomorrow was Sunday, a day of rest even for soldiers.

Nighttime passed slowly for Johnston's troops. After filling their cartridge boxes and checking their muskets for the umpteenth time, there was nothing to do but wait until dawn. It was always that way in the army: hurry up and wait.

Soldiers prepared for battle in various ways. Some preferred to be alone. Going off by themselves, they knelt in prayer, or lay dozing with their heads on their knapsacks. Others wrote to loved ones, or stared into the darkness, thinking their private thoughts. Most sat huddled in small groups, talking the hours away. They talked of many things: home, girls, the thrill of seeing the elephant for the first time. Youngsters bragged about "whupping" the "damnyankees." Yet there were long silences when mouths went dry and hearts beat faster. No one uttered the forbidden word: fear. To feel fear, Civil War soldiers believed, was to be a coward. This being the case, soldiers kept their feelings bottled up inside. To share them with others was to admit to being "unmanly."

"I have a great anxiety to see and be in a great battle," a Rebel wrote in his diary.[4] Many of his comrades, too, had anxiety, but for another reason. As battle approached, they threw away their dice and playing cards. Soldiers on both sides liked to gamble in their spare time. They would bet on anything from how far a frog would jump to who could spit closer to a louse on a tin plate. Yet they were also superstitious. Since gambling was sinful, there was no telling what might happen if you carried gambling tools into battle. God knew all, and nobody wanted to provoke Him when bullets flew.

By 4:00 A.M., April 6, the Rebel lines were forming. Then, as the sun began to rise in the east, Johnston gave the attack signal. "Tonight," he told his staff, "we will water our horses in the Tennessee River."[5]

It was a lazy morning in the Union camps. At 6:30 A.M., troops were still taking it easy. Many were fast asleep, while others dressed and cooked breakfast. Suddenly, a dull rumbling was heard to the west. *Pum. Pum. Pum. Pum.* The sound grew louder as it came closer. Men rose to their feet, staring at one another with puzzled expressions. Moments later, pickets, some bleeding from wounds, ran by, yelling at the top of their voices. Rebels! The Rebels were coming!

Drummers rapped out the "long roll," the call to arms. "Get a move on!" sergeants bellowed. "Fall in! Form line! Hurry! Hurry! Hurry!" Soldiers spilled out of tents, hastily pulling on pants and buttoning shirts. Mess kits were tossed aside and coffee pots kicked over as men grabbed their muskets. Then Johnny Reb appeared.

Those who were there that morning carried the image for the rest of their lives. It was an unforgettable sight, at once thrilling and terrifying. Masses of gray-clad soldiers swept through the woods and across the fields. "The Rebels out there are thicker than fleas on a dog's back," a captain yelled, scarcely able to believe his eyes. Leading each regiment was a standard bearer with a Confederate battle flag, a blue cross with thirteen white stars on a bloodred field.

The Southerners came with a war cry on their lips: *"Yip-yip-yip-e-e-e-e-e-e-e! Yah-ah-ah-yah-e-e-e-e-e-e-e!"* Known as the Rebel yell, the high-pitched wail was designed to make men forget their own fear while striking terror into the enemy. And it did. Henry M. Stanley, later famous as an African explorer, was nineteen when he fought with the 6th Arkansas Infantry at Shiloh. The Rebel yell, he wrote in his autobiography, "drove all sanity . . . from among us. I rejoiced in shouting like the rest."[6] Union men swore there was nothing like it this side of hell. You didn't hear the yell so much as *feel* it as icy fingers moving down your spine.

The Yankees gave ground. Some units fell back in good order, fighting for every inch of ground. The majority, however, retreated helter-skelter. At one place, a fleeing mob was overtaken by a single cannon drawn by a team of horses. It was a Confederate cannon, and its crew was up to mischief. Suddenly the gunners stopped their horses, unlimbered their weapon, and poured canister into the oncoming men. They kept on loading and firing, while the Yankees continued to rush past on either side. There were enough of them, a Rebel noted, "to pick up the gun, carriage, caisson and horses and hurl them into the Tennessee," but no one tried to disable the gun.[7] It was every man for himself.

Thinking they had already won, Rebel soldiers made their first mistake. The abandoned camps were chock-full of good things just waiting to be taken. Hungry men sat down to finish half-eaten breakfasts. And drink; whiskey from the medical stores caused many cases of "tanglefoot," falling over one's own feet. Privates made off with officers' uniforms, swords, and belts. Men gawked at pictures of Yankee sweethearts, joking as they read their love letters aloud. It was such fun that hundreds simply left the battle.

Johnston was furious. "None of that, sir," he scolded a lieutenant loaded down with loot, "we are not here to plunder!" Then, seeing that he'd hurt the man's feelings, he picked up a tin cup and said, "Let this be my share of the spoils today." He used it thereafter instead of a sword to direct the battle. It was still in his hand when he was shot that afternoon.

Meantime, a messenger reached Sherman with news of the attack. Sherman brushed it aside as yet another skirmish with enemy scouts. "You must be badly scared over there," he said with a sneer.[8] But this time he went to investigate. Riding to the edge of a field, he pointed a telescope at the woods beyond. Just then Rebel troops burst from the treeline, killing a man at his side. This was no raiding party. "My God," Sherman cried, "we are attacked!"[9] Then he whirled around, spurred his horse, and sped away.

Sherman changed in those few seconds. Normally a very nervous person, he thrived on danger. Strange as it may seem, battle calmed him as nothing else could. The hotter things got, the cooler and more clearheaded he became.

Shiloh saw Sherman at his best. He seemed to be everywhere at once, giving orders and rallying his men. Bullets missed him by a hair, but he ignored them. One nicked his hand, another passed through his coat, a third through his hat. Three horses were shot from under him. He picked himself up, found another mount, and kept going. Afterward, men would say he had ice water, not blood, in his veins.

Grant was having breakfast at Savannah when he heard the rumble of artillery. "Gentlemen," he said, setting down his coffee cup, "the ball is in motion. Let us be off."[10] Before leaving, he sent a note to Buell ordering him to go straight to Pittsburg Landing. He then boarded a steamer and headed upriver, arriving at 9:00 A.M.

Grant limped ashore and was helped onto his horse; a crutch was tied to the saddle, since his ankle had swelled to twice its size. Moving inland, he saw splintered trees, their trunks shot to pieces. Deep furrows, plowed by solid shot, crisscrossed in all directions. Leaderless troops, their eyes glazed in terror, hurried toward the rear. Wagons full of supplies were being driven toward the river, while others were trying to bring supplies to the front. In the confusion, Grant's men did not recognize him. A colonel, cursing like a lunatic, would not let him pass until he identified himself. A lieutenant yelled, "Git out of the way there! Ain't you got no sense?"[11]

At last he reached the front. Calmly, without raising his voice, Grant began to set things straight. Before long, ammunition wagons were moving in the right direction and cavalry patrols blocked roads with orders to shoot deserters. Not satisfied with reports, he visited every divisional commander to see what was happening with his own eyes. Most of all, he encouraged his troops merely by showing himself and refusing to act like a loser. But in the end, after Grant had done his best, the battle was the troops' to win or lose. It always is.

There are two ways of viewing a battle. Seen through the commanding general's eyes, battle is a matter of maps and plans, decisions and orders, based on an ever-changing situation. For him, therefore, every battle is different from every other. Seen through the eyes of the common soldier, however, all battles are alike. Certain things, of course, can never be exactly the same. Armies take different positions; generals make different moves that have different results. Even so, the soldier's battle is always about the basics: courage and fear, life and death. Seen in this light, Shiloh may serve as a "model" Civil War battle. What happened there happened everywhere to a greater or lesser extent.

Battle was (and is) as far from everyday life as can be imagined. In addition to war cries and shouted orders, the air crackled with gunfire. Each weapon had its special sound. Minié balls screamed, whistled, and whined as they sped to their targets. Firing was so heavy at Shiloh that swarms of bullets could actually be seen flying overhead. A bullet struck flesh with a *thud,* followed by a scream and a "goddamn," if the victim still had a voice. Cannon set off shock waves that struck the ears like a hard fist. Shells flew with a high-pitched *eeeowww;* solid shot skipped along the ground with a *thump, thump, thump.* Weapon sounds were not heard singly, but blended into a hellish din. Thirty years later, Private Sam Watkins, 1st Tennessee Infantry, still heard the noises of Shiloh when he closed his eyes: "The fire opened—bang, bang, bang, a rattle de bang, bang, bang, a boom, de bang, bang, bang, boom, bang, boom, bang, boom, bang, boom, bang, boom, whirr-siz-siz-siz—a ripping, roaring, boom, bang! The air was full of balls and deadly missiles."[12] Others reported a continuous rumble, grumble, and roar.

Greenhorns reacted with shock and dismay. Battle was not the game they had imagined when they enlisted. Those fellows over there, who didn't know you from Adam, were doing their best to *kill* you. That was hard to accept, and it caused some weird behavior. One Yank at Shiloh broke ranks and hid behind a tree. A comrade, knowing a good thing when he saw it, ran up and stood behind him. Before long, forty men formed a line snaking back from the tree, each gripping the waist of the fellow ahead. Meantime, their captain had completely lost his mind. He paced back and forth along the line, waving his sword and jabbering nonsense.

You lost track of time during battle. As you took up the rhythm of the work, your actions became automatic. Time stood still. Your musket became master, a living being demanding that you pour "food" down its throat.

Load. Ready. Aim. Fire. Reload.

Your ears rang each time you pulled the trigger. Your shoulders turned black and blue from the musket's recoil. The "fog of battle," clouds of smoke and dust, rolled across the battlefield, shrouding it in a gray mist. You coughed and wheezed; your eyes stung and tears ran down your cheeks. Your appearance changed so much that your mother might not have recognized you. As you tore cartridges with your teeth, powder spilled on your face, forming black rings around your mouth. The burnt powder from your ramrod came off on your hands; and when you brushed the sweat from your face, you blackened it completely.

Sweat flowed from every pore of your body. Battle is hard physical work, causing sweat even in cold weather; soldiers lost as much as five pounds in a big fight. Sweating brought unquenchable thirst. "I could have drunk out of a mud puddle—without stopping to ask questions," a Yankee private recalled.[13] Occasionally, we read of men who became so desperate that they drank their own urine.

Errors were common in battle, especially in loading muskets. Amid the noise and confusion, you might forget to bite off the end of a cartridge or insert a fresh firing cap. As a result, nothing happened when you pulled the trigger. If you didn't notice this, you rammed down another bullet, then another. After every battle, officers picked up discarded muskets for examination. Thousands contained anywhere from two to twenty-three unfired bullets. Even with their weapons loaded properly, some men forgot to remove the ramrod, turning it into an arrow. At Shiloh, a Yank realized his error only when he saw the ramrod quivering in a Rebel's body.

There was no such thing as getting used to combat. Fear, the unspoken word, was real. Fear is part of being human, a way of preparing to face danger. It is so powerful an emotion that the ancient Greeks considered it divine. In Greek mythology, the gods Phobus (Fear) and Pan (Panic) haunted the battlefield, tormenting the bravest warriors. We still call any abnormal fear a "phobia."

Battle meant constant fear. Some times were worse than others, but fear never left entirely. Shortness of breath, a sinking feeling in the stomach, a violent pounding of the heart, vomiting— all were common symptoms. Fear might be so strong that it froze you to the spot, shaking and unable to move. At Shiloh, a Yankee private's hair stood up on his head like porcupine quills. Men urinated in their pants or lost control of their bowels, reactions as old as warfare itself. In the fifth century B.C., Greek historians noted that warriors' cloaks became wet and changed color in battle. The playwright Aristophanes called war "the terrible one, the tough one, the one upon the legs."

The soldier's worst fear might not be of wounds or even death. It was the fear of fear, of showing cowardice. A coward was a wretch who betrayed his comrades and shamed his loved ones. Civil War soldiers knew what was expected of them. As a Yankee wrote his wife: "If I was to turn back now, many would say I was a coward. I would rather be shot at once than have such a stigma rest on me." A Rebel agreed: "I may run, but if I do I wish that some of our own men would shoot me down."[14] Parents warned their sons to be careful, but also that death was better than dishonor. They must be brave, do their duty, and never be a "yellow-belly." Women demanded courage, since a coward could not be a faithful husband or a good father. For many soldiers, therefore, honor became more precious than life.

There were still plenty of cowards. At Shiloh, Grant found thousands of soldiers frantic with fear. Perhaps a quarter of his army—eight thousand men—huddled beneath the riverbank or tried to paddle across the Tennessee on driftwood. Even officers panicked. One was found inside a hollow log; he had crawled in all the way, and, hugging him for dear life, were two common soldiers. Grant had a dozen officers arrested for cowardice, noting "These men are necessarily my enemies."[15] The Rebels, too, had their share of cowards. Deserters shot at General William J. Hardee when he ordered them back into the firing line. Some avoided danger by playing sick, getting lost, or claiming their weapons were damaged. Sam Watkins recalled a man "stepping deliberately out of the ranks and shooting his finger off to keep out of the fight . . ."[16]

What is amazing is not the cowardice, but the courage displayed at Shiloh. After the initial shock wore off, men pulled themselves together and did their duty. The Civil War soldier may have been inexperienced, but he learned quickly and, once aroused, fought with incredible courage. Courage, however, is not fearlessness; it is being able to go on despite your fear.

Combat was unpredictable. Nearly everyone had close calls, and there was no clear reason why one man should survive while his comrades fell all around him. There were times when nothing a soldier did, or did not do, made a difference. Chance alone decided life and death.

Soldiers' letters and diaries have countless examples of close calls. At Shiloh, a Yank tripped and fell forward. Just then a bullet hit the ground next to his nose and came out near his foot, clipping his boot as it continued on its way. Another Yank had a tall Kentuckian in his sights and was about to pull the trigger when his brother knocked his musket aside. "Hold on, Bill," he cried, "that's Father!"[17] Father had no idea how close he'd come to death. A comrade, taking cover behind a log, had a shell explode on top of him. All that remained was his musket and some bloody bits of cloth.

Weapons did not kill only the enemy. "Friendly fire"—being hit by your own side—is normal in combat. Roman legionnaires, fighting hand to hand, mistakenly killed friends with sword and spear. At Germantown in 1777, George Washington attacked the British in a thick fog. As one column advanced, a second column arrived and, taking the first for the enemy, opened fire, killing several Americans. At Shiloh, the Orleans Guard Battalion still had its prewar blue uniforms and was badly shot up by fellow Rebels. When the group returned the fire, it was told that it was shooting friends. "I know it!" cried the colonel. "But, dammit, sir, we fire on anybody who fires on us!"[18] In Vietnam a century later, American helicopters rocketed and machine-gunned their own ground troops.

Death came as a shock to greenhorns. Moments before, a comrade was alive and well. Then, in the blinking of an eye, he lay on the ground silent, motionless, mangled. That scene burned itself into memory. "I shall never forget how awful it felt on seeing for the first time a man killed in battle," a Yank recalled. "I stared at his body, perfectly horrified!"[19]

Men reacted differently to the emotional experience of death. Seeing comrades killed drove some into a frenzy. They wanted revenge, to do to the enemy what he had done to their friends. "I could have tore the heart out of the rebal [rifleman] could I have reached him," a Yank admitted.[20] Still others turned away and cried. Crying was not a sign of weakness, but a healthy way of dealing with stress. Soldiers also tried to deny death by avoiding the word altogether. Billy Yank and Johnny Reb never died; they "went to mother," "went to their last sleep," or were "gobbled."

During his inspection, Grant saw that the Confederates were forcing his army backward all along the line. If they broke through the center, the army would be split in half and each piece destroyed separately. But if the center held, he might carry out an orderly retreat, form a second line near the river, and wait for Buell.

Grant visited the center and ordered its commander, Major General Benjamin M. Prentiss, to "hold on at all hazards." If any position could be held, this was it. Prentiss occupied an old wagon road that had been worn into the earth by years of use. Though shallow, it formed a natural trench with dense underbrush on either side. Using this for protection, his men put up a fierce fight. Rebels said they fought like angry hornets; hence their position was named the Hornets' Nest.

Johnston's men charged the Hornets' Nest twelve times without success. Each time the Yankees crouched low, waiting to

strike. It was like Bunker Hill eighty-seven years before, with the Rebels playing the part of the Redcoats. "Boys, lay low," officers shouted. "Don't fire a gun until you see the whites of their eyes— then rise and give 'em hell!"[21]

Hell it was. As the Rebels drew near, they leaped up and fired. The Rebel lines rippled from end to end as bullets and canister tore through them. Soldiers fell in batches, one on top of another or in neat rows, as if on parade. Bodies lay in piles. They lay in weird poses, some headless, others cut in two with their guts spilling onto the ground. "Eyes [have never] rested on such a scene of human slaughter," noted Captain Andrew Hickenlooper, 5th Ohio Artillery. He was exaggerating, but not by much.[22]

A peach orchard lay close to the Hornets' Nest. Its trees were in full bloom, and whenever cannon fired, the shock waves sent petals fluttering down like pink confetti. Try as they might, the Rebels could not budge the Yankees. Johnston, however, would not accept failure. He rode among the shaken troops on his horse, Fire-eater. "Men, they are stubborn," he cried, touching their bayonets with his tin cup. "We must use the bayonet." Suddenly he turned and shouted, "I will lead you!"[23]

Giving the Rebel yell, they raced toward the peach orchard. They passed over ground littered with dead, dying, and wounded. Ignoring calls for help, they kept going until they took the position

An artist's conception of the "Hornet's Nest" at Shiloh. Union forces held the position for hours, delaying the Confederate advance and allowing Grant to regroup, until overwhelmed by enemy artillery fire.

at the point of the bayonet. Johnston rode back smiling, his clothes torn by bullets and the sole of a boot hanging by a thread. He flapped it about, laughing: "They didn't trip me that time!" The words had scarcely left his mouth when he slumped in the saddle. A bullet had cut an artery in his leg and he bled to death within minutes.

General Beauregard took command immediately. Determined to crush the Hornets' Nest, he massed sixty-two guns and unleashed a bombardment. The effect was devastating. Human bodies and clods of earth flew into the air. Chunks of flesh hung from tree limbs, dripping blood on those below. The defenders hugged the ground. A Yankee captain noted how "the shell and shot passed over us terrifically at about the height of a man's head from the ground while [lying] down . . . continued so long that it was a relief when the Rebels began to advance upon us."[24] The gunners had to cease fire for fear of killing their own men.

Confederate General Pierre Gustave Toutant Beauregard, "The Hero of Fort Sumter," took over command at the Hornets' Nest.

The advancing Confederates swung to the right and left, flanking the position. Those who saw them coming escaped moments before the trap closed. Most, however, were caught in the Hornets' Nest. At 5:30 P.M., Prentiss surrendered with 2,320 officers and men. It was the largest capture made by the Rebels in the Civil War. But it came too late.

The capture of the Hornets' Nest was no Southern victory. Acting on Grant's orders, Prentiss had stalled the enemy for seven hours, putting hundreds of troops out of action in the process. That delay bought time for Grant to build a defense line two miles to the rear. Units were reorganized and sent to new positions. Scores of cannon were assembled on a hill near Pittsburg Landing. The gunboats *Tyler* and *Lexington* anchored offshore and were cleared for action.

It was the Rebels' turn to face massed artillery. Advancing regiments met a line of cannon standing wheel to wheel. Grant's guns exploded with a hail of canister, grape, and solid shot. The noise, however, was drowned by the roar of naval guns hurling

thirty-two-pound shells. These burst overhead, showering the attackers with chunks of hot iron.

Yankees stationed near the guns also suffered. Each barrage
set off powerful shock waves. "Guns pounded away," a private
recalled. "The sensation at every shot was that of being lifted two
feet and slammed down with a good healthy whack."[25] Men bled
from their noses and ears; several had permanent damage to their
hearing.

At 5:00 P.M., Buell's Yankee advance units began crossing the
Tennessee River aboard steamers. Led by Brigadier General William "Bull" Nelson, a three-hundred-pound giant, they were eager
for action. "You have seen the elephant often, we want to see him
once, anyhow," his men called to Grant's troops.[26] Grant's men
waved them forward with a cheer. They had already seen the
elephant and knew what awaited the newcomers.

Nelson's men had much to learn. As they neared the front, two
of his aides, Captains Fisher and Carson, saw a cannonball flying
toward them. Fisher ducked. Carson didn't. "I heard a thud and
some dark object whizzed over my shoulder," Fisher reported. "It
was Captain Carson's head."[27] Those nearby swallowed hard; they
had already seen enough of the elephant.

Beauregard, meantime, was unaware of Grant's growing
strength. He only knew that it was getting dark and his army was
worn out after so many hours of fighting. At 6 P.M., he ordered a
ceasefire and withdrew to the Union camps to rest his men, taking
Sherman's tent for himself. Grant was so shaken, he believed, that
he could easily finish him off in the morning. That night, as the
rest of Buell's army crossed the river, he wired Jefferson Davis to
announce a magnificent victory, "thanks be to the Almighty."

It was after midnight when Sherman found Grant standing
under an oak tree, a lantern in his hand, a cigar clenched between
his teeth. It was raining, and his ankle throbbed.

"Well, Grant," he said, "we've had the devil's own day, haven't
we?"

"Yes," Grant replied, puffing away. "Yes. Lick 'em tomorrow,
though."[28]

The rain was falling harder when they said good-night. Spattered with mud, water running in streams from his hat and coat,
Grant took shelter in a log cabin nearby. He lay down on the floor,
trying to get some sleep, only to be wakened by screams. Army

surgeons had taken over the cabin and were operating on the wounded. Squeamish as ever, he found the sight "unendurable" and returned to his tree. He sat under its dripping branches, his coat collar pulled up around his ears, till dawn.

The night of April 6–7 was an ordeal for everyone. Though they were exhausted, few slept soundly. The rain, which had begun as a drizzle, became a violent thunderstorm. Lashed by cold winds, both armies were drenched. The Yankees were forced to lie on the wet ground. Some stuck their bayonets into the ground, leaned their chins on the rifle butts, and slept standing up.

The Rebels were better off, but not much. They crowded into the captured tents, sharing blankets as a way of sharing body warmth. One soldier, however, noticed that his companion lay still and was cold—very cold—but was too tired to pay attention until morning. He awoke to find that he had slept huddled against a dead Yankee. Many a youngster, having seen more than a youngster should in one day, awoke screaming from a nightmare.

Those out on patrol had wide-awake nightmares. Wherever they turned, they saw scenes of horror. Flashes of lightning lit up the battlefield, revealing blasted trees, smashed wagons, and overturned cannon. The ground was thick with the dead, making it impossible to avoid stepping on human flesh. Hogs from local farms rooted among bodies, eating arms and legs. Blood was spattered everywhere, forming puddles in the folds of the ground. Confederate W. G. Stevenson came to a small gully while on an errand. Suddenly his horse stopped and refused to go forward. Looking down, he saw the reason: the rain had washed leaves down the channel, exposing its clay floor and opening a pathway six inches wide. "Down this pathway ran a band of blood nearly an inch thick, filling the channel."[29] There were so many dead that their blood had mingled, forming a moving stream. The place of peace had become the place of death.

For the wounded, however, the battle was only just beginning. Today's soldier carries a first-aid kit of bandages, painkillers, and antibiotics. His Civil War ancestor had no first-aid kits, no first-aid training, and no corpsmen to give first aid. The walking wounded made their way to field hospitals on their own. The seriously wounded waited until the army got around to them. During the first night at Shiloh, hundreds of wounded dragged themselves to a pond near the peach orchard. Here enemies discovered their common humanity. Men of both armies lay side by side, quenching their thirst and helping each other bathe their wounds. And here

most died, also side by side. Their blood so colored the water that it is still called "Bloody Pond."

At Shiloh, nine-tenths of the wounded lay where they fell, unattended, for forty-eight hours. The survivors were packed into ambulances—small, springless wagons. Every bump on the uneven ground was torture as the wounded bounced up and down on the rough floorboards. "My God! Why can't I die?" men cried. "My God! Will no one have mercy and kill me?"[30]

Mercy killings occur in all wars. At Cannae in 216 B.C., the Carthaginians destroyed a Roman army in one of history's greatest battles. The Roman wounded, we are told, bared their throats and begged "who would to spill what little blood they had left."[31] In Vietnam two thousand years later, some wounded Americans, who could not be saved, were given overdoses of painkiller to end their misery. This was not considered murder (by the troops), but an act of kindness. We have no reason to believe it was different during the Civil War. Soldiers' letters tell of wounded men asking to be killed. Although the writers say they refused, one confessed it was only because "too many were looking."[32]

A field hospital was anything with a roof: tent, barn, private

A Union ambulance team demonstrates how wounded men are removed from the battlefield. The soldiers pictured here were known as Zouaves. Instead of the standard blue uniform, Zouaves wore colorful red outfits modeled on those of the Turkish army.

home, church, school. The wounded lay outside on stretchers or
on the bare ground, waiting their turn. If blankets were available,
they were covered. If not, they shivered from shock and loss of
blood; blood transfusions were unknown during the Civil War.
Soldiers feared hospitals no less than enemy bullets. Yankees
wrote home about those "infernal hells called hospitals," telling
how "I would rather risk a battle than the Hospitals." Rebels
agreed. "If a man Lives he Lives and if he Dies he dies. A Dog is
thought of more . . . than A Solger is hear," one wrote from a
hospital.[33]

Civil War weapons caused wounds as serious as any in the
twentieth century. Even doctors were amazed at their effects. Dr.
J. R. Weist, who served with an Ohio regiment, described a typical
day in a field hospital:

> Wounded men were lying everywhere. What a horrible sight
> they present! Here the bones of a leg or an arm have been
> shattered like glass by a minnie ball. Here a great hole has
> been torn into an abdomen by a grape shot. Nearby see that
> blood and froth covering the chest of one choking with blood
> from a wound of the lungs. By his side lies this beardless boy
> with his right leg remaining attached to his body only by a
> few shreds of blackened flesh. This one's lower jaw has been
> entirely carried away; fragments of shell have done this cruel
> work. Over yonder lies an old man, oblivious to all his sur-
> roundings, his grizzly hair matted with brain and blood slowly
> oozing from a great gaping wound in his head. Here is a
> bayonet wound; there a slash from a saber. Here is one bruised
> and mangled until the semblance of humanity is almost
> lost. . . . This one has been crushed by the wheel of a passing
> cannon. . . . Here are others whose quivering flesh contains
> balls, jagged fragments of shell, [and] pieces of iron. . . . The
> faces of some are black with powder; others are blanched from
> loss of blood, or covered with the sweat of death. All are
> parched with thirst, and many suffer horrible pain. . . .[34]

Doctors made their rounds, deciding which wounds to treat and
which to ignore. Deep wounds to the chest and stomach were always fatal; the best they could do was to make the patient as
comfortable as possible until death ended his agony. Those with
treatable wounds were put on an operating table, merely a kitchen
table or boards laid across cracker boxes. The surgeons looked like

butchers with their sleeves rolled up to their elbows and their aprons smeared with blood.

Flesh wounds were sewn up and the patient returned to duty. Those who were hit squarely, however, were in big trouble. A musket did not make a nice, neat wound; its soft lead bullet smashed bones and tore away muscles. For an arm or leg wound, there was only one remedy: cut it off. Surgeons deserved the nickname "sawbones," not because they liked amputating, but because they had no other choice. More limbs were removed during the Civil War than at any other time in American history. Surgeons worked around the clock, numb with fatigue, until they passed out. These men were haunted by their war experiences. S. Weir Mitchell, one of the finest physicians of the time, never got the Civil War out of his mind. As he lay dying in 1913, he kept mumbling: "That leg must come off—save a leg—lose a life."[35]

Ether and chloroform, unknown in past wars, put the patient to sleep. But if these were in short supply, the surgeon did without and his helpers made the wounded man "bite the bullet"; that is, they put a bullet or a wooden wedge between his teeth to keep him from biting off his tongue. Then they held him down as the surgeon went to work. Amputated limbs were tossed aside to await

Union wounded at Fredericksburg, Virginia, in May 1864. The woman sitting in the doorway is one of the hundreds of nurses who traveled with the Army of the Potomac.

burial. At Pittsburg Landing, a pile of arms and legs three feet high stood outside the door of the log-cabin hospital.

A successful operation did not bring an end to suffering. Upon awakening, the soldier was racked with pain. In one respect, he was better off than those in previous wars: pain could be controlled to a certain extent. The treatment, however, brought its own problems. Drugs made from the opium poppy were the only painkillers known during the Civil War. Opium pills were taken with water; morphine, a liquid made from opium, was injected. Both are powerful narcotics. As a result, soldiers became addicted; indeed, drug addiction used to be called "the army disease." Most men forced their bodies to become drug-free after a few weeks of stomach cramps and cold sweats. Yet there were others who became hooked for life.

Most physicians had never heard of germs, and few knew that they cause infection. Thus, they saw no need for cleanliness. Wounds were washed with sponges to give a better view, but the sponges themselves were not washed for days, and then in dirty water. Surgeons did not use rubber gloves, for they did not exist, nor did antiseptics and antibiotics. A surgeon cleaned his hands *after* an operation, not before; and if an instrument fell on the ground, he wiped it on his apron and kept working. Surgical knives might be sharpened on the sole of a boot and used, unwashed, on one patient after another. Bandages could be anything from bed sheets torn into strips to shirts, tablecloths, and rags from the ragbag. Bloodstained bandages, even those taken from the dead, were reused.

Under these conditions, it was impossible to escape infection. Doctors expected wounds to produce pus; they thought it part of healing, hence the name "laudable pus." A cloth bag filled with earth was used to wipe the pus away. For the wounded, therefore, it was always the survival of the fittest. If you were strong, your body fought off infection and you survived. If not, you died. It was that simple.

General Beauregard went to bed without taking proper steps to reorganize his army. That was an error, because thousands of men had become separated from their units during the day. They returned to the captured camps thirsty and hungry. Without officers, they went on a rampage, finishing what their comrades had begun earlier. Men sat in the mud, stuffing themselves with Yankee rations. Others took whatever they could carry and headed home.

Beauregard also failed to learn what the Yankees were doing. It was his own fault. The information was available; all he had to do was listen to his cavalry chief, Colonel Nathan Bedford Forrest. A born horseman, Southerners called Forrest the "Wizard of the Saddle"; Sherman dubbed him "that devil Forrest." Perhaps the best cavalry leader of the war, Forrest was utterly fearless; he often wept from excitement in battle. He also believed in keeping close watch on the enemy and then doing the unexpected.

Forrest sent patrols through the Union lines. Dressed in captured blue overcoats, they rode to the bluffs above Pittsburg Landing. There, through swirling mist and rain, they saw Buell's troops coming ashore.

Forrest could not pass this vital information to Beauregard, who had gone to bed without informing his staff of his whereabouts. After a futile search, the cavalryman reported to two corps commanders. The Confederates, he insisted, must attack at once or retreat to avoid fighting a superior enemy. If they waited till morning to fight, they would be "whipped like hell." The generals thanked him for the information and told him to keep up the good work. No action was taken.

Daybreak, Monday, April 7, 1862. Grant awoke under the oak tree and gave his orders. He now had seven divisions, forty-five thousand soldiers, half of them fresh. Thousands of deserters, having found their courage, were returning to duty as well. Their mission was simple: Go forward, overpower the Rebels, and regain their camps. Beauregard had about twenty thousand men to stop an avalanche.

The Yankees crossed the same ground they had fought over the previous day. It was heartbreaking. Sixteen-year-old John A. Cockerill saw a dead Rebel about his own age, with golden curls and delicate hands. "At the sight of the poor boy's corpse, I burst into a regular boo-hoo," he wrote his parents.[36] Groans and cries arose as the lines of battle passed. "O God, have mercy! O God, O God!" a wounded Yankee kept repeating. A Union captain found a Rebel covered with clotted blood from head to toe; he had spent the night with his head pillowed on the body of a mutilated comrade. "O God!" he moaned. "What made you come down here to fight us? We never would have come up there."[37]

The Confederates fought bravely, desperately, hopelessly. Grant's army was too strong; at best it could be checked only briefly. Rather than risk total disaster, Beauregard ordered a retreat. His army—what remained of it—headed back to Corinth.

To cover their retreat, the Rebels burned the Union camps, covering the area with a pall of smoke. That night the rain returned with a vengeance. It fell for hours, causing streams to overflow and creating knee-deep mud. About midnight, it turned to sleet. Hailstones the size of robins' eggs crashed to earth. Exhausted men sat down to rest for a moment, awakening hours later in icy pools of water. The wounded suffered as never before. A Tennessee soldier wrote from Corinth: "Every house between here and the battlefield is a hospital, and the whole road is lined with wagons freighted with dead and wounded."[38] During the following weeks, as many Rebels died in Corinth of disease as had fallen at "Bloody Shiloh."

Grant did not pursue. The roads were almost impassable, and there was no point in getting bogged down. Besides, his men were in no condition to go further. So long as the battle raged, the excitement kept them going. But as the action slowed, exhaustion took over. They were too tired, both physically and emotionally, to continue.

Four brigades did push ahead, not to fight, but to make sure that the Confederates had left the area. At one point they met the enemy's rear guard, 350 cavalrymen under Nathan Bedford Forrest.

Forrest led his men in a charge that broke through a forward unit. It was magnificent, exhilarating, and he wanted more. "Charge! Charge!" he cried, waving his sword. But his men, seeing more Yankees coming, backed off. Without realizing it, he galloped ahead alone, one against hundreds.

He rode smack into the enemy ranks. Forrest's men, watching from a ridge, were dumbfounded. During the next few minutes, he became their hero. As Yankee infantrymen swarmed around him, he slashed at their heads with his sword. A soldier put a musket to his side and pulled the trigger; the blast lifted him from the saddle and a bullet lodged against his spine. Despite the wound, Forrest wheeled about, reached down, and grabbed a Yankee by the collar. Then, with a mighty heave, he lifted the man up on the horse's rump as a shield. Reaching safety, he threw him off and sped away. So ended the Battle of Shiloh.

There is a saying: "To the victor goes the spoils." That may be true in politics, but not in war. The only spoils (loot) for the victors of Shiloh was the work of the undertaker. To the Union troops fell the duty of burying the dead, theirs as well as the enemy's. Always unpleasant work, it became downright revolting when the weather

Nicknamed the "Wizard of the Saddle," Confederate General Nathan Bedford Forrest was one of the most daring cavalry commanders in the Civil War, if not in the entire history of warfare. After the war, he headed the Ku Klux Klan, an organization that terrorized blacks and prevented them from gaining equal rights.

turned warm on April 8. Bodies swelled to twice their normal size, turned green, then black, and gave off a sickening smell of decay. The smell hung in the air and got into everything; soldiers even tasted it in their food.

Shiloh's dead were not buried in individual graves; there were too many of them for that. For Grant's dead, long trenches were dug and the bodies laid side by side and head to feet, to save space; Confederates were stacked in layers two to seven deep. No dog tags or other means of identification were issued to Civil War soldiers. Those who could be identified by comrades had their names written on wooden stakes driven into the ground. Most, however, remain nameless. In some Civil War cemeteries, three-quarters of the graves are marked "Unknown."

Shiloh was a growing-up experience for the survivors. They learned the lesson that every generation learns anew: war is about death, not glory. Seeing the elephant was not thrilling or glamorous. It was dirty and ugly. They came to realize that to fight *in* a "glorious" cause does not mean that the fight itself *is* glorious.

Grant was horrified by his victory. Sherman told his wife that "the scenes of this field would have cured anybody of war."[39] Private Sam Watkins spoke for the common soldier, North and South. Glory, he said, was a glittering lie: "[W]e soon found out that the glory of war was at home among the ladies and not upon the field of blood and carnage . . . where our comrades were mutilated and torn by shot and shell. And to see the cheek blanch and to hear the fervent prayer, aye, I might say the agony of mind were very different indeed from the patriotic times at home." Thus the boys of 1861 become the veterans of 1862.[40]

Shiloh was America's worst bloodbath to date. In killed, wounded, captured, and missing, the Union lost 13,047 men to the Confederacy's 10,694. These figures are higher than the total of American deaths from all causes in all the nation's previous wars.[41]

This battle was a turning point in the Civil War. Militarily, the Mississippi Valley was opened to invasion. What is more, both sides learned some harsh truths on its killing grounds. For Southerners, it exploded the myth that one Rebel could whip any number of Yankees. It was now clear that Southern independence, if it came at all, would demand greater sacrifice than anyone had imagined at the time of Fort Sumter.

Grant, like most of his countrymen, had believed the rebellion would quickly collapse. Shiloh proved him wrong. From then on, he recalled, "I gave up all idea of saving the Union except by complete conquest."[42]

IV ✧ VICKSBURG

See what a lot of land these fellows hold, of which Vicksburg is the key. . . . Let us get Vicksburg and all that country is ours. The war can never be brought to a close until that key is in our pocket.

—Abraham Lincoln, 1863

If Grant expected thanks for winning at Shiloh, he was wrong. Once the smoke of battle cleared, he more than anyone was blamed for the slaughter. In letters home, soldiers cursed his "imbecile character," "blundering stupidity," and "criminal carelessness" in letting himself be surprised. Newspapers called him "Ulysses *Surprise* Grant." Nonetheless, President Lincoln had the last word. As he told a politician who demanded Grant's dismissal: "I can't spare this man: he fights."

General Halleck thought he *could* spare him. Four days after the battle, he arrived from St. Louis to take charge in person. Grant became second in command, a polite way of pushing him aside. Whenever Halleck issued orders, he had others pass them along the chain of command. No one asked Grant's advice, nor did he have any real duties. He spent his time smoking cigars, reading newspapers, and making small talk with his staff. He hated every minute of it.

Meantime, the war continued. Grant had wanted to move on Corinth without delay. Halleck feared doing anything in haste. Advancing with the speed of a snail, he took six weeks to go from Pittsburg Landing to Corinth—less than a mile a day. The army, which had grown to 120,000 men, would set out at daybreak. But

75

before anyone had raised a sweat, Halleck ordered a halt to dig trenches. By the time he reached Corinth on May 30, Beauregard was gone. The only war "prizes" he took were a few Confederates too ill to be moved and some "Quaker cannon," dummy guns made of logs painted black.

Deeply discouraged, Grant asked for a thirty-day leave to think about transferring to another area or resigning from the army altogether. When Sherman learned of the request, he asked why. "Sherman, you know," Grant replied. "You know that I am in the way here. I have stood it as long as I can, and can endure it no longer."[1] Sherman, however, would not accept this explanation. He pointed out that if Grant left, the war would go on anyhow, and he would be forgotten. But if he stayed, "some happy accident" might change things for the better. Grant thanked his friend, promising not to leave without telling him first.

The "happy accident" came on cue. Early in July 1862 Halleck became general-in-chief of all Union armies and moved to Washington. Grant took over the Army of the Tennessee, all

Grant and his family at City Point. A devoted father and husband, whenever possible he tried to have Julia and at least one of their children with him.

Union forces between the Tennessee and Mississippi rivers, with headquarters at Corinth. Lincoln and Sherman, each acting without the other's knowledge, had saved him for the sake of the nation.

Grant sent for his wife and children at once. Ever the family man, he could not bear to be apart from them, even in wartime. First at Cairo, then at Corinth and a dozen other places, they joined him whenever the army was not in motion. Without Julia, he was careless about his health; a meal might be little more than pickles and cake, combined with cream, vinegar, and lettuce! She made sure he ate real food. Most of all, he needed her companionship. Every evening they would find a quiet place and sit silently holding hands. If an aide accidentally intruded, they would look as bashful as two teenagers caught necking.

Julia had no fear of taking the children into a war zone. Being with the army, she told her father-in-law, was good for them and Ulysses. Old Jesse grumbled, but Julia was a strong-minded person, and there was no arguing once she had made up her mind. The children went along.

An old campaigner at twelve, Fred strutted about with a sword attached to his belt. He and Ulysses, Jr., would wrestle their father, tripping him up and rolling with him on the office floor. Nellie and Jesse, the youngest, would hang onto his neck while he was writing and scatter his papers. Yet if Papa told them to behave, they obeyed at once. The soldiers, many with children of their own, adored them. Battle-hardened veterans watched their language around Grant's "young 'uns."

Julia's three slaves were another matter. While the family lived in Illinois, she had to do without them. But Mississippi was a slave state, and she had a legal right to bring her property to Corinth. Black Julia, however, soon ran away. The general was delighted. He refused to search for her, saying he wished the others would follow her example. It is not known if they did. He never spoke of them for the record, nor did they come forward to speak for themselves. It would be interesting to know what they thought of their mistress.

Grant had many responsibilities. Militarily, he had to prepare for the next campaign. He was also responsible for civilian affairs, particularly the illegal cotton trade. A Union naval blockade of Southern ports had left the South with a fortune in unsold cotton. Purchased at ten cents a pound in Tennessee, it could bring eighty cents in Boston. Since the Union needed cotton for its own textile industry, a limited number of traders were allowed to buy it legally. Most simply smuggled it across the lines.

Jewish traders were among the lawbreakers. Although a tiny minority, Grant singled them out for special treatment. He issued an order condemning "the Jews as a class" and expelling them from his area within twenty-four hours. This bigoted act aroused a storm of protest in the North. An astonished Lincoln canceled the order, explaining it was wrong to punish an entire group for the sins of a few. Once again the president showed himself a true statesman. By saving Grant from his own stupidity, he allowed him to look down the Mississippi River toward the greatest challenge of his career.

Gaining control of the Mississippi was a key Union objective. The "Father of Waters" linked the Confederacy's western areas to those in the east. The area west of the Mississippi included Texas, Arkansas, and part of Louisiana and made up half the Rebels' territory. Texas, with its long Mexican border, was the South's gateway to the world. Foreign merchants landed war supplies in Mexico. From there they were taken overland, across the Mississippi, to the Rebel armies. Losing control of the river, therefore, would split the Confederacy in half and cut a vital supply line. It would also create a second front in the Confederate rear. So far Virginia had been the main scene of action, with the Rebels more than holding their own. But the Confederacy could not win a two-front war. Pressed eastward from the Mississippi and westward from Virginia, they would be crushed as if between gigantic millstones.

Late in April 1862, with burial details still busy at Shiloh, a naval squadron led by Admiral David Glasgow Farragut captured New Orleans at the mouth of the Mississippi. Sailing upstream, he then took Baton Rouge, the Louisiana state capital. This gave the Union control of the entire river, except for a 250-mile stretch between Port Hudson, Louisiana, and Vicksburg, Mississippi. Port Hudson, though well defended, could not hold out against a determined assault. Vicksburg was something else.

Founded in 1814 by Newet Vick, a preacher turned merchant, Vicksburg had a population of five thousand at the start of the Civil War. A natural fortress, it stood on a high bluff on the eastern side of a hairpin curve in the river.[2] The bluff bristled with artillery. Heavy guns at the top commanded the channel for miles in either direction; more guns were placed midway to the top and along the water's edge. Thus, any ship trying to pass would face a "layered" defense. If it were fast enough, and lucky enough, a ship might get through at night. But if it were too slow, or its engine broke down, even the strongest ironclad would be blown to bits. It was suicide for wooden transports to challenge the guns. Even if troops could land safely, they would be trapped between the bluff and the river. The defenders could then easily pick them off from above.

Vicksburg's land-side defenses were equally impressive. Steep, rugged hills guarded its northern approaches. Further north lay the Yazoo Delta, a maze of swamps, woods, and muddy creeks called bayous. More swamps lay to the south of the city, and more hills to the east. Jefferson Davis had reason to call Vicksburg "the Gibraltar of America." Like the British fortress in Spain, it seemed impregnable.

Grant faced two main problems. First, he must put a large army—and its supplies—on the same side of the river as the Rebels. Second, he must defeat them and take their city. It was the most difficult assignment ever faced by a Civil War general. He would find the solution only after months of trial and error.

He began by setting up two supply bases in Tennessee. One base, at Grand Junction, was under his command; the other, at Memphis, on the Mississippi, was commanded by Sherman. Grant planned to attack through central Mississippi, not to take Vicksburg, but to draw away large numbers of its defenders. Meantime, Sherman would sail down the river and march in by way of the northern hills. It was a good plan—on paper. But like so many other good plans, it ran into unforeseen difficulties.

Grant was deep in Rebel territory when Nathan Bedford Forrest led twenty-five hundred horsemen through western Tennessee. Wherever the "devil" passed, he left smoking bridges, torn-up railroad track, and cut telegraph wire. Another force under Earl Van Dorn struck Grant's supply base at Holly Springs, Mississippi. Everything of military value—ammunition dumps, provisions, railroad trains—went up in flames. Had he attacked a day sooner, he would have taken Julia Grant, who had just passed through. In any case, Grant lost his supplies and was forced to return to Grand Junction. But because he also lost his telegraph line, there was no way to cancel the rest of the plan. Sherman attacked on December 29, only to find the Rebels ready and waiting. His report said it all: "I reached Vicksburg at the time appointed, landed, assaulted, and failed."[3]

To avoid sailing in front of the gun batteries defending Vicksburg, Grant has runaway slaves dig a bypass on a peninsula opposite the city. The plan failed when the Mississippi flooded the half-completed ditch.

Grant tried again. Late in January 1863, he landed forty-five thousand men on the western side of the Mississippi. Vicksburg was located on a hairpin curve in the river that formed a narrow peninsula pointing toward the northeast. Army engineers began to dig a canal across the base of the peninsula to allow ships to bypass the city. But the Father of Waters was not very cooperative. Early in March, a sudden rise in the water level ruined the engineers' work. The project had to be abandoned.

The navy thought it had a better idea. Spring rains had flooded the Yazoo Delta, exposing Vicksburg to an "amphibious" attack from the north. Grant gave the idea his blessing, and eleven gunboats set out on March 14, followed by transports carrying a division of Sherman's troops.

Steaming through Steele's Bayou, the fleet moved easily, apparently undetected. Gradually, however, the channel narrowed,

leaving little room between the ships and the shore. Ironclads struck low-hanging tree limbs, toppling smokestacks and smashing deck gear. Admiral David Dixon Porter, the expedition leader, was astonished at the wildlife that fell from above. The moment a vessel struck a tree, swarms of rats, raccoons, snakes, and lizards were shaken onto the decks. Sailors had to be posted with brooms to sweep them overboard.

By the third day, rudders became fouled in submerged roots and vines. Ships were immobilized until crewmen, standing up to their necks in muck, cut them loose, only to be stuck again minutes later. Finding it impossible to move forward, Porter had to return to the Mississippi. But since the channel was too narrow to turn around, he ordered the ships to back out. They were moving slowly when the sound of axes and falling trees echoed through the woods. Rebel work parties were sealing the escape route!

The army became the navy's only hope. Unless troops arrived soon, Rebel infantry would close in, forcing the warships to surrender. Porter scribbled a message: "Dear Sherman: Hurry up, for Heaven's sake. I never knew how helpless an ironclad could be steaming around through the woods without an army to back her."[4]

Union steamboats land troops and supplies for an attack through the swamps north of Vicksburg. After repeated failures, Grant crossed the Mississippi south of the city, cutting it off and forcing it to surrender. His victory split the Confederacy in half and gave the Union control of the entire length of "The Father of Waters."

The message was given to an escaped slave, who delivered it for fifty cents.

Sherman's troops made a night march with candles in their hands. They arrived at daybreak, wet, tired, and angry. And just in time to drive off the Confederates. The sailors—"Jack-tars"—heard plenty of catcalls on the way back:

"Hello, Jack, how do you like playing mud turtle?"

"Where's all your sails and masts, Jack?"

The Jacks were not amused.

By late March, Grant had formed another plan, his masterpiece. Porter would run his ships past the batteries while the troops marched down the west bank to meet them below the city. They would then be ferried across, land at a point beyond the swamps, and come up on Vicksburg from the rear.

His commanders thought the plan suicidal and told him so. Porter noted that the clumsy ironclads could make only one trip; if they tried to go back upstream, the swift current would slow them down, making them perfect targets for Rebel guns. Sherman worried that, once across the river, the army would be cut off from its supply base, violating a basic rule of warfare. Grant, however, believed that great risks must be taken to win great victories. The operation would go ahead as planned.

Porter gathered a fleet of eight ironclads and three transports filled with supplies. Each ironclad had a coal barge lashed to its port (left) side for added protection, but low enough to give its guns a clear field of fire. The wooden transports had bales of wet cotton stacked around their boilers. Departure was set for 10 P.M., April 16, 1863. The ships would move in single file, slowly and without lights, carried along by the current. They would go to full speed only if discovered by the enemy.

Vicksburg felt secure behind its defenses. A ball was to be held that night in a house atop the bluff. All the belles would be there, dressed in their elegant gowns. They expected to dance the night away, safe in the arms of dashing officers in gray.

Grant's headquarters ship rode at anchor in midstream, out of range of the Rebel guns. It was not there to take part in the action, but to give spectators a clear view. Army and navy officers crowded the deck, eager for the "show" to begin. He and Julia stood silently, hand in hand, at the ship's rail. Their children stood nearby; all, that is, except little Jesse, who sat on a colonel's lap. History was about to be made, and their parents wanted them to be able to tell their own children about it.

For a long time all they could make out were lights twinkling on the Vicksburg bluffs. Looking upstream, they saw only darkness. Slowly, a shapeless mass, blacker than the night itself, slid past the headquarters ship. Behind it came yet another mass, then another close behind. Rounding the hairpin curve, they drifted toward Vicksburg.

A single musket shot, fired from a Rebel patrol boat, broke the silence. Instantly signal rockets rose from the bluff and abandoned houses along the shore burst into flame; these had been filled with barrels of tar and brush to form giant torches. The fires made the river almost as bright as day, ideal for gunners on both sides.

Veterans were impressed by the amount of metal that flew through the air. Civilians were terrified. Julia whispered, "Our men are all dead men." A nurse standing nearby agreed: "No one can live in such a rain of fire and lead."[5] Jesse cringed at each explosion, clinging to his colonel's neck until Papa sent him to bed.

An artist's view of Grant's fleet running the Rebel defenses at Vicksburg on April 16, 1863. By moving at night, the ships were able to avoid the full fury of the guns placed on the cliffs and along the shore of the Mississippi River.

Meantime, the Vicksburg belles ran into the night in their elegant gowns, trembling with fear, and dropping to the ground each time a shell whooshed overhead.

The action lasted two and a half hours, until the last ship joined the troops downriver. It was a brilliant success. The only vessel lost was the transport *Henry Clay*. One sailor died, accidentally shot by a ship's guard; eight others were slightly wounded. A few nights later, five more transports ran past the city.

The next step was to land troops at Grand Gulf, thirty miles below Vicksburg. However, the Grand Gulf defenses proved to be too strong. After a five-hour duel, Porter's gunboats were forced to steam away. All were damaged, some severely.

Grant ordered scouts to row across the river to find another landing site. They returned with a slave kidnapped from a plantation. The man turned out to be an encyclopedia of local information. The general told him what he needed, pointing to his map. Each time he touched a spot, the man shook his head. "Dar is only one way, General, and dat is by Bruinsburg, eight miles furder down," he said at last. "Dar you can leave de boats and walk on high ground all the way. De best houses and plantations in all de country are dar, sah, all along dat road."[6] Grant was thrilled. Not only had he found a landing point, but a solution to his supply problem. Those Rebel plantations were exactly what he needed. Mississippi's slave owners would feed the very troops who were coming to conquer their state. Soldiers call this "foraging," or "living off the country." Civilians use another term: looting.

On April 30, Grant's army landed at Bruinsburg without opposition. Traveling lightly, its few wagons carrying only ammunition and three days' rations, it moved inland. The slave had been right. This was rich country, and it "contributed" generously to the Union cause. Rickety farm wagons and expensive carriages were loaded with hams and chickens, sacks of corn and sweet potatoes, baskets of fruit and vegetables. Livestock was shot and barbecued over fires made of rails torn from plantation fences. Foragers raided Brierfield, Jefferson Davis's own plantation, taking everything of value. They even gave one of the Confederate president's best horses to Grant. He called it Jeff Davis and rode it throughout the campaign.

Foragers seldom found men of military age on a plantation. That was to be expected. Even so, they expected nothing like the women who remained behind. Southern country women were different from those they had left at home. Yes, some were pretty. But how they dressed! "The women wear their dresses without any hoops & they come only about 3 inches below their knees . . . [and] their shoes look like [bread] trays," a Yankee wrote from near Vicksburg.[7] At a time when using tobacco was not "ladylike," they smoked, snuffed, and chewed the weed. "There are some nice looking girls, but they will chew tobacco, sweet little things," another Yankee reported. "Don't you think that I, for instance, would *look,* or rather *make* a nice show, riding along in a carriage with a young lady, me spitting tobacco juice out of one side of the carriage, and she out the other. Then we would each of us take a cigar and have a real old fashioned smook together. Wall, ain't that nice, Oh Cow!"[8]

Instead of moving on Vicksburg at once, Grant headed for Jackson, the state capital thirty-five miles to the east. An army under General Joseph E. Johnston—no relation to Albert Sidney—was gathering there. The Yankees could never attack Vicksburg with that army loose in their rear.

Grant won five battles in less than three weeks. On May 1, he beat the Confederates at Port Gibson, on May 12 at Raymond, and on May 14 at Jackson. Not that he intended to hold Jackson. With Johnston's force out of the way, he turned toward Vicksburg, leaving Sherman to finish the job. Sherman burned everything of military value, and much else besides. Jackson became the first American city burned by Americans. Acting on Grant's orders, Sherman was applying the lesson of Shiloh: complete conquest.

Two battles were fought on the road to Vicksburg. On May 16, Grant won at Champion's Hill after an all-day fight. The victory cost 2,441 Union casualties; the Rebels lost 3,840 men. The following day, Grant lost 279 men to the enemy's 1,700 at Big Black River, ten miles from the city.

Fred Grant was among the wounded at Big Black River. Although the other children had gone home with Julia, Fred stayed with the army. Apart from an old horse, a gift from some officers, he had no special privileges. His father, busy with the war, let him go where he pleased, when he pleased, trusting to his good sense to avoid trouble. In following the retreating Rebels, he suffered a flesh wound in the leg. It hurt. "I am killed!" he screamed. A kindly soldier came to see what was the matter. "Move your toes," he ordered. Fred did, smiling to find that he would live after all.[9]

Caught between Porter's gunboats and Grant's army, Vicksburg was cut off from the Confederacy. Another commander might have been tempted to surrender. But General John C. Pemberton was not made that way. A native of Pennsylvania, with two brothers in the Union army, "Pem" had fought in Mexico and against the Plains Indians. Grant had known him in Mexico. This Yankee turned Rebel was a fighter. "I knew he would hold on to the last," Grant recalled.[10]

Pemberton had spent months strengthening Vicksburg's land defenses. His main line was built along the crest of an eight-mile ridge fronted by deep gullies. Forts mounting heavy guns stood on the ridge and were in turn linked by trenches. A trench was no mere slit in the ground. Eight feet deep, solidly built of logs and banked-up earth, it had a heavy log running along the top. This "head log" was raised a few inches above the dirt to allow riflemen to shoot through the slit without showing themselves. An abatis, a tangle of felled trees with sharpened branches facing outward, lay about twenty yards in front of the trenches. Beyond this were hundreds of *chevaux-de-frise,* logs pierced with rows of sharpened stakes three feet in length. Finally, there were entanglements of telegraph wire to trip attackers; barbed wire did not appear until after the Civil War. Soldiers lived in bombproofs, deep holes roofed with logs and sandbags.

Fired up by their victories, Yankee soldiers wanted to attack at once. Their general disagreed. Vicksburg's defenses, Grant believed, could not be pierced by a single, bold charge. They would have to be worn down by weeks of shelling. And that would involve plenty of hard work under the Mississippi sun. Knowing that his men would resent the work so long as they hoped for an easier way, he decided to let them try an assault.

On May 19, Grant hurled his army against the Confederate defenses. The result was a bloody mess. Another attack, on May 22, was bloodier still. The advancing Yankees were mowed down by invisible marksmen; all they could see were puffs of smoke rising from the distant trenches. Enemy fire was so heavy, a soldier wrote, that "the very sticks and chips scattered over the ground [jumped] under the hot shower of Rebel bullets."[11] The attackers took shelter in the ravines, only to have the Southerners roll down artillery shells with lighted fuses. Two days of fighting had claimed thirty-two hundred dead, wounded, and missing; Rebel losses were under five hundred.

Yankee wounded lay on the battlefield for another three days. They screamed in pain and thirst, but Grant sent no help. Although the Rebels rescued a few of them at night, most died. Their bodies lay rotting in the hot humidity. The odor drifted toward Vicksburg, causing people to say that the enemy hoped to stink them out.

Grant would not ask for a truce to aid his wounded or bury his dead. It was a question of principle—and arithmetic. Soldiers' lives were important to him, as they are to any decent person. Yet he was not just *any* person. He was an army commander and, for him, the mission must come first. Asking for a truce might be taken in two ways. True, it could be seen as a kindly act. On the other hand, it could be mistaken for weakness and lack of resolve. Any hint of weakness would discourage his own men, endangering the mission. It might also encourage the enemy to fight harder, costing many more lives. Thus, Grant refused to act until Pemberton made the first move. Only on May 25, after the Confederate general asked for a truce "in the name of humanity," did he agree. By then, however, it was too late for hundreds of men.

Grant now began a full-scale siege. Siege craft was a special branch of military science. Taking a fortress meant building a position much like the target itself. A line of trenches was dug facing the fortress, complete with forts, obstacles, and bombproofs. The object was to bring artillery as close to the fortress as possible. And since the defenders also had artillery, it could not be done in the open.

This was work for the army's "sappers." Sappers dug saps, or approach trenches. Starting at the main trench line, they dug zigzag trenches in toward the fortress. As they dug, they rolled "bullet-stoppers" ahead of them, large barrels filled with earth to protect them against snipers. Once the saps were far enough from the main trench, they dug to the right and left, forming a new trench parallel to the main line. Guns were then brought up to bombard the fortress at closer range.

The sappers, meantime, started all over again. Gradually, the lines tightened until the fortress was being blasted day and night at close range. Sappers also dug tunnels, or "mines," under enemy strongpoints, filled them with explosives, and blew them up. Finally, the infantry raced forward with bayonets.

Trench life was hard on everyone at Vicksburg. By June, temperatures reached 100° Fahrenheit in the shade. Soldiers found it impossible to stay clean in the damp heat. Any water they had was used for drinking, not washing. Unable to wash or change their clothes, they became food for the insects. Besides the usual six-legged pests—lice and fleas—they were tormented by swarms of mosquitoes. Yankees said Mississippi mosquitoes were the nastiest in creation. They bit through the thickest shirts. They flew into soldiers' eyes, noses, and ears. An officer wrote his wife in Ohio: "I am now suffering terribly from the effects of mosquitoes & other bugs—I am full of bites all over. . . . I have to stop writing after every sentence I write to scratch myself & drive off the bugs."[12]

Grant's lines came to within six hundred yards of the enemy positions. They were so close that Southerners admitted "a cat could not have crept out . . . without being discovered."[13] Danger lurked everywhere. Even when it was quiet, watchful eyes, snipers' eyes, scanned the opposing lines. Snipers compared themselves to fishermen: they set out "bait" and nabbed anyone foolish enough to take it. A favorite trick was to place a cap on the end of a ramrod and raise it inches above the trench. A curious fellow had only to pop his head up for an instant and he was a goner. Another trick won the hatred of soldiers on both sides. There was an unwritten law that forbade shooting at latrines. Nevertheless, snipers would shoot men as they squatted over a slit trench to answer the call of nature. Soldiers agreed that snipers were beasts. One Yankee recalled, "I hated sharpshooters, both Confederate and Union, in those days, and I was always glad to see them killed."[14]

Grant showed no concern for his personal safety and would gallop along the front line alone, within range of the enemy guns. On one occasion, Rebel snipers began popping away as he and an aide were walking in a trench. The aide begged him to take cover, insisting that he, an aide, could easily be replaced, but the general was irreplaceable. Grant peered through his field glasses; then, when he was good and ready, strolled to the rear. Another time, he was sitting on a log writing a message when a shell exploded a few yards away. He looked up for a moment, brushed the dirt off the paper, and continued as if nothing had happened. Some wounded men were lying nearby when that shell exploded. "Ulysses don't scare worth a damn," one piped up.[15] He didn't, and his courage made him a hero in the eyes of his men. Shiloh was forgotten, or at least forgiven, by his actions at Vicksburg.

The armies were not always active, or active everywhere at once. There were lulls in the fighting, especially at night. During those quiet times, Yankees and Rebels teased each other by shouting across the lines. "I say, Johnny Reb, why don't you wear better clothes?" Yankees called. "We uns don't wear our best clothes when we go to kill hogs," Rebels replied.

> *Rebel: When is Grant going to march into Vicksburg?*
> *Yankee: When you get your last mule and dog eat up.*

Another question brought a yes from everyone. "Ain't you tired of this thing?"[16]

Once in a while, soldiers forgot they were enemies. At Vicksburg and elsewhere, they arranged informal truces on their own. This is not as strange as it might seem. Despite their differences, these men were very much alike in certain ways. They spoke the same language, had a common history, and held the same ideas of fair play. It was only natural for them to put the war aside if they could safely do so.

When the firing died down, a soldier might call out to ask for a truce. Two men would then lay down their muskets and meet between the lines. There they traded tobacco—scarce in the North—for coffee—precious in the South. Comrades joined in, until scores of men stood about shaking hands, swapping things, and talking. They spoke about everything from the weather to past fights and home. At Vicksburg, when a homesick Rebel got choked up and said, "I want to see my ma," everyone understood.[17] Another time, Yanks and Rebels discussed the war, not as politicians, but man to man. They agreed that "if the settlement of this war was left to the Enlisted men of both sides we would soon go home."[18] Yet truces did not mean they were going soft. Once they returned to their lines, they reached for their muskets. The killing continued.

Grant could afford to take heavier losses than the enemy. Although Pemberton had thirty-one thousand men, his own force rose to seventy-seven thousand as reinforcements arrived by ship. The majority were veterans, "reg'lar great big hellsnorters," noted one Rebel. Furthermore, Grant had 220 pieces of artillery of various types. In addition to field guns, there were scores of mortars, short-barreled cannon used to lob shells, called "bombs," over and behind enemy positions. The navy landed several monster guns that fired 166-pound shells two miles.

The bombardment of Vicksburg lasted forty-seven days and nights. The laws of war allowed defended towns to be shelled so long as civilians are not deliberately harmed. The town and its defenders are legitimate targets, but not its inhabitants. If they get in the way, that is their hard luck, and not the attacker's fault. They are innocent, but inevitable, victims of the violence that is war.

No American city had ever taken such a pounding as Vicksburg. Solid shot turned houses into heaps of rubble. Exploding bombs made holes in the ground ten feet across by seventeen feet deep. Shells exploded overhead, spraying chunks of metal in a wide circle. The noise and flashes set dogs running up and down the streets, howling as if they had lost their minds. Horses tied to trees reared on their hind legs, whinnying and wild-eyed with fear.

Everyone in Vicksburg had their own siege story to tell. Emma Balfour's story was typical. A doctor's wife, she kept a diary of her experiences. On May 31, 1863, she wrote:

> The shelling from the mortars was worse than usual last night. . . . I could hear the pieces falling all around us as the shells would explode, and once I thought our time had come. . . . The mortars [fired] all night. . . . At 12 o'clock the guns all along the lines opened and the . . . shells flew as thick as hail around us! . . . We had gone upstairs determined to rest lying down but not sleeping, but when these commenced to come it was not safe up-stairs so we came down to our dining room and lay down upon the bed there, but soon found that would not do as they came from the southeast as well as east and might strike the house. Still from sheer uneasiness we remained there until a shell struck in the garden against a tree, and at the same time we heard the servants all up and making exclamations. We got up thoroughly worn out and disheartened and after looking to see the damage, went into the parlor and lay on the sofas there until morning, feeling that at any moment a mortar shell might crash through the roof. . . . We have slept scarcely none now for two days and two nights. Oh! it is dreadful. After I went to lie down [after watching the shells] I could see them just as plainly with my eyes shut as with them open. They come, gradually making their way higher and higher, tracked by their firing fuze until they reach the greatest altitude, then with a rush and whiz they come down furiously. . . .[19]

The family of the Reverend Dr. William Lord took shelter in the basement of his church. During a bombardment, Dr. Lord sat quietly, smoking his pipe and reading his Bible. His wife and their four children were huddled in a corner. Their slaves hid in the coal bin, praying for divine protection. Lida, the Lords' youngest, began to cry when an explosion rocked the building. Her mother held her close, trying to comfort her. "Don't cry, my darling, God will protect us," she said. "But, momma," the child sobbed, "I's so 'fraid God's killed too!"[20]

Vicksburg went underground. As the shelling increased, people tunneled into the hillsides for protection. For a hundred dollars, laborers dug two-room caves with ceilings and walls supported by wooden beams and lengths of railroad track. Each cave housed a family; larger caves, built by the city, held as many as two hundred people. Simply furnished, the caves had mattresses, bedding, and a few chairs. Rattlesnakes liked these dark places, and more than one person awoke to find a reptilian bedmate snuggled up to them. The worst discomfort, however, was the poor ventilation. Summer nights were stifling, and the air became so foul that candles went out. People lay awake, bathed in sweat, listening to the exploding shells.

Cave dwellers organized their lives around the Yankees' routines. The shelling usually stopped for short periods in the morning, afternoon, and evening, as the guns cooled and the gunners ate their meals. At these times, it was safe to leave the shelters. Women shopped, cooked, and did the laundry. Children played amid the rubble.

Vicksburg's women helped the war effort in countless ways. Volunteers nursed the wounded, rolled cartridges, and knit clothing for the soldiers. During battles, women climbed the hills to cheer on their defenders by waving handkerchiefs. Some even went out during the bombardments. Shells were exploded by burning fuses that left a smoky trail by day and a fiery trail at night. The idea was to walk in the middle of the street. When you saw a shell coming, you ran in the opposite direction. If it burst overhead, you

The caves of Vicksburg. During the siege, the city's inhabitants went underground to escape the constant shelling.

stood still; the fragments always fell ahead of the person beneath. Grant's men admired these brave women. According to a sergeant, "were they but on our side how we would worship them."[21]

Shells took a steady toll, though not as heavy as might be supposed. It is unclear how many civilians died in the shelling. At most, it was a dozen, among them several children. Two white youngsters were blown to bits when shells entered their caves; another, a black girl, was killed while playing with a dud shell that exploded in her hands. Many others were wounded.

Grant kept up the pressure. Each day more guns appeared in his frontline trenches. Meantime, a tunnel was dug under a Confederate fort and filled with twenty-two hundred pounds of gunpowder. On June 25, sappers detonated the mine. A low rumbling came from deep within the earth. Moments later, the fort vanished as tons of soil shot skyward, along with men and equipment. A black laborer named Abraham flew clear into the Union lines. He was not hurt badly, but stunned by his experience. Asked how high he had flown, he replied: "Dun know, massa, but t'ink 'bout t'ree mile."[22] The Union attack, however, was repulsed with heavy losses.

By then much of Vicksburg lay in ruins. Its streets, Sergeant Willie Tunnard recalled, were barricaded:

> The avenues were almost deserted, save for hunger-pinched, starving and wounded soldiers, or guards lying [about], indifferent to the screaming and exploding shells. . . . Palatial residences were crumbling into ruins, the walks torn by mortar shells, the flower beds . . . trodden down, the shrubbery neglected. . . . Fences were torn down and houses pulled to pieces for firewood. Even the enclosures around the remains of the revered dead were destroyed, while wagons were parked around the graveyard, horses trampling down the graves, and men using the tombstones as convenient tables for their scanty meals. . . . Lice and filth covered the bodies of the soldiers. Delicate women and little children, with pale, careworn and hunger-pinched features, peered at the passer-by with wistful eyes from the caves in the hillsides.[23]

Vicksburg was a dying city.

When the siege began, Jefferson Davis called his military advisers to Richmond to work out a rescue plan. Everyone agreed that a good offense was the best defense. The only question was where to attack. Pete Longstreet wanted to invade Tennessee, forcing Grant to split his force. Robert E. Lee disagreed. Sending reinforcements south, he argued, would weaken his own Army of Northern Virginia. He had another idea. By invading the North itself, he would ease the pressure on Vicksburg and end the threat to Richmond. With luck, he might even capture Washington or other Northern cities. Lee's plan was adopted, and soon his army was in Pennsylvania, heading for a sleepy crossroads called Gettysburg. Meantime, two smaller forces struck Grant on the Vicksburg front. They failed, thanks to his Negro regiments. By now, thousands of blacks were demanding freedom with guns in their hands.

The slaves saw the Yankees as liberators. Wherever they appeared, slaves ran away from their owners. They clogged the roads, a swarm of humanity pouring into the Union lines. They came in such large numbers that soldiers declared they looked "like on-coming cities." They came as to a jubilee, the adults cheering "Massa Linkum's sojers," the little ones singing and skipping along.

They were not welcome. The army had plenty to do without having to look after homeless fugitives. Nor did Grant see himself as a liberator. Before setting out for Vicksburg, he had come down hard on escaped blacks. Those already within his lines, he declared, would be allowed to stay so long as they behaved themselves. But newcomers would be expelled without question. Once, when a runaway begged for help, he said: "Can't help you, sir. We're not here to look after Negroes, but after Rebels. You must take care of yourself."[24] Some generals returned fugitives to their masters.

Leaders of the free black community objected to this policy as both cruel and self-defeating. Slavery, Frederick Douglass insisted, was "the very stomach" of the rebellion. The South could not wage war without slave labor. Slaves freed white men for the army, rather than tying them down to other vital tasks. Slaves grew most of the South's food. Slaves worked in factories and railroads, dug trenches, built forts, and hauled ammunition to the front. Black men did camp chores, allowing soldiers to rest; they even loaded and cleaned cannon during battle. At least half the nurses in Confederate military hospitals were black women.

Not only were slaves essential to the Rebels, they aided their enemies in countless ways. Black people gave Union agents information they would not have been able to gather on their own. Union troops could count on blacks to carry messages and serve as guides. Just as the Underground Railroad once helped fugitive slaves go north, it aided Yankee soldiers in the same way. It would have been impossible for escaped prisoners to make their way back to Union lines without the aid of friendly blacks. Blacks fed them, hid them, and led them to safety at great risk to themselves. It was a matter of honor, something they had to do regardless of reward or danger.

Although the war was not being fought to free the slaves, freeing them was clearly necessary to winning the war. Abolishing slavery would cripple the Confederate war effort by encouraging blacks to leave their masters and join the Union armies. Blacks had already fought in the American Revolution and the War of 1812. They had enlisted in the navy from the start of the Civil War; by the time it ended, one-fourth of all Union sailors (twenty-nine thousand men) were blacks. Four black sailors won the Congressional Medal of Honor for outstanding courage.

Nevertheless, many Northerners—perhaps a majority—opposed the use of black soldiers. Racial prejudice ran as deep as ever. Many whites still believed they were racially superior. They insisted they were fighting for the Union, not for the sake of "inferior" blacks. Or, as someone said in Ohio: "We want you damned niggers to keep out of this; this is a white man's war."[25]

Many northerners also believed that blacks were too cowardly to make good fighting men. President Lincoln himself was clear on this point: he feared that if he armed blacks, the weapons would soon be in Rebel hands. To be sure, he blamed blacks for the war itself. "Had it not been for the presence of your race upon this Continent, there would have been no war between the North and the South," he told black leaders during a visit to the White House in August 1862.[26]

Lincoln changed his mind a month later. Putting aside his prejudices, he decided to abolish slavery out of military necessity. On September 22, the Emancipation Proclamation declared that as of the New Year, slaves in the Confederacy "shall be then, henceforward, and forever free." Note: "Forever free" did not include all slaves, but only those in areas where the Union armies had no control. Slaves in loyal slave states, like Kentucky, and in Rebel areas occupied by Union forces, were not included.

Yet there is more. Lincoln's action had turned the Civil War into more than a struggle to preserve the Union. It became a crusade for human rights. This was recognized on January 31, 1865, when Congress passed the Thirteenth Amendment to the

Constitution abolishing slavery throughout the United States.

Slaves learned of the Emancipation Proclamation by word of mouth, or the grapevine, as they called it. They saw it as a gift of God brought by His messenger, Abraham Lincoln. Never mind Lincoln's motives; it was his action that counted with them. As one fugitive put it: "Dey can't sell my wife and child any more, bress de Lord. No more dat! no more dat! no more dat, now!"[27] That was all he needed to know.

The army began to recruit black troops into segregated regiments led by white officers. Blacks needed little encouragement to enlist. Putting on Yankee blue made one a different person. "I felt freedom in my bones" was how Elijah Marrs explained it. A song, sung to the tune of "Yankee Doodle," said it another way:

> *Captain Fidler's come to town,*
> *With his abolition triggers;*
> *He swears he's one of Lincoln's men,*
> *"Enlisting all the niggers."*
>
> *You'll see the Rebels on the street,*
> *Their noses like a bee gum;*
> *I don't care what in thunder they say,*
> *I'm fighting for my freedom![28]*

About 180,000 blacks served in the Union armies, nearly 10 percent of the total force. Of these 68,178 died in battle, of wounds or disease. Seventeen black soldiers earned the Congressional Medal of Honor.

Members of the United States 107th Colored Infantry, a few of the nearly two hundred thousand black men who served in the Union armies during the Civil War

Rebels hated blacks who wore blue. The Confederate Congress declared that captured blacks would be returned to slavery or executed as criminals, according to the laws of their states; their white officers would be executed for inciting rebellion. Soldiers' families were, in fact, whipped or sold to slave dealers in distant states. In retaliation, Lincoln ordered that for every Union soldier killed in violation of the laws of war, a Rebel prisoner of equal rank was to be executed without trial. Furthermore, for every Union soldier enslaved, a Rebel prisoner would be put to hard labor.

Union soldiers at first opposed the formation of all-black regiments; indeed, some threatened to mutiny if made to serve alongside their "inferiors." But the grumbling soon quieted down. Most Yanks, no matter how they felt about slavery, realized that blacks had a vital role to play in the war. Either blacks worked for the enemy, or they worked and fought for the Union. It was that simple. Besides, blacks were just as good at stopping bullets as whites. An army song was titled "Sambo's Right to be Kilt." Sung with an Irish brogue, it made sense to the ordinary Billy Yank:

> Some tell us 'tis a burnin' shame
>   To make the naygers fight;
> An' that the thrade of bein' kilt
>   Belongs but to the white;
> But as for me, upon my soul!
>   So liberal are we here,
> I'll let Sambo be murthered instead of meself
>   On every day of the year.[29]

Grant easily adjusted to the new situation. Although no abolitionist, he had no love of slavery, either. His aim had always been to whip the Rebels and save the Union. If the Rebels could not be beaten in any other way than by abolishing slavery, then that was it!

He supported Lincoln's policy in every way. Not only did he open his lines to slaves, he encouraged them to come. Runaways were set to harvesting the cotton crops on abandoned plantations and preparing them for shipment to Northern factories. Able-bodied men became laborers, building roads and fortifications. They were paid for their work either in money or food and shelter. Black soldiers were welcomed, whether whites liked it or not. The general simply ordered it to be so, and so it was.

The black soldier first proved himself during the Vicksburg campaign. On May 27, 1863, two black regiments led an attack on Port Hudson. Although repulsed with heavy losses, they showed great promise as fighting men. Ten days later, Confederate forces attacked Grant's outposts at Milliken's Bend and Young's Point on the Mississippi twenty miles above Vicksburg. These outposts, vital communications links for the army at Vicksburg, had to be held at any cost. Their defenders, mostly blacks, knew their duty and did it splendidly, driving the enemy back in furious bayonet charges.

Such bravery changed many minds, black as well as white. Former slaves gained confidence. "I feel that I am as much a man as any one" was the way one put it.[30] They also earned the respect of their white comrades. Take, for example, Captain M. M. Miller, a Union man from Louisiana. Miller wrote his aunt: "I never more wish to hear the expression, 'the niggers won't fight.' Come with me 100 yards from where I sit, and I can show you the wounds that cover the bodies of 16 as brave, loyal and patriotic soldiers as ever drew a bead on a Rebel."[31] A few days later, Grant asked Washington to send as many black regiments as it could to the Vicksburg front.

Conditions inside Vicksburg went from bad to worse. By June, food supplies were running low, making prices skyrocket. Not everyone suffered, however. Certain shopkeepers, tempted by quick profits, charged whatever they could get. Soldiers and civilians survived as best they could. Things that would not have been thought fit for animals before the siege became regular parts of the diet. Bread made of ground peas and cornmeal was mushy on the inside, its crust harder than the hardest hardtack. Mule meat was a bargain at under five dollars a pound. A restaurant boasted an all-mule menu; among its delicacies were Mule Tail Soup, Stuffed Mule Head, Mule Ears, Mule Liver, Mule Foot Jelly, and Mule Salad.

Rats also went into the cooking pots. A visitor from New Orleans, trapped by the siege, noted in her diary that "rats are hanging dressed in the market for sale with mule meat. There is nothing else."[32] So many rats were caught that they became scarce by the end of the siege. Rat meat wasn't too bad, if we are to believe Sergeant Osborn H. Oldroyd, a Yankee who was curious about the taste. "I once made a hearty breakfast on fried rats and found the flesh very good."[33] Most people found it awful.

Hunger, not artillery shells, sealed the fate of Vicksburg. On June 28, a letter signed "MANY SOLDIERS" was slipped under Pemberton's door. The writer was blunt. His comrades, he noted, had fought courageously and would gladly do so until kingdom come. But they were starving, unable to keep body and soul together. The general must do right by his troops. "If you can't feed us, you had better surrender us, horrible as the idea is."[34] If he did not act quickly, the army would take matters into its own hands, the writer promised. It would mutiny.

Pemberton swallowed his pride and asked for surrender terms. This time, however, Grant did not live up to his nickname. Instead of demanding unconditional surrender, he was more generous than the Rebels had dared to hope. Vicksburg's defenders would not be sent to prison camps. They would be paroled; that is, set free after promising not to fight until informed that a Union captive had been released by the Confederacy, freeing both to return to duty. Officers would be allowed to keep their pistols and swords; cavalry officers could keep one horse.

Grant was not being generous out of the goodness of his heart. Goodness and necessity went hand in hand at Vicksburg. In the first place, it would have been too costly to ship his captives up the Mississippi River to Illinois, then overland by train to prison camps in the North. Moreover, the Rebels had fought bravely, and he did not want to humiliate them. He believed that by leaving them with their self-respect, it would be easier for them to become good citizens after the war.

The bluecoats followed their general's lead. They did so not because of orders, but out of admiration for the enemy. The formal surrender took place on the morning of July 4, Independence Day. Grant's army was drawn up in battle formation, watching as the Rebels marched out of their trenches to stack their weapons. They stood silently, scarcely moving a muscle. Later, some Yanks confessed to resisting an impulse to salute those men in gray. Not a jeer or taunt came from the blue ranks. The only sound was from a division that could no longer contain its feelings. Its members did not give a victory shout, but, according to Confederate officer S. H. Lockett, "a hearty cheer . . . for the gallant defenders of Vicksburg!"[35] Brave men had been conquered, and they were to be treated as they deserved.

Yankees began to mingle with Rebels the moment they marched into Vicksburg. It was like a meeting of old friends rather than former enemies. Soldiers swapped stories about the siege and introduced themselves to fellows who, until then, they had known only from the distance. "See here, mister—you on that little white horse!" a Union private called to a Confederate officer. "Danged if you ain't the hardest feller to hit I ever saw; I've shot at you more'n a hundred times!"[36] Best of all, the Yankees shared their rations. "I myself," Grant wrote, "saw our men taking bread from their haversacks and giving it to the enemy they had so recently been engaged in starving out. It was accepted . . . with thanks."[37]

Yet nothing could take away the pain of defeat. In addition to 30,000 prisoners, the Rebels gave up 172 cannon and 60,000 muskets. This was the largest army ever captured before the final surrender of Confederate forces at the end of the war. For over four generations, Independence Day would not be celebrated at Vicksburg. It took the Allied victory in Europe in 1945 to make the city part of a truly united nation.

As the Confederate flag was being lowered at Vicksburg, at Gettysburg the Rebel Army of Northern Virginia began its retreat after a three-day battle. It had been a slaughter, especially the third day, when 7,500 men were lost in a single charge led by General George E. Pickett. It broke General Lee's heart. "This has been a sad, sad day for us," he told an aide. "Too bad! *Too bad! Oh! Too bad!*"[38]

The Confederacy had gambled and lost. News of the twin disasters shattered Southern morale. Countless people, realizing that the tide had turned against them, lost hope in their ultimate success. Gettysburg was not only a defeat for their finest army, but for Lee, their best and most beloved general. Vicksburg, however, was more than a Southern defeat. It was a smashing victory for the North.

On July 9 the Confederate commander at Port Hudson learned of the fall of Vicksburg. Rather than continue a hopeless struggle, he surrendered his six thousand men to Major General Nathaniel P. Banks. Exactly one week later, a Union steamboat docked at New Orleans without having been fired upon during its voyage down the Mississippi. The Confederacy was now split in two and the mighty river entirely under Union control. Or, as Abraham Lincoln, put it, "The Father of Waters again goes unvexed to the sea."[39]

Equally important was the president's faith in the man from Galena. Despite setbacks, Grant had kept plugging away. That stubborn little fellow was the man to watch. "Grant is my man," said Lincoln firmly, "and I am his the rest of the war."

He's the quietest little fellow you ever saw. . . . The only evidence you have that he's in any place is that he makes things git! Wherever he is, things move!

—Abraham Lincoln on

U. S. Grant, 1864

After the fall of Vicksburg, Grant sailed down the Mississippi to New Orleans. He had returned the Father of Waters to the Union and wanted to celebrate. Union sympathizers in one river city after another greeted him with banquets and receptions. Outside New Orleans, the military governor held a parade in his honor. For more than an hour, troops marched past him, cheering, waving, and tossing their caps in the air.

Grant was elated as he rode into the city afterward. He rode a borrowed horse, a skittish, high-spirited animal with a mind of its own. Suddenly, the shriek of a steam whistle frightened the horse. It reared, brushed against a wagon, and fell on top of its rider.

The general awoke in a hotel room with doctors surrounding his bed. "My leg," he recalled, "was swollen from the knee to the thigh, and the swelling, almost to the point of bursting, extended along the body up to the arm-pit. The pain was almost beyond endurance."[1] He lay in that room for two weeks, unable even to turn without help. When he became well enough to travel, he was carried to a steamboat, which took him back to Vicksburg and Julia.

The Grants were living in a twenty-six-room house high on the Vicksburg bluffs. As usual, Julia and the children had joined him at the first opportunity. Despite Ulysses's pain, his return there was a joy, his first vacation in years. There was a garden, and shade trees, and cool breezes off the river at night. From August through September 1863, Julia nursed him and made him laugh at her jokes. Nellie sat at his bedside for hours, glad to have Papa to herself. Fred and Ulysses, Jr., dashed about as usual, making sure to tell him their latest news. Little Jesse was a "toy, a delight," to his father. But it could not last. The country was at war and duty called.

Army planners had chosen Chattanooga, Tennessee, as the next major objective. Known as the Gateway to the Deep South, the city is located in a gap cut by the Tennessee River through the Cumberland Mountains in the southeastern part of the state. The fall of Vicksburg had already split the Confederacy in half. By seizing Chattanooga, Union forces would be in a position to move into neighboring Georgia, splitting it into thirds.

The offensive began in September. It was spearheaded by the Army of the Cumberland under Major General William S. Rose-crans. A classmate of Grant's at West Point, "Old Rosy" was an able soldier. In a series of brilliant maneuvers, he forced Confederate General Braxton Bragg to abandon Chattanooga. Bragg withdrew twelve miles to the south, to Chickamauga Creek in Georgia, where he was reinforced by troops sent by rail from the Army of Northern Virginia.

Chickamauga is Cherokee for "River of Blood." On September 19 and 20, it lived up to its name. Rosecrans's army was beaten and would have been destroyed but for George H. Thomas, one of its corps commanders. As the Rebels moved in for the kill, Thomas rallied his troops on a low hill at the center of the battlefield. He told a colonel that the hill must be held to the last man, if that's what it took. The colonel replied, "We'll hold it, General, or we'll go to heaven from it." Many brave men did leave the world from that hill. But the position held like a rock, covering the army's retreat. From that day forward, Thomas was known as the Rock of Chickamauga.

Rosecrans retreated into Chattanooga to

Known to his men as "Old Rosy," General William S. Rosecrans commanded the Union forces routed at Chickamauga Creek in September 1863.

await reinforcements. He did not have to wait long. They came from the Army of the Potomac, the Union's largest force, and were led by Major General Joseph Hooker. The Army of the Potomac had been based at Washington since 1861 to protect the capital and fight the enemy on the Virginia front. Its men were veterans of a dozen pitched battles, including Gettysburg. Within ten days, twenty thousand of them were in Chattanooga. Now, for the first time, the Union's eastern and western armies were acting together.

Not that they liked the idea. These men had little in common, apart from their loyalty to the Union. Easterners thought of their western cousins as wild frontiersmen who had never done "a lick" of real fighting. Westerners thought of easterners as city slickers who would have turned tail at Shiloh or Vicksburg. "What elegant corpses they'll make in those good clothes," they jeered at the newcomers. "Tramps," sneered the easterners in return.

One thing did unite them: hunger. With forty thousand men in town, supplies were being eaten up faster than they could be replaced. By early October, the Confederates had dug in along Missionary Ridge to the east and Lookout Mountain to the south, all but isolating the city. Rosecrans still had a railroad running down from the north, but it ended at Bridgeport, Alabama. To reach Chattanooga, wagon trains had to make a sixty-mile detour over rugged mountain roads with little grass for livestock. As a result, thousands of dead horses and mules lay by the roadside, next to abandoned wagons. Cattle arrived in such poor shape that soldiers called them "beef dried on the hoof."

Food was so scarce that men followed the supply wagons to pick up any scraps that might fall from them. Guards had to be posted at the feed troughs to prevent soldiers from stealing the animals' food. A Kansas infantryman told how "the hungry and tired men haunted the slaughterhouses in crowds, and snatched eagerly for the hoofs, tails, heads, and entrails of the animals that were butchered, cooking and eating with avidity garbage they would before have shrunk from in disgust. . . . One of the regiments of our Brigade caught, killed and ate a dog which wandered into the camp."[2] He did not say if they enjoyed it.

Yet Chattanooga was not another Vicksburg. In trying to starve out the Yankees, the Rebels were starving themselves as well. Although there was plenty of food available in the area, the Confederate supply system was so inefficient that very little reached the front.

Instead of a square meal, Johnny Reb had a visit from Jefferson Davis. Apparently, he believed that seeing him would nourish his men's spirits, if not their bodies. One morning, thousands of hungry troops were ordered into line of battle to be reviewed by their president. As he galloped along with his staff officers, all sleek and well fed, the soldiers let him know just how they felt. "Send us something to eat, Massa Jeff," they begged with mock humility. "I'm hungry! I'm hungry!"[3] About this time, the 1st Tennessee learned that Pemberton's men had been eating rats at Vicksburg. Hungry enough to try anything, Sam Watkins and his friends caught a big old rat with their bare hands. They skinned it, washed and salted it, and fried it in pork fat. It smelled so good that "our teeth were on edge; yea, even our mouth watered to eat a piece of rat."[4] Watkins's friends ate their fill, but he lost his appetite at the last moment. Both sides were in a tight spot at Chattanooga.

In mid-October, Grant received a telegram from General Halleck. He was to go by steamer to Cairo, Illinois, then by train to Lexington, Kentucky, to meet an official who had special orders for him. The "official" turned out to be Secretary of War Edwin M. Stanton. The orders gave Grant command of the Military Division of the Mississippi, that is, all Union forces between the Allegheny Mountains and the Mississippi River. His command consisted of the Army of the Tennessee, the Army of the Cumberland, and the Army of the Ohio. He was to use these forces to break the siege of Chattanooga.

General George H. Thomas, "The Rock of Chickamauga," was a Virginian who remained loyal to the Union, becoming one of its most effective generals.

Grant's first action was to replace Rosecrans with Thomas as chief of the Army of the Cumberland. His order to Thomas was short and sweet: hold Chattanooga until he arrived. Thomas pledged to hold out until Grant came or everyone starved.

Thomas was to become an important member of Grant's team. A Virginian by birth, he was a Union man and a West Pointer to his fingertips. As a boy, he had visited the quarters of his parents' slaves to swap jokes and eat possum. His parents forbade him to have anything to do with slaves, but he disobeyed; he even taught black youngsters the lessons he learned in school.

At the start of the Civil War, he sided with the Union, an action that did not make him popular at home. His sisters turned his picture to the wall, burned his letters, and demanded he change his name. They told neighbors that if George ever set foot in the house, they would tell him where to put his sharp Yankee sword.

With his leg still swollen, Grant's trip to Chattanooga was an endurance test. He went by train to Bridgeport, then across the mountains on horseback. He traveled over rugged trails, pain following him every inch of the way. Arriving on October 23, he had to be lifted from his saddle, gritting his teeth to keep from crying out. It had rained, and he was soaked to the skin. But instead of changing clothes, he went directly to Thomas's headquarters. There he drew a chair up to the fireplace and began to question Thomas's staff. Each answer only provoked further, deeper questioning. If no one knew an answer, an officer was detailed to get it immediately. Before long, he knew as much about Chattanooga as anyone.

That night Grant wrote orders covering every aspect of his new command. He rarely used a secretary, preferring to write everything in his own hand. General Horace Porter, an aide, described how he wrote swiftly, never pausing over a word or phrase, seldom making a correction. Finishing a page, he pushed it off the table onto the floor and went on to the next. If he had to go to another table to get a paper, he moved across the room without straightening himself, and returned to his seat with his body still bent over at the same angle. At last he picked up the pages, put them in order, and handed them to an aide for distribution. The orders were as clear as their author was clearheaded. No matter how quickly he wrote, no one had to read them a second time to understand their meaning.[5]

Each day Grant went to see for himself how things were going. There was no telling where he might appear, or when. He would ride up to a work detail, watch it for fifteen minutes, then ride off without saying a word. Or he sat with men around a campfire to chat about home and listen to their gripes. They spoke freely, since few had ever seen Unconditional Surrender Grant in person. He looked like one of them, with scuffed boots, mud-spattered pants, and coat open at the neck. A soldier noted how "he walked with his head down and without the slightest suggestion of a military step. Neither his face nor his figure was imposing."[6] Soldiers knew who was in charge only when he gave an order. There was something in his voice that told them he was the boss.

One day Grant was riding alone beside a creek that flowed between the lines. Union outposts were on his side of the creek, Confederate outposts across the way. As he neared a Union outpost, a picket recognized him. "Turn out the guard for the commanding general!" he cried. Soldiers raced from their tents and sprang to attention.

"Never mind the guard," Grant said, and they returned to their tents.

Hearing the call, the Rebels had turned out as well. There, only a few feet away, they saw the enemy leader—a perfect target! But they would not dream of shooting. It was one thing to shoot an enemy in battle; that was in the line of duty. However, to shoot an unarmed man at point-blank range was murder. Instead, they decided to have some fun. "Turn out the guard for the commanding general—General Grant!" one called. The Rebel honor guard faced the Union commander, snapped to attention, and presented arms. He tipped his hat and went on his way.[7]

Grant's first move was to break the siege. Thomas had already worked out a plan, but had not yet put it into effect. The plan called for a surprise attack on Brown's Ferry on the Tennessee River a few miles below the city. The ferry was lightly defended, as was a mountain road that ended at a dock across the river. Best of all, it was beyond the range of Confederate artillery on Lookout Mountain. After studying the plan, Grant gave Thomas the go-ahead.

On the night of October 26, Union troops drifted downstream on pontoons, wooden floats over which planks could be laid to form a bridge. A second force marched overland to attack enemy outposts guarding the approaches to the ferry. Surprise was complete. Brown's Ferry was taken in a dawn attack and the Rebels driven off. Even before the guns fell silent, engineers were anchoring pontoons and nailing down planks. Troops then crossed the bridge and dug in on the other side. The new supply line, dubbed the Cracker Line by hungry Yankees, began operating the next day.

Reinforcements poured in during the weeks that followed. Grant's warmest welcome went to seventeen thousand men from the Army of the Tennessee under General Sherman. His friend had gone through a great deal since Vicksburg. After the siege, he, too, had brought his family to the conquered city for a long visit, only to have his son Willie, age nine, die of typhoid fever. Like Fred Grant, Willie had taken a keen interest in the army. During parades, he liked to sit behind his father on his horse. The troops made him an honorary sergeant—"Sergeant Willie"—and gave him a uniform. Willie strutted around camp, saluting the men and being saluted by them in return. Sherman blamed himself for Willie's death, saying he should have died in his son's place.

He was still grieving when Grant welcomed him to Chattanooga.

"How are you, Sherman?" he said, offering a cigar.

"Thank you, as well as can be expected," replied a somber Sherman.

"Take the chair of honor, Sherman," said Grant, pointing to a rocker with a high back.

"The chair of honor? Oh, no! That belongs to you, general."

"I don't forget, Sherman, to give proper respect to age," said Grant, a twinkle in his eyes. (Sherman was two years older.)

"Well, then, if you put it on that ground, I must accept," Sherman answered, a small smile on his face.[8]

This was more than a polite exchange. Without saying it in so many words, Grant had let his friend know that he understood his sadness, but that they must get down to business.

Grant's "business" was to whip the Confederates. By opening the Cracker Line, he had turned Chattanooga from a city under siege into a base for attack. His next move was to be a "double envelopment," a military term for surrounding an enemy position from two directions at once. Sherman was to strike the Rebel right at the northern end of Missionary Ridge while Hooker struck the Rebel left at Lookout Mountain. Thomas, meantime, was to put pressure on the center of Missionary Ridge to keep the enemy from reinforcing either flank.

The Confederates occupied strong defensive positions. At Missionary Ridge, they held a six-mile line atop a steep slope four hundred feet high. Trenches were dug at the crest and foot of the ridge, with rifle pits halfway up the slope. From the fifteen-hundred-foot peak of Lookout Mountain, Rebel gunners commanded the plain below.

Attacking such positions was extremely dangerous. Men racing uphill tire easily and are good targets for those firing from above. Nevertheless, Grant had certain things in his favor. Enemy morale was low. Not only were Confederate troops hungry, ammunition was in short supply. Unless there was a pitched battle, soldiers were under orders not to fire without an officer's permission. Anyone who disobeyed was fined twenty-five cents for each bullet and given extra duty.

Braxton Bragg was the Confederates' chief morale problem. "Not a single soldier in the whole army ever loved or respected him," noted Sam Watkins.[9] Bragg was not a person a soldier *could* love or respect. Hot-tempered and foul-mouthed, he had always had an evil reputation in the army. He was so unpopular that, during the Mexican War, a bomb had been placed under his bed; luckily, for him, it was a dud. Yet he did not change his ways. Before Chickamauga, for example, a private was arrested for desertion after being refused leave to visit his sick mother. Bragg had him shot. Even Chickamauga wasn't a "victory" his men wanted to repeat. It cost the army 18,454 casualties, better than a third of its strength. As Johnny Reb saw it, Bragg was more dangerous than "a passel of Yankees."

The Battle of Chattanooga began at Lookout Mountain. On November 24, Hooker's men, outnumbering the enemy six to one, started up the slope. It was so steep that they had to grab bushes to keep their balance. Men slipped, fell backward, and kept rolling until stopped by a tree or rock. Those who could, picked themselves up and started up again. Many lay still, because the Rebels were no longer saving ammunition. Musket fire was so intense that one Yank thought "it was raining bullets." Yet those watching from below had no idea of what was happening. They could hear the crack of muskets and the boom of cannon, but they saw nothing. A fog had settled over the mountain, shrouding it in mist. Next morning all was clear, revealing the Stars and Stripes flying from the mountaintop. The "Battle Above the Clouds" had ended in a Union victory.

On November 25 Hooker came down from the mountain, trying to slip behind Missionary Ridge. He moved quickly, until stalled by a wrecked bridge. In the meantime, Sherman was having his hands full at the northern end of the ridge. Four times he attacked, only to be forced back with heavy losses. At 3:00 P.M., after eight hours of fighting, he asked Grant for help. It was time to use Thomas's troops.

Braxton Bragg won a major Confederate victory at Chickamauga in 1863 but failed to follow up his success. Instead, he besieged the Union army in Chattanooga and merely waited for Grant to break his lines at Missionary Ridge.

The Army of the Cumberland was itching for a fight. Ever since the siege began, outsiders had poked fun at the Cumberlands' poor showing at Chickamauga. The men were angry; the defeat at Chickamauga had not been their fault, they insisted. Just wait till next time!

That morning, the assault regiments were joined by men who were not expected to take part in battle. Cooks, clerks, and orderlies grabbed muskets and crowded into the front line. As the men of the 6th Indiana put it, "We were crazy to charge."[10]

"Crazy" was the right word for what followed. Grant had ordered the Cumberlands to take the trench at the base of Missionary Ridge, regroup, and await further instructions. As things turned out, they would disobey every part of the order except the first.

At Grant's signal, eighteen thousand men set out from the Union lines, a blue tidal wave rolling across the plain. Bragg stood atop Missionary Ridge, watching them with amazement. Trying to take the ridge was like trying to walk up a straight wall, he thought. His boys would slap them down the moment they came into range.

As Bragg watched, a local woman came up to him. "Oh, General," she pleaded, "the Yankees are coming. What shall I do? Where shall I go?"

"Woman, are you mad? There are not Yankees enough in Chattanooga to come up here," he said with a sweep of his hand. "Those [down there] are all my prisoners."[11]

He had spoken too soon.

The blue wave spilled into the trench. The defenders backed up the slope toward the rifle pits, firing while their comrades above cut loose with everything they had. At once the Yankees found that the trench offered no protection. It was like shooting fish in a barrel, as Rebel marksmen scoured it with bullets from end to end. The only cover was behind the bodies of the dead.

The Yankees felt helpless and angry. If they stayed put, they would all be killed sooner or later. They could retreat, but that meant recrossing open ground they had already paid for in blood. There was only one thing to do: get the enemy before he got them. And that meant storming Missionary Ridge.

Yet they were paralyzed without orders. Company leaders— captains and lieutenants—had not been told what to do in such an emergency. Field officers—colonels and generals—had no authority to advance further. Grant's order was precise: take the trench and hold on. Military law was equally precise: disobeying a lawful order in battle meant the firing squad.

It was not a conscious decision to take Missionary Ridge, or one reached after deep thought. It was a gut reaction. Ignoring the danger from above, a few men climbed out of the trench and ran forward. Their courage was infectious. Soon others were following them by tens, by companies, by whole regiments. There had never been anything like it in American history. Officers shouted for them to come back, cursing and waving their swords, but no one obeyed. Their only choice was to follow their men or be left behind.

Grant and his staff were at an observation post on a small hill in front of Missionary Ridge. When the charge began, he demanded an explanation. "Thomas, who ordered those men up the ridge?" he asked harshly. Thomas had no idea; it wasn't he. Turning to Thomas's aide, Gordon Granger, he snapped: "Granger, did you send them up?" "No," Granger replied, "[but] when those fellows get started all hell can't stop them."[12] Hell indeed! Grant mumbled that someone would surely catch hell if they failed.

A divisional commander, Major General Philip Sheridan, tried to halt the charge, but wound up joining it. Before moving out, he raised a silver whiskey flask, threw back his head, and drank deeply. "Here's to you!" he called to a Confederate officer watching from above. No gentleman, the Confederate ordered a volley from a gun battery. Shells exploded near Sheridan, showering him with clods of earth. He was more insulted than hurt. Brushing dirt out of his eyes, he barked, "That's damned ungenerous; I'll take those guns for that!"[13]

The Yankees pressed forward, shouting, "Chickamauga! Chickamauga!" as if the very word had power. Feverishly, the Rebels fired and reloaded. They lit the fuses of shells and rolled them down the slope. They even rolled down boulders and threw rocks. Still, the men in blue kept coming.

They stormed the rifle pits and raced for the trench above. The Confederates panicked. Men who had never turned their backs on the foe suddenly gave in to fear. Thousands ran down the other side of the ridge and into the woods beyond. Left behind was a trail of muskets, knapsacks, and blankets—anything that might slow them down.

Reaching the top of the ridge, the Yankees were astonished at the sight. "My God, come and see 'em run!" they yelled to one another. An Indiana soldier recalled, "It was the sight of our lives—men tumbling over each other in reckless confusion, hats off . . . running wildly."[14]

Rebel officers could not halt the rout. Poor Bragg! Sam Watkins saw him riding among the fleeing men, frantic with rage. "Here is your commander," he kept shouting. "Here is your mule," soldiers shouted back. "Bully for Bragg, he's hell on retreat."[15] Bragg was later removed from his post and never again held an important battlefield command.

The Cumberlands were thrilled. They had pulled off one of the boldest charges in the history of warfare. They laughed and wept and shook hands. Rank was forgotten as privates and colonels hugged one another. Phil Sheridan kept his word: the moment he reached the top, he leaped on a captured gun and wrapped his legs around its barrel, crowing with delight. "What do you think of this, General?" someone asked Gordon Granger, who arrived shortly afterward. Granger growled, "I think you disobeyed orders, you damned rascals!"[16] But there were tears in his eyes. The Battle of Chattanooga was over.

Casualties were heavy: 5,815 Union and 6,667 Confederate soldiers killed or wounded in two days of fighting. After Missionary Ridge, piles of arms and legs the size of small haystacks were seen outside the hospital tents. Grant, who had planned a different kind of battle, got the credit nevertheless. The exact details of the victory made no difference to a grateful nation; what counted was the victory itself.

Grant seemed to have everything one could wish for in a commander. He was smart. He was bold. He was lucky. He was a winner. It was only natural that the war should be turned over to him.

In February 1864 Congress restored the rank of lieutenant general. Although others had held it as an honorary title, only two men, the nation's greatest soldiers, held it permanently. The first, George Washington, had once commanded all the armies of the United States. U. S. Grant was now Washington's equal. But instead of Washington's thousands, he commanded hundreds of thousands: 533,000 to be exact, the largest military force ever assembled in the New World. His salary was $8,640 a year, a large sum in those days. The position also entitled him to wear three stars on his uniform.

Grant received his commission in a White House ceremony

held on March 9. After the ceremony, the president took him aside for a private talk. Lincoln explained that he was no military man. Although he had never wanted to interfere with the conduct of the war, incompetent generals had forced him to make certain decisions. All he had ever wanted was a commander who would take responsibility and call on him for help as needed. Grant had proven himself trustworthy. He did not want to know Grant's plans, or the details of his campaigns. The general, for his part, promised to "do the best I could with the means at hand, and avoid as far as possible annoying him or the War Department."[17]

Grant had intended to direct the war from the West, but visiting Washington changed his mind. It became clear that he would have to be in close touch with the capital for the rest of the war. But being in touch with the capital did not mean being imprisoned in it. Life in Washington would be an endless struggle between his job and his social obligations: banquets, receptions, visits to and from Very Important People. Grant called these obligations "the show business" and refused to go along; he even got out of a dinner party Mrs. Lincoln planned to give in his honor.

Since his was to be a fighting command, not a desk job, Grant made his headquarters with the Army of the Potomac at Brandy Station, Virginia, fifty miles from the capital. General George Gordon Meade, the hero of Gettysburg, was still the army's head, but Grant directed its operations.

Grant replaced Henry Halleck as general-in-chief. Although he had reason to dislike Halleck, the Union cause was uppermost in his mind. Halleck, he knew, was a superb desk officer. Very well, he would let him do what he did best: push papers. Halleck became the army's first chief of staff, a post created specially for

President Lincoln in a photograph dating from the summer of 1863, soon after Grant's capture of Vicksburg and Robert E. Lee's defeat at Gettysburg

him. While Grant saw to the fighting, he managed the army's day-to-day affairs. Troop replacements, transportation, supplies: these and a thousand other details were left to Old Brains. It was an ideal arrangement. By freeing Grant from paperwork, it left him time to plan future campaigns. Nevertheless, Grant still remembered Halleck's behavior after Shiloh. Determined to clip his wings once and for all, he forbade him to interfere with combat operations. Halleck followed his orders to the letter.

Grant met Sherman in Cincinnati, Ohio, on March 18. He had gone west to turn over command of the Military Division of the Mississippi and discuss future operations. What he had in mind was nothing less than a revolution in the way war was waged.

For centuries, commanders had thought in terms of the knockout battle. Their goal was to win a war through one mighty effort. Experience showed that single battles had, indeed, changed the history of nations. That is what happened when Andrew Jackson defeated the British at New Orleans in January 1815; it happened again five months later at Waterloo in Belgium, where Napoleon lost both a battle and an empire.

Grant realized that the Civil War did not follow the old pattern. Shiloh, Vicksburg, Gettysburg, and Chattanooga were defeats for the Confederacy. Yet they had not brought victory to the Union. Nor would the capture of Richmond. Grant had assured Lincoln that with enough men and supplies, he could take the Confederate capital. Still he knew that this would be a sideshow, not the heart and guts of the war. The enemy could lose any number of battles and cities and still go on fighting. Victory, in this case, required something else.

The Civil War was the first modern war. In it we see the outlines of the world wars of the twentieth century. Like them, it was not merely a struggle between armies, but between entire societies. The Southern people stood behind the Southern armies. Those armies were not made up of mercenaries serving for pay, but of the people's own flesh and blood. The people in turn fed the fighting men and provided the tools of war. More, they encouraged them, giving them a cause to fight for. It followed that the war would end only when the society that supported it was conquered. That is what Grant meant when, after Shiloh, he gave up any idea of saving the Union except by complete conquest. "I therefore determined," he recalled, "to hammer continuously against the armed force of the enemy and his resources, until by mere attrition . . .

there should be nothing left to him but . . . submission . . . to the constitution and laws of the land."[18]

Mark these words: *to hammer continuously . . . until by mere attrition.* Grant meant to operate on two levels at once. Unity of command came first. Until he took charge, the Union's eastern and western armies had acted independently, "like a balky team" of horses, no two pulling together.[19] This enabled the Confederates to shift troops from one front to the other. As a result, it was impossible to make a breakthrough on either front. Those days were over. Grant would make the Union forces act together, each action serving a common end. Their aim was to hammer the enemy without letup, preventing it from sending reinforcements to trouble spots. As long as the Confederate armies existed, there was no point in capturing towns unless that would cut their communications or deprive them of supplies.

Attrition, Grant's second aim, is the wearing down of resistance by steady pressure. He not only targeted the Southern armies, but the Southern people and their will to fight. They had to feel the hardships of war in their daily lives, even in their homes. When they could bear no more, they would beg their leaders for peace. Thus, by 1864, the general-in-chief was planning for total war. Today, it is called "the American way of war."

Grant told Sherman what this meant in practical terms. The Confederates had two main armies: one in Georgia under Joseph Johnston and Robert E. Lee's Army of Northern Virginia. Grant would hurl the Army of the Potomac against Lee. If he managed to take Richmond, all well and good; but his true objective was the Southern heartland. That is where Sherman came in. Advancing from Chattanooga, he must smash Johnston's army, plunge deep into enemy country, and destroy its resources. Meantime, Grant would keep Lee pinned down, unable to reinforce Johnston. Lee would have to keep facing north while Sherman cut the Confederacy to shreds behind his back. Or, as Abe Lincoln explained it: "Grant has the bear by the hind leg while Sherman takes off the hide."[20] Great battles had still to be fought, thousands killed, wounded, and driven from their homes. But the Union had a plan at last. It was a harsh plan, but that is war.

On May 4, 1864, U. S. Grant crossed the Rapidan River, bound for Richmond. Let us leave him there for the time being and follow Sherman on his famous march.

VI ✦ THE LAND DEVOURED

We have devoured the land. . . . All the people retire before us, and desolation is behind. To realize what war is one should follow our tracks.

—William Tecumseh

Sherman, 1864

Next to his chief, U. S. Grant, William Tecumseh Sherman was the Union's best fighting general and one of the most remarkable men of the day.

Sherman was born February 8, 1820, in Lancaster, Ohio, the son of a state supreme court judge who died when the boy was nine. The judge's sudden death left his wife with a large family and a small income. Unable to support them, she sent some of her eleven children to live with relatives and friends. "Cump," as he was known in the family, moved in with Thomas Ewing, a wealthy lawyer who had been his father's best friend. He got along well with the Ewings; indeed, he later married his foster sister, Ellen.

Ewing used his influence to have Cump appointed to West Point when he turned sixteen. He graduated sixth in the class of 1840 and was posted to various units in Florida, Alabama, South Carolina, and Georgia. During the Mexican War, he served in California, but saw no action. Growing tired of the army, he resigned after thirteen years. Like Grant, he could not adjust to civilian life. Whatever he tried—banking, real estate, law—came to nothing. The future looked bleak until he became headmaster of the Louisiana State Seminary of Learning and Military Academy in October 1859.

Sherman admired Southerners, finding them cultured, gra-

General William Tecumseh Sherman was Grant's friend as well as his most trusted commander. While Grant pounded Lee in Virginia, Sherman threatened the Confederate rear by marching through Georgia and the Carolinas.

cious people. His ideas about slavery would have warmed the heart of any racist, and he expressed them in coarse, brutal language. "I would not if I could abolish or modify slavery," he said a month after arriving in Louisiana.[1] Slavery, he insisted, was vital to the Southern way of life; abolishing it would ruin the whites without helping the blacks. It was not only a matter of economics, but of scientific fact, he believed. To him, black people were an inferior race. He had not made them that way; Mother Nature had. "Iron is iron and steel is steel, and all the popular clamor on earth will not impart to one the qualities of the other. So a nigger is not a white man, and all the Psalm singing on earth won't make him so."[2] He also said that "the Negro . . . must be subject to the white man, or he must . . . be destroyed. Two such races cannot live in harmony save as master and slave."[3]

Sherman loved the South but hated secession. Secession, he felt, was worse than murder. It was treason, rebellion, the end of law and order. And it meant war. "This country will be drenched in blood," he told a professor who favored secession. "God only knows how it will end. . . . Oh, it is folly, madness, a curse against civilization. . . . You speak so lightly of war. You don't know what you are talking about. War is a terrible thing. . . . At best war is a frightful loss of life and property, and worse still is the demoralization of the people. . . . You are bound to fail."[4] When Louisiana seceded in January 1861, he resigned as headmaster. Having to leave his students hurt him deeply; he had grown fond of them, but could not live among rebels.

He rejoined the Union army as a colonel and quickly rose to the rank of brigadier general. During the fall of 1861, while stationed in Kentucky, he predicted the war would last several years and that it would take two hundred thousand men to beat the Confederates in the West. Hardly anyone expected a long war at this time. His ideas seemed so outrageous that people began whispering behind his back. The poor fellow, they said, had lost his mind. Those whispers reached an Ohio newspaper, which announced, "GENERAL W. T. SHERMAN INSANE." As if that wasn't enough, his son Tommy came home in a state of shock; a boy in the street had told him that his father was crazy.

Sherman was transferred to Paducah, Kentucky, to serve under Grant. Although they had known each other at West Point, their friendship dates from this time. Grant had faith in "crazy Sherman"; Sherman defended Grant against charges that he was a drunkard. He said of their friendship: "Grant is a great general. He stood by me when I was crazy, and I stood by him when he was drunk. And now, by thunder, we stand by each other always!"[5] They were closer to each other than to their own brothers. The record shows that though they might disagree, no harsh words ever passed between them.

Yet they were different in many ways. Grant was slightly built, calm, and quiet. Sherman stood six feet tall, had a big red nose, small bright eyes, and a receding hairline crowned by a tuft of tangled red hair. His wrinkled face sported a short beard, also red. Like Grant, he was careless about his appearance, only more so. His crumpled, sweat-stained uniform looked as if he had slept in it for years. He wore shoes rather than boots, and a single spur.

Friends compared Sherman's mind to "a splendid piece of machinery with all the screws a little loose."[6] A bundle of nervous energy, he could not be still for any length of time. His fingers were constantly tugging at his beard, buttoning and unbuttoning his coat, and drumming on everything within reach. He spoke rapidly, spitting out words like shotgun pellets. In giving orders, he would grab an aide by the shoulders and push him away without pausing for breath. He seldom slept more than three hours a night, usually waking up at three or four in the morning. Dressed in red flannel drawers and a woolen shirt, he walked around the campfire in circles, his hands clasped behind his back, his mind racing.

Sherman believed a general had to command his soldiers' hearts and minds as well as their bodies and legs. He did this simply by being himself. Outgoing by temperament, he would talk to privates about farming and junior officers about strategy. He spoke to them as equals, man to man. Nor was he shy—about anything. When things were quiet, soldiers would dive into the nearest creek for a wash and a swim. Their general joined the fun, stripping naked and splashing around like one of the boys. Soldiers adored him. They called him Uncle Billy and took off their hats as he rode by. A private expressed their feelings in a letter home: "I am very tired of war But the Countrey Needs my help and I Never will turn my Back on it. I am a awful Cow hart [coward] you know But I Shall Die before I will Leave as true a Solger as Billie Sherman."[7]

Sherman's objective was Atlanta. Founded in the 1830s, it had a population of twenty thousand at the start of the Civil War. Besides being a railway center, its factories, machine shops, and warehouses were essential to the Confederate war effort. Blacks worked in Atlanta's war industries and slave traders prospered. Slave markets clustered near the railroad station, their signs announcing "Slaves Bought and Sold Here," "Slave Auction Rooms," and "The Great Slave Mart." In the rear of each auction house were jail cells and whipping posts.

The Union force numbered one hundred thousand men and was the healthiest army in American history up to that time. Sherman had thought of everything. Since he would be operating far from his Chattanooga base, he could not afford to be burdened by the sick. His surgeons, therefore, were ordered to give everyone a more thorough examination than they had received when they enlisted. Those with any health problems were left behind. As a result, no more than 2 percent of his men fell ill during the campaign. This figure was amazingly low; there had never been anything like it in an American or European army.

Chattanooga became a vast supply dump. Everything from beans to bullets to bandages was collected, checked, and rechecked by Sherman's quartermasters. If there were slipups, those in charge answered to Uncle Billy. He did not want excuses, as one fellow discovered the hard way. Sherman grabbed him by the collar, shook him vigorously, and roared: "I'm going to move on Joe Johnston . . . and if you don't have my army supplied, and keep it supplied, we'll eat your mules, sir—eat your mules up!"[8]

The Union lifeline was a single-track railroad between Chattanooga and Atlanta. Trains were reserved for the military; under no circumstances could they carry civilians. This rule applied, above all, to newspaper reporters. Grant and Sherman held different views on the press. Grant believed in freedom of the press even in wartime; he allowed newsmen to write whatever they wished, provided they did not reveal military secrets. Sherman believed newsmen to be less trustworthy than rattlesnakes.

It was not just the "crazy Sherman" incident that made him bitter. He knew from experience that reporters "leaked" valuable information. They did so not because they were spies, but for the sake of a juicy story. Still, the effect was the same; the enemy learned the information, endangering his men's lives. Certain reporters actually stole army papers and hung around officers' tents to overhear conversations that could be used in their articles. Reporters were, to Sherman, "the damned newspaper mongrels," traitors to their country.[9] Upon hearing that three had died in an explosion, he cried, "Good! Now we'll have news from hell before breakfast."[10] He had no doubt that they were in hell, the newsman's true country.

Sherman invaded Georgia three days after Grant crossed the Rapidan. Opposing him were Joseph E. Johnston's combined armies of Tennessee and Mississippi. Johnston had replaced Bragg after the disaster of Missionary Ridge. The moment he arrived, things began to improve. He walked through the camps, smiling and shaking hands with every soldier he met. More, he made sure they had new clothing and plenty of food. In their eyes, "Old Joe" was a saint. "He was loved, respected, admired; yea, almost worshiped by his troops," recalled Sam Watkins. "I do not believe there was a soldier in his army but would have gladly died for him. With him everything was his soldiers. . . . His soldiers were to him his children. He loved them. They were never needlessly sacrificed."[11]

Johnston's sixty-five thousand men were outnumbered by Sherman's army. Knowing that a slam-bang battle meant certain defeat, Johnston planned to remain on the defensive. He would retreat slowly, falling back to defense lines prepared earlier by slaves. He would bide his time, hoping one day to catch the enemy off balance and destroy him. Uncle Billy, however, had his own plans. He intended to "flank" the Confederates; that is, slip behind them, ease them out of their trenches, and smash them in the open.

For seven weeks the campaign resembled an elaborate dance—to the music of muskets and cannon. It began with the two armies facing each other. The Yankees stepped to their right and forward. The Confederate rear guard then blocked the advance while their main force stepped backward. Sherman's tactics led to fights at Resaca, Cassville, and New Hope Church. Men died, but the flanking, shooting, and retreating continued at their own leisurely pace.

Joseph E. Johnston, one of the Confederacy's best-loved generals, served in both the eastern and western theaters of operations.

Confederates came to believe that Sherman could not be stopped no matter what they did. His skill at flanking seemed miraculous. A prisoner sighed, "Sherman'll never go to hell; he will flank the devil and make heaven in spite of the guards."[12] News that Nathan Bedford Forrest had destroyed a tunnel in the Yankee rear left Johnston's troops cold. "There isn't no use in that," they said. "Sherman carries duplicates of all the tunnels."[13]

Johnston finally halted at Kennesaw Mountain, twenty miles north of Atlanta. He was well dug in there, with trenches and rifle pits supported by plenty of artillery. This time Sherman decided to attack head-on, rather than flank the position. Why he did so is still a mystery. But whatever his reason, it was wrong. Dead wrong.

The assault began on the morning of June 27. This was no replay of Missionary Ridge. Sherman's troops came in human waves forty deep. They came slowly, deliberately, as the redcoats had done at Bunker Hill. "They seemed to walk up and take death as coolly as if they were automatic men, and our boys did not shoot for the fun of the thing," said Sam Watkins.[14] Nor did they miss very often; a Rebel had only to aim at the crowd to hit someone. The Yankees lost 2,500 killed and wounded in less than an hour;

Rebel losses were 808. Sherman never admitted his mistake, but he never repeated it, either.

Next day, both sides declared a truce to bury the dead; it was hot—110° Fahrenheit in the shade—and a terrible odor hung in the air. After finishing their grisly work, the burial details hung around to trade and talk. Once again, they found the enemy to be people like themselves. "It seems too bad that we have to fight men that we like," a Yankee wrote his parents. "Now these Southern soldiers seem just like our own boys. . . . They talk about . . . their mothers and fathers and their sweethearts just as we do."[15]

There were some emotional reunions that day. A huge Rebel sat under a tree with his arm around the shoulder of a young bluecoat. The Rebel cried, then laughed, then kissed the Yankee again and again.

"Why, you seem to be taken by that boy. I suppose he is some old friend of yours," an officer said.

"Old friend, sir! Why, he is my son!"[16]

Sherman returned to flanking after Kennesaw Mountain. Johnston retreated, this time into the defenses around Atlanta. Although Johnston had delayed Sherman's advance two months and kept casualties low, Jefferson Davis was not satisfied. He wanted an aggressive general, one who would take the fight to the enemy. On July 17 he removed Old Joe from command. It broke his army's heart. Sam Watkins saw "thousands of men cry like babies—regular old-fashioned boohoo, boohoo, boohoo."[17]

His replacement was John Bell Hood of Texas. At thirty-three, Hood was a handsome man, over six feet tall, with broad shoulders, a full beard, and soft blue eyes that melted women's hearts. Gettysburg had left him with a crippled left arm, and he had lost his right leg at Chickamauga. These days he had to be tied to his horse, but he was still a bold, reckless fighter. Rebel soldiers knew his reputation and feared a bloodbath. Sherman knew it, too, and was delighted. He wanted an opponent who would fight in the open—and lose.

Hood did as expected. He fought three major battles in eight days: Peachtree Creek (July 20), Decatur (July 22), Ezra Church (July 28). These battles cost the Confederates over eighteen thousand men, three times the

Undaunted by crippling wounds, John Bell Hood led Confederate forces during the Atlanta campaign. An aggressive fighter, his men accused him of taking needless chances with their lives.

Union total and twice as many as Old Joe had lost in ten weeks.
That was too much for his soldiers. Calling Hood "butcher,"
hundreds deserted after Ezra Church. Thousands of civilians fled
Atlanta by road or packed into rickety trains. They knew all about
Vicksburg and feared a siege.

Atlanta was a fortress. Like Vicksburg, it was protected by
trenches, forts, abatis, and wire entanglements. But unlike Vicksburg, these covered too large an area to be encircled by Union
forces. At no time was it cut off from the outside world. A railroad
to the south kept Hood's army supplied with food and ammunition.

Unable to starve Hood out, Uncle Billy dug trenches in an arc
north and west of the city and set up heavy artillery. The bombardment continued without letup, forcing civilians into shelters
built in their yards and gardens. Yet a month of shelling produced
no results. Meanwhile, Grant had bogged down outside Petersburg, Virginia, and Lincoln had serious political troubles. This
was a presidential election year, and the Democrats spared him
no insult. Lincoln, they claimed, had betrayed the nation; he was
willing to spill the last drop of white blood to free the blacks. He
was even accused of being partly Negro himself. "Abe Lincoln,"
said the New York *Freeman's Journal,* "is altogether an imbecile. . . . He is brutal in all his habits. . . . He is filthy. He is ob-
scene. . . . He is an animal."[18] Sherman's failure to take Atlanta
might cost Lincoln the election and with it the Union cause.

The morning of August 26 was strangely still at Atlanta. Yankee guns were silent and no one moved in the trenches. Cautiously,
Rebel patrols inched forward to see what that meant. The trenches
were empty! Sherman had pulled out during the night! Atlanta
was safe!

It was a trick. Sherman had, indeed, left with his army. But
instead of retreating, he hurried southward, toward Hood's railroad. His move brought on another battle, and another Confederate defeat. On the night of September 1, Sherman heard distant
explosions. With his railroad cut, Hood was abandoning Atlanta.
The explosions came from eighty carloads of ammunition set afire
to keep them out of Yankee hands.

Sherman arrived in the morning. He had already telegraphed
Lincoln: "Atlanta is ours, and fairly won!" Not only had he taken
the city, he had assured the president's victory in the November
elections. Lincoln promptly announced a day of national
thanksgiving.

Sherman planned to turn Atlanta into a military base, which

Outside Atlanta. William Tecumseh Sherman views the besieged city from one of the Union gun emplacements.

meant removing the remaining inhabitants, about sixteen hundred people. They could go wherever they pleased, so long as they left quickly. Expelling them would not only make the city easier to defend, but send a message to their countrymen. Southern civilians must learn that the Union meant business, and that they had better give up before it was too late. If they kept on with the war, he would keep up the pressure until they changed their minds.

The expulsion order was issued on September 8. Atlanta's mayor and two city councilmen begged Sherman to reconsider. He refused. His letter to them was as blunt as the man himself. It told of war as it really is, not as civilians imagined it to be. War is no spectator sport. It is a horrible ordeal, and those who unleash it should learn its reality firsthand:

You cannot qualify war in harsher terms than I will. War is cruelty, and you cannot refine it. And those who brought war into our country deserve all the curses and maledictions a people can pour out. I know I had no hand in making this war, and I know I will make more sacrifices today than any of you to secure peace. But you cannot have peace and a division of our country. . . .

You might as well appeal to the thunderstorm as against these terrible hardships of war. They are inevitable, and the only way the people of Atlanta can hope once more to live in peace and quiet at home is to stop the war. . . .

We don't want your Negroes or your horses or your houses or your lands, or anything you have. But we do want, and will have, a just obedience to the laws of the United States . . . and if this involves the destruction of your improvements, we cannot help it. . . .

The South began the war. . . . I myself have seen . . . hundreds and thousands of women and children fleeing from your armies and desperadoes, hungry and with bleeding feet. . . . Now that war comes home to you, you feel very different. . . . I want peace, and believe it can only be reached through union and war. . . . But, my dear sirs, when peace does come, you may call on me for anything. Then will I share with you the last cracker, and watch with you to shield your homes and families against danger from every quarter. Now you must go. . . .[19]

Sherman knew he was causing hardship, but felt he had no choice. He was fighting a new kind of war, a people's war in which it seemed impossible to separate the innocent from the guilty. Indeed, by supporting the Confederate cause even with a smile, *every* Southerner was an enemy, he believed. As he told General Halleck, "We are not fighting armies, but a hostile people, and must make old and young, rich and poor, feel the hard hand of war, as well as their organized armies."[20]

Nevertheless, Sherman did not enjoy their suffering. As the refugees left Atlanta, he took a little girl in his arms and patted her cheeks. He had daughters of his own and knew how she must feel. Calling her "poor little exile," he said he was sorry to drive her from her home, but that it had to be done. "I have been forced to turn families out of their houses and homes," he wrote his thirteen-year-old daughter Minnie. "Think of this, and how cruel men become in war when even your papa has to do such acts. Pray every night that the war may end. Hundreds of children like yourself are taught to curse my name, and every night thousands kneel in prayer and beseech the Almighty to consign me to perdition."[21]

The Confederates still had plenty of fight in them. After losing Atlanta, they began attacks on Yankee supply lines stretching all the way back to Chattanooga. Nathan Bedford Forrest swept through western Tennessee, tearing up railroads and destroying Union outposts. Hood marched his army toward Tennessee in the hope of drawing Sherman after him. Sherman took the bait for a while. The Rebels led him on a merry chase, but refused to make a stand. All he could show for his efforts were thousands of exhausted men and a few hundred dead ones.

Sherman asked permission to try something different. He wanted to send George Thomas back to Tennessee with thirty thousand men to deal with Hood. Meantime, he would lead the rest of the army across Georgia and come out at Savannah on the coast. True, this meant ignoring the enemy in his rear and abandoning his supply line. But his army was more than a match for anything the Confederates could send against it. As for food, he would follow his chief's example at Vicksburg: live off the country.

His army would be an immense eating machine, taking the food needed by the Army of Northern Virginia and destroying the rest. He would smash everything of military value, making Georgians sick of war and all Southerners feel helpless at the sight of his army moving through their heartland. "I can make the march and make Georgia howl!" he wrote Grant.[22]

President Lincoln had his doubts about the plan, but he trusted Grant, who trusted Sherman. Grant advised his friend to do a thorough job. Uncle Billy must "clean the country" of transportation and supplies. The South should be taught such a lesson in total war as to make future generations tremble at the thought of rebellion.

Sherman's march to the sea began on November 15, 1864, a week after Lincoln's reelection. He watched from the roadside as his army streamed out of Atlanta. It consisted of 62,000 soldiers, 25,000 horses and mules, 65 cannon, 2,500 wagons, and 600 ambulances. The men were in high spirits. Bands played popular tunes like "Farewell, Farewell, My Own True Love," "When This Cruel War Is Over," and "Oh, Jenny, Come Tickle Me." Whenever they struck up "John Brown's Body," thousands of voices took up the chorus: "Glor-y, glor-y, halle-lujah! Glor-y, glor-y, halle-lujah!" Sherman had never heard it sung with such spirit. Nor had his men ever greeted him so warmly. "Uncle Billy, I guess Grant is waiting for us at Richmond!" they shouted.

Toward evening, when they were well clear of the city, a red glow lit the northern sky. Atlanta was burning.

Sherman had ordered the destruction of buildings used for military purposes; the others were to be spared, and no private homes touched under any circumstances. But once the fire began, it went out of control. Many of the fire-setters were drunk, which made them careless with matches. In any case, there had been nothing like it since the British burned Washington in 1814. It was the "grandest and most awful scene," an officer wrote. "First bursts of smoke, dense, black volumes, then tongues of flame, then huge waves of fire roll up into the sky. Presently the skeletons of great warehouses stand out in relief against . . . sheets of roaring, blazing, furious flames. . . . [As] one fire sinks, another rises . . . lurid, angry, dreadful to look upon."[23] Sherman spent the night organizing fire-fighting teams. By morning, however, Atlanta lay in ruins. Of its four thousand houses, barely four hundred survived the inferno.

The march settled into a daily routine. Reveille sounded between 4:00 A.M. and 6:00 A.M., depending on the distance to be traveled that day. After breakfast, the troops packed their gear before the buglers sounded assembly, where an officer read out the marching orders and any special instructions from Uncle Billy. Then they took their places and set out.

The army moved in four columns, each twenty-five miles long, on parallel roads from five to fifteen miles apart, traveling about ten miles a day. Wagons and guns used the roads, the troops marching on either side. To avoid ambushes, cavalry patrols ranged ahead and along the flanks of the columns. The cavalry was led by Hugh Judson Kilpatrick, described by Sherman as "a hell of a damned fool." But he was a fighting fool, just the sort of man he needed. Kilpatrick's troopers called him "Kill Cavalry," because he kept them going until almost dead from exhaustion.

Each division detailed men for special jobs. Engineers built bridges and "corduroy" roads; that is, they cut down trees and laid the logs side by side, like the ridges in corduroy cloth, to give a roadbed a firm foundation. The engineers were equally skilled at destroying things, particularly railroads. A company would spread out along one side of a length of track, two men to a tie. At a "Yo heave!" everyone lifted at once. As the track came up, they flipped it over, knocking the rails loose. The ties were then piled up, set on fire, and the rails laid across the top. The red-hot rails were then bent around trees to form "Sherman's neckties." Once bent out of shape, rails had to be rerolled at a steel mill. And since the South had only one mill left in 1864, in Richmond, Georgia's railroads were put out of action for the rest of the war.

Before leaving Atlanta, Sherman issued Field Order No. 120, commanding the army to "forage liberally on the country during the march." Each morning, all brigade commanders were to send search parties, led by an officer, to collect food from civilians living along the line of march. Foragers were not to enter private homes, threaten civilians, or loot.

Field Order No. 120 was made to be broken. We cannot say whether Sherman wanted this and was just covering himself with a written order, but he must have known that, with so many troops away from the marching columns, it was impossible to keep track of them at all times. In addition to the regular foragers, thousands of others set out on their own each day; nobody tried to stop them, much less arrest them for desertion. These were called "bummers," from the German *bummler*—tramp. As the march continued, the word became respectable. All foragers became known as bummers; Sherman called himself an "old bummer." After the war, bummer was shortened to "bum."

The bummers had a jolly time in Georgia. With most white men away in the Confederate army, they found only women, children, old folks, and slaves on the plantations. Even when on their best behavior, bummers were pretty scary. Their visit to the Burge Plantation near Covington was typical. On November 19, 1864, Mrs. Dolly Sumner Lunt, the owner's widow, was out walking with her nine-year-old daughter, Sadai. Seeing smoke in the distance, she took Sadai by the hand and ran for the house.

They reached home moments ahead of Sherman's men. Years later, Mrs. Lunt told what happened in a book, *A Woman's Wartime Journal*. Without saying a word, bummers began looting her plantation:

> . . . like demons they rush in. My yards are full. To my smoke-house, my dairy, pantry, kitchen, and cellar, like famished wolves they come, breaking locks and whatever is in their way. The thousand pounds of meat in my smoke-house is gone in a twinkling, my flour, my meat, my lard, butter, eggs, pickles of various kinds . . . wine, jars, and jugs are all gone. My eighteen fat turkeys, my hens, chickens, and fowls, my young pigs, are shot down in my yard and hunted as if they were Rebels themselves. . . . Sherman himself and a greater portion of his army passed my house that day. All day, as the sad moments roll on, were they passing not only in front of my house, but behind; they tore down my garden palings, made a road through my back-yard and lot field, driving their stock and riding through, tearing down my fences and desolating my home—wantonly doing it when there was no necessity for it. Such a day, if I live to the age of Methuselah, may God spare me from ever seeing again!

Frantic, she begged a guard for help. "I cannot help you, Madam; it is orders," he replied coldly. Not only did his friends take her food, they looted her "boys'" (slaves') cabins, shouting that "Jeff Davis wanted to put them in his army, but that they should not fight for him but for the Union." Mother and daughter were crying when the Yankees left. Even Sadai's favorite doll had been stolen![24]

People tried to hide their valuables before the Yankees came.

Bummers, however, knew all the tricks. Floorboards were pulled up, walls broken open, and searchers sent into the nearby woods. They looked for anything unusual, such as freshly turned soil, which they probed with ramrods. Freshly dug graves always attracted their attention. Often they struck it rich, coffins filled with food or a family's money and silver. At other times they found a corpse; we know of bodies being dug up four times by different bands of bummers.

Finding nothing made them suspicious. In that case, the bummers had ways of loosening a person's tongue. They might tickle a man with bayonets, or place a pistol to his head and promise to blow his brains out if he didn't come clean "right quick!" Some gave in after being hung by the neck for a few seconds; others had only to see the rope to tell everything. One fellow had three hundred dollars in gold hidden in his garden. He was very fat and gave in immediately. "I'm dogged," he said, "if I'm going to risk my weight on a rope around my neck just for a little money!"[25]

A Yankee captain named George Pepper admitted that bummers were "possessed of a spirit of pure cussedness."[26] Nasty for the sake of being nasty, they enjoyed ruining plantation houses. The nicer the house, the more shocking their behavior. They smashed antique pianos and furniture with rifle butts. They cut open feather beds and scattered the contents. They broke into trunks, searching for expensive clothing; it was great fun to dress up as Southern belles. One bearded "lady" pranced about in a low-cut evening gown and a pearl necklace around his throat. Another fellow wore a lace wedding dress with a long train.

After they had their laughs, the bummers rejoined the army with wagons full of loot. Whatever was not needed, or could not be carried away, was destroyed. Cotton was burned and thousands of cattle and hogs slaughtered and left to rot. Plantation dogs, especially bloodhounds used to track runaway slaves, were routinely shot. Chickens were always fair game. A popular story told of an Irishman's encounter with an "unpatriotic" hen. "I found this hin laying eggs for the Ribil Army," said he, "and I hit her a whack that stopped that act of *treason* on the spot." Later, that same fellow had a run-in with a goose. "Oh! bedad S-r-r-r, this goose came out as I was wending my way along *peaceably* and hissed at the American flag and bejabez I shot him on the spot."[27] Plantation buildings were also burned, but this did not happen often.

Yankees described the march as "a holiday excursion." It was not really a campaign in a military sense. There was little danger; most soldiers never saw an armed Rebel, much less traded shots with one. With Hood off in Tennessee, only two small forces stood in Sherman's way. The Georgia militia were untrained civilians led by inexperienced officers. Confederate cavalry were too few to stop the invaders and too many for the local people. Having received no army rations for months, the horsemen had to live off the land or starve. They, too, looted plantations. More than one plantation owner was ordered to hand over his or her valuables to men in gray. Some Texans held the town of Rome hostage until it paid a ransom.

One battle was fought during the march to the sea. In late November, three thousand militiamen attacked a Yankee brigade near Griswoldville. It was a slaughter. Afterward, bluecoats were horrified at what they had done. An officer described a field littered with six hundred dead and wounded. These were not the soldiers he expected to find, but elderly men and boys in their early teens. "I hope we will never have to shoot at such men again," he wrote. "They knew nothing at all about fighting and I think their officers knew as little."[28]

Unable to beat Sherman in the open, Rebel leaders turned to guerrilla warfare. *Guerrilla* is Spanish for "little war"—war fought by roving bands of civilians behind enemy lines. Jefferson Davis called on Georgians to ambush Yankee patrols, fell trees across the roads, and burn hay that could feed horses. Southerners knew about this kind of fighting. During the Revolution, Francis Marion led guerrillas against the British in South Carolina. His skillful use of hit-and-run tactics, hiding in swamps to avoid enemy patrols, earned him the nickname "Swamp Fox."

The Swamp Fox would have met his match in Uncle Billy. The Yankee general was an old hand at dealing with guerrillas. After Shiloh, he had taken command at Memphis, Tennessee, an area infested with guerrillas. Peaceful farmers by day, at night they raided his outposts and shot at Union steamers on the Mississippi. Sherman did not consider a guerrilla a soldier. For him, a soldier must serve in a regular army, wear a uniform, and fight like a man. A soldier was not a "bushwhacker," a sneak who killed and vanished into the darkness. If civilians wished to fight, let them join the Confederate army, he said. If not, let them say their prayers!

Sherman believed in "hard war." He had a rule: *"In war everything is right that prevents anything."*[29] In keeping with this rule, he ordered ten pro-Confederate families expelled from Memphis for every steamer fired upon. When a boat was hit near Randolph, Tennessee, he burned the town in reprisal. When transports were shot at from a plantation, he landed troops to burn every building and field for miles around. If the attacks continued, he promised to fill boats with captured guerrillas and use them for target practice. He would stop at nothing to discourage guerrillas.

His Special Field Order No. 127 directed commanders to "deal harshly" with civilians who interfered with military operations. Their homes, barns, cotton gins, storehouses, and fields were to be burned at the slightest provocation. This did not mean that someone had to be caught doing anything wrong. Everyone was held responsible for guerrilla activity in an area. If they knew of guerrillas and did not report them, they were as guilty as the guerrillas. And if they knew no guerrillas, they were guilty of not trying to detect criminals, a duty of all law-abiding citizens. In effect, they were all hostages to the behavior of others.

Uncle Billy was willing to kill hostages to save his troops. Some of his men, he knew, were bound to be captured. But once they were disarmed, he expected them to be treated as war prisoners. Several bummers, however, were shot or had their throats slit upon surrendering. These men were killed in cold blood and had signs left on their bodies: "DEATH TO ALL FORAGERS." Foraging is legal in warfare. Even if bummers had committed crimes, they were entitled to a trial. These deaths were murder. In reply, Sherman ordered commanders to shoot a Confederate prisoner for each Yankee body they found.

Confederate use of torpedoes, or land mines, was treated in a similar fashion. Mines were buried artillery shells rigged to explode when stepped on. Like foraging, mine-laying is now an accepted tactic of warfare. In twentieth-century wars, millions of mines have been planted in every possible location. As a result, people are killed years after a war ends. But in Sherman's day, mines could be used only in front of trenches and forts. To bury them in roads far from defended places was considered a crime.

After the fall of Atlanta, Rebels mined a stretch of railroad north of the city. Sherman had no intention of allowing the enemy to wreck his trains and get away without a scratch, so he ordered a carload of Confederate prisoners to be pulled ahead of a train. Nothing happened, except that the prisoners had the scare of their lives. The mining, apparently, had stopped.

Another time Sherman saw a lieutenant whose horse had

stepped on a torpedo. The horse lay dead; the soldier's left leg was torn off at the knee. "This is not war, but murder!" the general roared.

Sherman ordered Confederate prisoners to clear the road of mines—or die trying.

"You can't send us out there to be blown up—in the name of humanity, General!" one pleaded, speaking for his comrades.

"Your people put 'em there to assassinate our men," he said, pointing to the wounded lieutenant. "Is that humanity?"

"It wasn't us, General. We don't know where the things are buried."

"I don't care a damn if you're blown up," said Sherman. "I'll not have my own men killed like this."

One prisoner was freed to warn his comrades about planting mines in the future. The others used shovels and their bare hands to uncover seven more explosive devices.[30]

Sherman's policy was clearly one of terrorism, that is, using fear as a weapon, largely against civilians and prisoners, to crush opposition. And it worked. Fear ruled in Georgia during that fall of 1864. People were so terrorized that, with few exceptions, they dared not resist.

Town after town fell without a struggle. At Milledgeville, the state capital, militiamen fled before Uncle Billy arrived. His troops used the opportunity to have a little "fun" before moving on. Officers repealed Georgia's act of secession after a mock debate in the statehouse, while their men looted the building. Millions of dollars in Confederate money was flung to the wind or used to light pipes and kindle fires. Thousands of books, some of them centuries old, were tossed from the windows of the State Library. That was too much for Major James Connolly of the 123d Illinois Infantry. He wrote his wife: "I don't object to stealing horses, mules, niggers and all such *little things,* but I will not engage in plundering and destroying public libraries."[31]

The town, however, escaped the torch. Dreadful as it was, Yankee terrorism was not that of the twentieth century. Today's terrorist aims to destroy people, usually helpless civilians. Sherman's aim was to destroy enemy morale and property rather than people. True, civilians went hungry and lived in fear, but few (if any) were killed. Southern women described his bummers as dirty, foul-mouthed thieves, yet, one recalled, "they generally spoke to us as 'lady' and, although they swore horribly, they seldom swore *at us.*"

Moreover, they "abstain[ed] from *personal insult,*" a polite term for rape.[32] Army records show that two women were raped during the entire march. Undoubtedly other cases went unreported, but we shall never know how many. Sherman said he knew of no cases of murder among his soldiers, a view supported by historians.

Sherman freed more slaves than any other Union general. No doubt he would have been shocked had he known that this would happen when he left Atlanta. The war did not change his racist views; if anything, it strengthened them. He opposed putting blacks into the army, because he did not think them clever enough. "I like niggers *well enough* as niggers," he wrote a friend, "but when fools and idiots try to make niggers better than ourselves, I have an opinion."[33] Still, he was a practical man. Like Grant, he saw the need to end slavery in order to win the war.

Black people were equally practical. Whatever Sherman's reasons, they knew he was destroying slavery, and that was good enough for them. Everywhere he went, blacks hailed him as a red-haired, red-bearded Moses come to lead them to the Promised Land. The story of Moses and the flight of the Hebrews from Egyptian bondage had always been a favorite among slaves. It was more than history; it was God's promise that someday all people would be free. Now God, through Sherman, was keeping His promise. "He's the Angel of the Lord!" blacks shouted when he appeared.[34] A young woman held up her baby as he passed, crying, "Dar's de man dat rules de world!" An old man could not take his eyes off the general. "I have seen the great Messiah and the army of the Lord!" he shouted.[35]

Sherman's army *did* seem almost biblical. Blacks sat on rail fences, watching the columns pass hour after hour. They had never seen anything like it. So many men and so many guns! A white-haired man was cheering and saluting when a boy rode up to him on a mule. The boy said that another column, equally large, was marching on a road nearby. The man raised his arms and shouted, "Dar's millions of 'em, millions!" then asked a soldier, "Is dare anybody lef' up Norf?" A few days later, a lieutenant saw him hobbling along, trying to keep up with the soldiers. "Uncle," he asked, "how far are you going?" The old fellow thought that an odd question. "Why, I'se jined," he replied.[36]

Thousands of blacks "jined" the march. They fell in behind the columns, following the freedom road. Newsman David P. Conyngham described the scene:

Colonies, squads, whole families, from the feeble old folks, supported on their canes and tottering under heavy bundles, down to the muling infant in the mother's arms, while her back was burdened with a heavy bundle, fell in. The young and the old left home, at a moment's notice, to go they knew not where . . . in search of freedom. Black children of all ages and sizes . . . toddled along in rags and filth, urged on by the application of the maternal rod. Babies squealed in their mothers' laps [in] old buggies and wagons that they took from massa. . . . Mules and horses carried hampers and bags, stuffed with children and wearables, balanced on each side. It was no unusual sight to see a black head, with large staring eyes, peeping out of a sack at one side, and a ham [or side] of bacon or a turkey balancing it at the other. . . .[37]

Uncle Billy was not happy about this at all. Blacks, he said, must not slow down his army or give it additional mouths to feed. Only young, strong men able to work could be taken along; the others should stay behind until the war ended. He explained his reasons to black ministers, urging them to spread the word among their people, but he did not try to keep the refugees away by force.

One officer, however, acted on his own. General Jefferson C. Davis—no relation to the Confederate president—ordered a pontoon bridge taken up after his troops crossed a creek, stranding hundreds of refugees on the far bank. Confederate cavalry charged and drove them into the water, drowning hundreds. Davis was not punished, although fellow officers called him a cowardly brute. Still, blacks continued to follow the freedom road, and twenty-five thousand were said to be with Sherman's columns at any given time. He once measured them not in numbers, but in *miles*.

On December 13 they reached the coast. Eight days later, Savannah fell and Sherman wired Lincoln, offering it as a Christmas gift for the nation. The march to the sea was a success. In less than a month, he had led an army across 285 miles of enemy territory. At little cost to himself, he destroyed railroads, locomotives, rolling stock, bridges, tunnels, cotton gins, and public buildings. He took at least twenty-one million pounds of food and animal feed valued at $100 million, of which his army used $20 million worth and destroyed the rest. Those supplies would be sorely missed by the Army of Northern Virginia.

Sherman himself received a Christmas present from Tennessee. On December 15 George Thomas routed John Bell Hood at

Nashville. More than ten thousand Confederates surrendered on the spot, while many others fled in panic. "You go to hell. I've been there," a private yelled to an officer who ordered him to stop.[38] Hood was so agitated that he stood by helplessly, pulling his hair and crying as if his heart would break. The remnants of his army kept running until they reached Tupelo, Mississippi. Scores of men deserted each day until the Army of Tennessee vanished as a fighting force.

The next campaign fit in perfectly with Grant's master plan. Sherman was to march to Virginia by way of the Carolinas. By going overland, rather than by sea, he could destroy more of the South's resources and wreck the railroads that supplied the Army of Northern Virginia. Once Sherman got moving, Robert E. Lee would not know where to turn; indeed, anything he did in one place was bound to weaken him elsewhere. If he turned to face Sherman, Grant would break through in Virginia. But if he continued to face Grant, his army would starve while Sherman hammered from the rear.

Sherman invaded South Carolina early in February 1865. South Carolina was better known as the "hell-hole of secession." Had it not been for this state, there might never have been a Civil War. She had been first to secede, first to raise the banner of revolt, first to insult the Stars and Stripes. To make matters worse, during the march to the sea South Carolinians bragged about whipping Sherman if he dared set foot in their state. His men welcomed the challenge. As one explained, "Here is where treason began, and, by God, here is where it shall end!"[39]

Yankees planned a painful end, a fiery end. From the commanding general down, they meant to burn South Carolina. Sherman set the tone. As "Kill Cavalry" Kilpatrick, set out, Sherman asked to be kept informed of the cavalry's progress. When Kilpatrick asked how, he replied, "Oh, just burn a barn or something. Make a smoke like the Indians do."[40]

Georgia had gotten off easily, compared to its neighbor. In Georgia, few towns were burned. In South Carolina, few towns were spared. Wherever Sherman passed, plumes of smoke marked his route by day and tongues of fire by night. Among the towns either partially or completely burned were Robertsville, Grahamville, McPhersonville, Barnwell (renamed "Burnwell" by the Yankees), Blackville, Orangeburg, Lexington, Winnsboro, Camden, Lancaster, Chesterfield, Cheraw, and Darlington. In addition, pine forests were put to the torch, blazing out of control for days. The air reeked of burned wood and pine resin. "Sometimes the world seemed on fire. We were almost stifled by smoke and flames," a Yank reported.[41]

The worst destruction was in Columbia, the state capital. Sherman took Columbia on February 17; by next morning three-quarters of it lay in ashes. His veterans boasted of what would happen days before they arrived. As they marched, they chanted:

Hail Columbia, happy land;
If I don't burn you, I'll be damned![42]

The Confederates had already made a start. Before leaving, they set fire to hundreds of bales of cotton in the downtown business district. The first Yankees to arrive doused the cotton with water, but it continued to smolder. Meantime, others broke into warehouses in search of loot. They found plenty to steal—and to drink. Barrels of whiskey were rolled into the streets, their tops bashed in, and everyone invited to drink free of charge. Many soldiers had not eaten since breakfast, and the whiskey went down like liquid fire.

Yankees went on a drunken rampage. Joined by escaped prisoners of war and blacks, they set their own fires at the very time a strong wind was fanning the smoldering cotton. The fires grew larger, hotter, leaping from street to street and house to house. Seventeen-year-old Emma LeConte, the daughter of a college professor, watched from her window. "My God! What a scene!" she thought.

> Imagine night turning into noonday, only with a blazing, scorching glare that was horrible—a copper colored sky across which swept columns of black rolling smoke glittering with sparks and flying embers, while all around us were falling thickly showers of burning flakes. Everywhere the palpitating blaze walled the streets as far as the eye could reach—filling the air with a terrible roar. On every side the crackling and devouring fire, while every instant came the crashing timbers and the thunder of falling buildings. A quivering molten ocean seemed to fill the air and sky. The Library opposite us seemed framed in gushing flames and smoke, while through the windows gleamed liquid fire. . . .[43]

Sober Yankees tried to control the flames. These were the exceptions; their comrades thought no fire too hot for South Carolinians. "Serves 'em right" was heard often that night. "Did you think of this when you hurrahed for Secession?" a soldier shouted to a man watching his shop burn. "How do you like it, hey?"[44]

Sherman agreed. Years later, he admitted: "Though I never ordered it and never wished it, I have never shed many tears over the event, because I believe it hastened what we all fought for, the end of the war."[45]

The loss of Columbia forced the Rebels to abandon Charleston the following day. Sherman had bypassed the coastal city and was about to cut it off during his swing northward into North Carolina. Nevertheless, much of the city burned when cotton and other supplies were set on fire by the retreating troops. Once again the Stars and Stripes flew from Fort Sumter in the harbor.

By this time, Confederate General Joe Johnston had been recalled to face his old enemy. But the Confederates simply did not have the men to halt the Union steamroller. By early April, Sherman reached Goldsboro, North Carolina, only two hundred miles south of Richmond. He was preparing to move against Johnston when Grant sent word that Lee had surrendered at Appomattox Court House, Virginia.

VII ✧ GRANT AND LEE

The art of war is simple enough. Find out where your enemy is. Get at him as soon as you can. Strike him as hard as you can, and keep moving on.

—Ulysses S. Grant

Brandy Station, Virginia, March 1864. It was one of those early spring days, cool and damp, when the first crocuses peek out from beneath last year's fallen leaves. Two privates were standing guard as U. S. Grant rode by, the usual cigar clenched between his teeth. Silently, they followed him with their eyes until he was gone. Then one turned to the other and asked: "Well, what do you think?" Pausing to reflect, his friend replied at last, "He looks as if he meant it."[1]

Grant certainly did mean "it." The moment he arrived, things began to change in the Army of the Potomac. Reinforcements poured in, bringing regiments up to full combat strength. Newcomers as well as veterans drilled until they could go through the routines in their sleep. Freight trains and wagon trains arrived loaded with food, uniforms, tents, blankets, medical supplies, and ammunition. On the whole, a soldier wrote, "We all felt at last that *the boss* had arrived."[2]

Much as they admired Grant, Yankees were not looking forward to the next campaign. The Army of the Potomac had invaded Virginia four times. Each time it was defeated, or had to retreat after a costly stalemate. By 1864, it had an inferiority complex; even high-ranking officers expected defeat. Nothing, it seemed, could reassure them or raise their spirits. Yes, they knew Grant's reputation. True, he was the conqueror of Vicksburg, the savior of Chattanooga, Billy Sherman's friend, and Abe Lincoln's man. Even so, his aides heard the same remark from officers throughout the army: "Well, Grant has never met Bobby Lee yet."[3] He might whip a hundred Braxton Braggs and still not amount to much in their eyes. What really mattered was how he did against the Confederacy's first team: General Robert E. Lee and the Army of Northern Virginia.

Born in 1807, Robert E. Lee was the son of "Light Horse Harry" Lee, a revolutionary war hero. After four years at West Point without a demerit, he graduated second in the class of 1829. Two years later, he married Martha Washington's great-granddaughter, with whom he had seven children. A devoted father, he had a way with children—other people's as well as his own. He enjoyed helping them with their lessons and teaching them to ride, swim, and ice-skate. During long tours of duty, he wrote them of his love and how much he missed them. He also wrote about his pets. "My rattlesnake, my only pet, is dead," he told daughter Mildred. "He grew sick and would not eat his frogs and died one night."[4]

After the Mexican War, Lee became superintendent of West Point, then colonel of a cavalry regiment. The 1850s were troubled times, the issues of slavery and secession dividing the nation as never before. Unlike Grant and Sherman, Lee denounced slavery in the harshest terms. The six slaves given him by his father-in-law were freed long before the Civil War. "In this enlightened age," he wrote, "slavery as an institution is a moral, political evil in any country."[5] So was secession, the worst tragedy he could imagine. Secession was worse than murder; for while a murderer killed individuals, secessionists destroyed an entire nation. As the war clouds gathered, he told his son Custis, in January 1861: "Secession is nothing but revolution."[6] If he owned every one of the South's four million slaves, he said, he would gladly set them free to save the Union.

Considered the nation's best soldier, Lee was offered command of the Union armies by Lincoln after Fort Sumter. He refused and joined the Confederates instead. In doing so, he knew he would be fighting for slavery and secession, the very things he despised. Bad as these were, however, they were lesser evils, to him. "Virginia," his father once said, "is my country; her I will obey" at any cost.[7] It was the same for him. In order to serve the Union, he would have to fight Virginia. And fighting Virginia meant fighting

After Appomattox. On April 17, 1865, eight days after surrendering to Grant, Robert E. Lee posed for a picture in Richmond. His eldest son, Major General Washington Curtis Lee, stands on the left; Colonel Walter Taylor, his aide, is on the right.

his neighbors, his relatives, even his own children. These were not things he could do and remain true to himself. Had he decided differently, the Civil War might have been shortened by years and thousands of lives saved; and perhaps the world would never have heard of U. S. Grant.

The two men were alike in certain ways. Both hated war. Lee was horrified at the sights and sounds of the battlefield. "What a cruel thing is war . . . to fill our hearts with hatred instead of love for our neighbors, and to devastate the fair face of this beautiful world," he said.[8] Yet, like Grant, he was a master at his craft.

Lee could put himself in an opponent's place and see his next move before he saw it himself. If you tangled with Bobby Lee, you knew you were fighting for your life. You could always count on him to be daring and to do the unexpected. He put his whole self into a battle. Sometimes he became so excited that he shook his fist at the enemy, whom he called "those people"; Grant was always "that man." Totally fearless, he believed that God would not take him away before his time.

Lee's main task was to defend Virginia. This he did to perfection, not losing a single battle in his home state. Only when he invaded the North was he defeated. His first defeat came at Antietam Creek, in Maryland, in 1862; the second was at Gettysburg the following year. Nevertheless, his soldiers never lost faith in him. And why should they? He lived as they did; his dinner often consisted of cabbage boiled with a little salt. Soldiers' lives were precious to him, and he mourned the dead as if they were his own children. Losing them, he said, "causes me to weep tears of blood and wish that I could never hear the sound of a gun again."[9] Often, when he spoke to a soldier, he called him "my son" or "my dear boy." Men referred to him as "Uncle Robert" and "Marse [Master] Robert."

Lee became the idol of the Confederacy. Gentle, generous, and gallant, he could do no wrong in Southerners' eyes. Soldiers worshiped him. Churchgoers prayed for his safety. Parents made him a role model for their youngsters. Indeed, there was so much praise that he became almost godlike. "Mama, I can never remember," a little girl asked, "was General Lee in the Old Testament or the New Testament?"[10] A woman later recalled how, as a child, she saw a fatherly figure with white hair and a white beard: *We had heard of God, but here was General Lee.*"[11]

Grant knew that Richmond was one of the most heavily defended places on earth. If Lee chose to stay put, there would be no chance of blasting him out. But by crossing the Rapidan River and moving south, Grant thought he might slip between Lee and Richmond, easing him out of his trenches and forcing him to fight in the open. Since Lee had 66,000 men to Grant's 122,000, the odds were in the Union's favor. With luck, Grant might finish him off well before Sherman reached Atlanta.

Lee realized what his opponent had in mind. He also knew that Grant's plan had a weakness. Once across the Rapidan, the Yankees would have to cross some dangerous ground before moving into open country. That area, known as the Wilderness, was a twenty-square-mile tangle of trees, vines, bushes, swamps, and streams. The place was so overgrown that it was impossible to see more than a few yards in any direction. Union regiments and wagon trails would be strung out along two narrow dirt roads. Lee meant to let them get into the Wilderness, then spring an ambush. He would hit them on the left (northern) flank, break through, and get behind them. Grant would have to retreat or be cut off in the middle of nowhere.

On the evening of May 3–4, the Army of the Potomac crossed the Rapidan and plunged into the Wilderness. It marched all day without finding a trace of the enemy. Lee's scouts, however, followed its every movement. The Army of Northern Virginia was at home in these parts. Exactly a year ago, it had surprised the Yankees at the crossroads of Chancellorsville, where there was only one house, an inn. In two days' fighting, the Union lost seventeen thousand men. Regarded as "Lee's masterpiece," the battle is still studied at West Point.

Now the Yankees were back at Chancellorsville. On their first night out, they camped on the old battlegrounds. Reminders of the battle were to be seen everywhere. Trees were scarred and riddled with bullets. The ground was strewn with bloodstained clothing, rusty gun barrels, and broken equipment. Worse, they had bedded down in the middle of a vast graveyard—an *open* graveyard. The dead had been buried in shallow graves by the victorious Confederates. But in the year that followed, wind and rain unearthed many bodies, while animals scattered the bones. Private Frank Wilkeson was haunted by the scene:

> Many polished skulls lay on the ground. Leg bones, arm bones, and ribs could be found without trouble. Toes of shoes and bits of faded, weather-worn uniforms, and occasionally a grinning, fleshless face peered through the low mound that had been hastily thrown over these brave warriors. . . . We sat on long, low mounds. The dead were all around us. Their eyeless skulls seemed to stare steadily at us. The smoke [of campfires] drifted to and fro among us. The trees swayed and sighed gently in the soft wind. . . . As we sat silently smoking . . . an infantry soldier who had . . . been prying into the shallow grave he sat on with his bayonet, suddenly rolled a skull on the ground before us, and said in a deep, low voice, "That is what you are all coming to, and some of you will start toward it tomorrow."[12]

Lee struck next morning, May 5. In that awful Wilderness, 188,000 men tore at each other with a fury rare even in this, our most ferocious war. It was blindman's bluff—with guns. Clouds of smoke rolled among the trees, so that men seldom had a target to shoot at. They simply shot into the smoke or by "earsight"; that is, toward the sound of gunfire, hoping it was the enemy's. Battle cries and cries of pain mingled with the *whoosh, ping, bam* of bullets and shells. There was so much flying lead that one soldier thought he could catch a pot full of bullets if he held it up at the end of a pole. Even hardened veterans were amazed. Among them was a wounded Texan who had been taken prisoner. When asked what he thought of the battle, he snapped, "Battle be damned! It ain't no battle. . . . It's all a damned mess. And our two armies ain't nothing but howlin' mobs!"[13]

Both sides had a common enemy: fire. Muzzle flashes from thousands of muskets set fire to the brush in dozens of places. Flames spread among the fallen leaves, traveled along vines, and leaped from tree to tree. Ammunition wagons exploded. The wounded—men shot through the legs or in the guts—watched in terror, unable to escape. A blanket of smoke drifted ahead of the flames, smothering the wounded. At least they died before the fire reached them. Now and then the screams of men being burned alive rose above the din of battle. The odor was nauseating, a mixture of burned wood, gun smoke, and roasted flesh. As at Shiloh, wounded enemies helped each other as best they could. Yankees and Rebels shared their canteens; those who could crawl dragged those who couldn't out of harm's way.

Caught off guard, Grant refused to give way. Once the initial shock wore off, he fed more and more troops into the battle. Lee had not expected such a reaction. Never before had he met such a stubborn, aggressive opponent. In the past, Yankee generals had retreated after such a terrible fight. But Grant hung on like a bulldog. All day he attacked and attacked, not giving Lee a chance to maneuver or regroup his forces. The Confederates had lost the initiative, and the Yankees were calling the shots.

At dusk, the armies pulled back for the night. They lay down amid scenes of incredible horror. Bodies lay thick on the ground, often mangled beyond recognition. The wounded moaned outside the hospital tents. The breeze carried the stench of death and the screams of the dying; enemy snipers were everywhere, making it too dangerous to go out after the wounded. No one, least of all Grant, could be unaffected by such scenes. Officers noticed him wince as he passed the dead and wounded. "I cannot bear the sight of suffering," he'd say, turning his face away.[14]

War councils were held in both camps toward midnight. It was decided that tomorrow, May 6, would be the day of reckoning. Grant told his aides that he would attack at 5:00 A.M. Lee ordered his own attack for the same hour. Thus, each commander was expecting to attack, not to be attacked. It would be like express trains racing toward each other on the same track.

The attacks began on schedule. The previous day's slaughter was repeated, only on a larger scale. Grant pushed his troops forward, using his numerical advantage for all it was worth. Lee sat on his horse, Traveller, in a clearing, watching his men fall back with the Yankees close behind them. His only hope was Pete Longstreet's corps, which was expected any moment after an all-night march. Messages were sent urging Longstreet to hurry. Hurry! There was not a second to lose!

Suddenly, Lee saw hundreds of men racing from behind with muskets at the ready.

"Who are you, my boys?" he called at the top of his voice.

"Texas boys," they shouted. They were the spearhead of Longstreet's corps.

Nicknamed "Lee's war horse," James Longstreet was one of the ablest Confederate generals, as well as a friend of U. S. Grant.

"Hurrah for Texas!" Lee cried. Then he raised himself in his stirrups and yelled, "Texans always move them!"

Coming from Lee, those words were pure electricity. The Texans gave a cheer heard a mile away and surged forward. At that moment an officer rode by. Hearing Lee's shout and the Texans' reply, tears began to roll down his cheeks and he exclaimed, "I would charge hell itself for that old man!"

By now bullets were zipping within inches of Lee's head. He ignored them. "Charge them!" he called, his face flushed. "Charge! Charge, boys!" Then he spurred Traveller forward. He was going to lead the charge in person!

The Texans could scarcely believe their eyes. Lee's was the one life they could not afford to lose. Thousands might fall and the battle continue, but if he went down all was lost. "Go back, General Lee! Go back!" a soldier shouted, and instantly others took up the cry.

Lee kept going as if in a trance. At that point the soldiers took matters into their own hands. A sergeant grabbed Traveller's reins while others spread their arms to block the way. "Lee to the rear! Lee to the rear!" they shouted. "Go back, General Lee! Go back! We won't go on unless you go back!" At last he heard them. Turning Traveller around, he rode to the rear. His parting words were "Charge them!"[15]

They did, driving the Yankees back. Longstreet then led an all-out assault that broke the enemy line. He was advancing steadily when he and an aide came under "friendly fire." The aide died instantly; Longstreet received a neck wound that put him out of action for five months. With him down, the advance ground to a halt by midafternoon. General John B. Gordon of Georgia led another attack at dusk. Hundreds of Yankees were captured, including two generals, but resistance stiffened and could not be broken before darkness ended the fighting.

Gordon's attack was only a mile from Grant's command post. Officers were dashing about, acting as if the Rebels were already there. Not Grant. Quietly puffing his cigar, he listened to reports and gave the necessary orders. Only once did he show any emotion. A brigadier general came up to him shouting, "General Grant . . . I know Lee's methods well by past experience; he will throw his whole army between us and the Rapidan, and then cut us off completely from our communications."

Grant had heard a lot about Bobby Lee recently—too much,

in fact. But this was the last straw. He took the cigar out of his mouth and gave the general a piece of his mind: "Oh, I am heartily tired of hearing what Lee is going to do. Some of you always seem to think he is suddenly going to turn a double somersault, and land in our rear and on both of our flanks at the same time. Go back to your command, and try to think of what we are going to do ourselves, instead of what Lee is going to do."[16] The fellow left without saying another word.

Generals, even great ones, are still human beings; they, too, have a breaking point. Grant had been under terrific strain for two days. It finally caught up with him as the fighting died down. After attending to some last-minute details, he went to his tent, threw himself on his cot, and burst into tears. Officers standing outside were embarrassed at hearing their chief cry, but that was just what he needed to relieve the tension. After a while, he came out and sat by the fire as if nothing had happened.

A mile away Lee, too, sat by a fire, surrounded by his aides. They sat silently, thinking about what had happened since dawn. Finally, General Gordon broke the silence, saying that Grant was bound to retreat. Lee knew better. He had tested this Yankee and knew he was different from the rest. "Grant is not a retreating man," he said. "Gentlemen, the Army of the Potomac has a head."[17] He had met his match. For two days, Grant had held him in place and put him on the defensive. From now on, Grant would be calling the shots and Lee would have to react. Although no one could have known it then, the Wilderness was the beginning of the end for the Army of Northern Virginia.

The armies spent the next day resting, tending to their wounded, and burying their dead. The casualties were horrendous. Union losses totaled 17,666; the Confederates lost at least 7,500 men. President Lincoln was stunned. "My God! My God!" he moaned. "Over twenty thousand men killed and wounded in a few days' fighting! I cannot bear it! I cannot bear it!"[18] Unable to sleep, he paced the darkened White House, head bent, black rings under his eyes, staring at the floor.

On the night of May 7–May 8, the Army of the Potomac started to leave the Wilderness. The soldiers were in a sour mood as they slung their packs and stepped into line. Once again, it seemed, they were retreating after a fight with Bobby Lee. Once again, it seemed, men had bled and died for nothing.

They marched until they came to a familiar crossroads. If they turned left, they would be heading north, retreating; a right turn would take them south, deeper into Confederate territory. They turned south. At that moment they realized what Lee already knew. The Army of the Potomac was advancing. That stubby little man watching from the roadside was in a class by himself. With Grant in charge, there would be no turning back—ever. Their spirits rose. Soldiers began to sing "John Brown's Body," "Yankee Doodle," and a black spiritual: "Ain't I glad to get out of the wilderness!"

William Tecumseh Sherman called this "the supreme moment" in his friend's life. To have turned back might well have destroyed Northern morale and caused Lincoln's defeat in the November election. Grant's move had saved the Union.

Grant's objective was the crossroads at Spotsylvania Court House ten miles to the southeast. By moving fast, he still hoped to slip between Lee and Richmond, forcing a showdown in the open. Lee, however, learned of the move and got his men to the crossroads ahead of the Yankees. By the time the Yankees arrived, the Confederates held a line of trenches in the shape of an upside-down *U,* known as the "Mule Shoe." A mile deep and a half-mile wide, it was as strong a position as the Yankees had ever seen.

Grant decided to hit the top of the *U* on both sides at once. A hard blow, he believed, would split it wide open, as an iron wedge splits a log. Once inside, the Yankees could drive down the center, cutting Lee's army in half and attacking each half from behind.

The attack began at 4:30 A.M. on May 12. It was pitch-dark, and a heavy mist clung to the ground. Masses of troops moved ahead slowly, quietly, their officers leading by compass. By the time the defenders realized their danger, their trenches were over-run. Twenty guns and three thousand Confederates were captured within a few minutes. The survivors fled to the rear, running as if Satan himself were after them. When an officer cried, "Halt!" a soldier called back, "[I'll] give any man fifty dollars to halt me, but I can't halt myself!"[19]

Fortunately, John Gordon's division had been held in reserve midway down the Mule Shoe. Gordon's men, all seasoned veterans, were forming line of battle at the very moment Lee rode up on Traveller. As in the Wilderness, he tried to lead the counterattack. And once again the soldiers stopped him. They surrounded Traveller so closely that he could scarcely raise a leg. It seemed, to some, that they would pick up horse and rider and carry them to the rear.

"General Lee," Gordon cried, "you shall not lead my men in a

charge. No man can do that, sir. Another is here for that purpose. These men behind you are Georgians, Virginians, and Carolinians. They have never failed you on any field. They will not fail you here. Will you, boys?"

"No, no, no; we'll not fail him!" they cried. "General Lee to the rear! General Lee to the rear!"[20]

Lee got the message. As he turned away, Gordon's men swept forward. They delivered a hard blow, but not the knockout blow their commander intended. The Yankees fell back to the tip of the Mule Shoe, faced about, and continued to fight from the captured trench. They were determined to break through once again; the Confederates were equally determined to hold on. Lee was building another trench line in the rear, across the base of the *U*. Until it was finished, those up front must either retake the trench or prevent another advance.

At one place, the trench made a small bend, or angle. This was

The ultimate sacrifice. A dead Confederate soldier at Spotsylvania Court House, Virginia, 1864. His shirt is not Confederate gray, but Yankee blue. Clothing was so scarce in Lee's army that soldiers were forced to strip the enemy dead.

to become famous as the Bloody Angle of Spotsylvania. The closest, nastiest fighting of the Civil War took place on this spot. There had never been anything like it—not Shiloh, not Gettysburg, not the Wilderness. Those who lived through it called it the worst day of their lives. Many said they never expected to be believed when they told of the horrors of the Bloody Angle, because they could hardly believe it themselves.

Each side poured in troops until the trench and the area on either side of it were jammed with men bent upon killing one another. A cold rain had begun to fall, and they stood up to their knees in bloody water. Swarms of bullets cut down whole stands of trees; an oak two feet thick was felled by minié balls. Bodies were hit so often they disintegrated, becoming blobs of shapeless flesh. Soldiers in the rear, unable to get a clear shot, passed their muskets to those in front. Men leaped on top of the trench and fired down as fast as friends could hand them a loaded gun. Each man fired a few times before he fell and another took his place. Skulls were bashed in with clubbed muskets and men stabbed with bayonets.

A Union officer named Francis Walker described how the mud was churned into a reddish brown soup with the dead and wounded piled three deep. "Some of these helpless wounded were pressed so heavily by the dead that they themselves died of suffocation. And there were points where the gathering corpses impeded the fighting and had to be flung to the rear."[21] Strange as it may seem, exhausted men sometimes stepped out of the firing line, flopped down in the mud, and slept as bullets whizzed overhead. Not even exploding artillery shells could wake them.

It went on like this for nineteen hours. Finally, around midnight, it ended. The new Confederate trench line was finished, and Lee's men quietly pulled back. The exhausted Yankees slept where they were, in the mud, amid the dead and dying. Grant's losses were about 6,800 killed, wounded, and missing; Lee lost at least 5,000 killed and wounded, plus another 3,000 captured and missing. "Missing" meant one of two things: the soldier had deserted, or was blown to bits and unrecognizable.

Grant spent a week trying to move around the Confederate right flank. Marse Robert, however, blocked each move, daring Grant to attack his trenches while refusing to give battle in the open. By late May, Grant wanted no more of Spotsylvania. Again he moved his army southward, this time to Cold Harbor, a dusty crossroads only ten miles east of Richmond. And again he found that Lee had beaten him to the punch. The Army of Northern Virginia was dug in along a chain of hills. These were quite low, but there was hardly a square inch in front of them that could not be hit from head-on and both sides at once.

Grant decided to attack without delay. Cold Harbor was to be an old-fashioned slugging match. It would involve no skill, no maneuvering, just slam-bang frontal assaults. Heavy casualties were to be expected, but, Grant felt, these were part of the cruel arithmetic of war. A breakthrough would shorten the war and save more lives in the end.

His men knew what was coming and acted accordingly. The night before the attack, many pinned their names to their uniforms so they could be identified and their people notified in case they were killed. One Yankee wrote a final entry in his diary: "June 3. Cold Harbor. I was killed."[22] The diary, torn and bloodstained, was later found by a burial squad.

At 4:30 A.M. on June 3, three Union corps stepped out in battle formation. It was a stunning spectacle, sixty thousand men advancing in waves twenty-eight feet deep. Rebel infantrymen stood

The high command of the Army of the Potomac. Grant is bending over the bench, discussing his next move with General George Gordon Meade, the victor of Gettysburg. The picture was taken at Masaponax Church, Virginia, May 21, 1864.

in their trenches, staring in amazement. This was not war, they thought; it was murder.

The blue waves came to within thirty paces of the trench line. And then it happened. Thousands of muskets blazed as one. Cannon spewed double charges of canister and grape. Yankees toppled over in droves, whole companies mowed down in the blinking of an eye. Men literally exploded in a crimson spray. "Heads, arms, legs, and muskets were seen flying high in the air," recalled Colonel P. D. Bowles of the 4th Alabama infantry.[23]

After a minute or two, the survivors retreated, leaving the fallen behind. After another minute or two, another wave came forward, then another. These, too, melted away in a blast of fire and lead. "I could see the dust fog out of a man's clothing in two or three places at once where as many balls would strike him at the same moment," an Alabamian recalled. "In two minutes not a man was left standing. . . . The stench from the dead between our lines and theirs was sickening . . . but we had the advantage, as the wind carried it away from us to them. The dead covered more than five acres of ground about as thickly as they could be laid."[24]

Even then, one could appreciate a brave enemy. A Yankee flag

One of the fruitless charges at Cold Harbor. The artist took liberties with truth, since the Union troops hardly saw their enemies, let alone came close enough to take their cannons.

bearer, a sergeant, kept walking toward the flashing muskets, head erect, eyes fixed straight ahead. He was alone, the rest of his regiment having been shot down. The Rebels held their fire, shouting: "Go back! Go back! We don't want to kill you! Go back!" The sergeant turned and, seeing that he was alone, saluted the men in gray. Then calmly, taking his own sweet time, he rolled up the flag and walked away. The Rebels leaped on top of their trench, tossed their hats in the air, and cheered until he reached safety.[25]

Grant ordered more attacks, but his soldiers had had enough. They hugged the ground, digging shallow holes and piling the dead in front, like sandbags. Whenever an order came, they fired a little faster, but no one stood up, much less charged. At night they turned their holes into deep trenches. Half an hour of fighting had cost the Yankees 7,000 killed and wounded, or nearly four men a second, as compared with less than 1,500 for the Rebels. Some regiments were practically annihilated. The 25th Massachusetts, for example, started with 310 men; it lost 210, or 68 percent, of its members within minutes.

Grant sat silently during his evening staff meeting. At last he lifted his head and said, "I regret this assault more than any one I have ever ordered. . . . No advantages have been gained sufficient to justify the heavy losses suffered."[26] It was the only mistake he ever admitted. Thousands had died for a few feet of barren ground—died for nothing. Cold Harbor was never mentioned at headquarters again.

The Army of the Potomac had suffered 55,000 casualties in twenty-nine days (May 5–June 3), an average of 1,896 every day and almost equal to Lee's entire army. Public opinion held Grant responsible for the tragedy. Unconditional Surrender Grant became "Butcher Grant" in the eyes of many of his countrymen. He was accused of wanting to bleed his way to victory. It was said (and still is by some) that he was merely a slugger, willing to take heavy losses to hurt the enemy even slightly. Since the North could easily replace its losses and the South could not, he thought the North was bound to win—or so the argument goes.

Not so. Grant accepted losses if they were necessary for victory, but he did not deliberately sacrifice the lives of his men. Lee, who "wept tears of blood" for the Rebel dead, was actually the greater killer. On average, he lost 149 killed and wounded out of every thousand men sent into combat; Grant lost 113. Given the fact that Grant was always on the offensive, and that the attacker

U. S. Grant poses for a picture outside his tent at Cold Harbor, Virginia, where his army suffered terrific losses.

normally loses more than the defender, his casualties were not especially high.[27] Even so, no army could survive many Cold Harbors. He had to try something different.

Grant decided on a bold plan. He would take his army from just northeast of Richmond to Petersburg, twenty miles to its south. Since Petersburg was at the junction of five railroads, its loss would cut Lee's supply line from the south and west, forcing him out of his trenches. And with Petersburg gone, the Confederates must abandon their capital, a key manufacturing center and symbol of Southern resistance.

Each time Grant moved, Lee had always managed to keep a step ahead of him. To take Petersburg, therefore, Grant needed a head start. He had to slip away from Cold Harbor without Lee's knowledge, cross the James River, and reach his objective before its defenses could be reinforced. Lee had always feared such a move. "We must destroy this army of Grant's before he gets to the James River," he told an aide. "If he gets there, it will become a siege, and then it will be a mere question of time."[28]

On June 13, the Confederates awoke at Cold Harbor to find

the Yankee trenches empty. The Army of the Potomac had moved out during the night, leaving only the cavalry to screen it from Lee's patrols. Moving swiftly, the army reached the James at a place where the river was a half-mile wide and without a bridge. That did not faze Grant's engineers. Within eight hours, they threw a twenty-one-hundred-foot pontoon bridge, the world's longest, across the river. By the time Lee learned the Yankees' whereabouts, they were crossing the James and racing toward Petersburg. The soldiers were elated. As they marched, they told one another that, this time, the end of the war was really in sight.

General William F. ("Baldy") Smith reached Petersburg on June 15 with nearly eighteen thousand men. The town's defenses were manned by twenty-five hundred Rebels under P. G. T. Beauregard. Although they occupied deep trenches, they were too few to resist odds of better than seven to one. Petersburg was as good as lost.

Smith hit the thinly held line with everything he had. The line broke, sending the defenders scurrying a mile to the rear. Hundreds of Rebels were captured, along with two artillery batteries seized by a division of black soldiers, an outfit with little combat experience. Petersburg was Smith's for the taking, had he not lost his nerve at the last moment. Overestimating the enemy's strength, he decided to wait for reinforcements rather than go in for the kill.

The reinforcements, two veteran divisions, soon arrived. Seeing the blacks hauling away their prizes, they put two and two together. If inexperienced troops could break the Rebel line, then veterans like themselves could easily finish the job. "Put us in," they begged Smith, "and we'll end this damned rebellion tonight!"

Smith refused. Instead of renewing the assault, he sent them to occupy the captured trenches. They were not pleased. As they turned in for the night, they could hear digging; the Rebels were preparing new trenches a mile away. "The rage of the enlisted men was devilish," a soldier wrote. "The most bloodcurdling blasphemy I ever listened to I heard that night. . . . The whole corps was furiously excited."[29] Next morning, Lee's army arrived after an all-night march. Thanks to Smith's timidity, the war would last another ten months and cause thousands of additional casualties.

Grant had run out of bold ideas. Four times he had tried to slip around Lee's right flank. Having failed each time, he decided on a full-scale siege. Compared to Petersburg, the sieges of Vicksburg and Atlanta would almost be child's play. Petersburg became the largest battlefield in history. It covered an area of 170 square miles, forming a maze of connected trenches and forts protected by wire entanglements, abatis, and *chevaux-de-frise*. The world had never seen anything like it before; nor would it again until the First World War fifty years later.

Petersburg pointed to the future in more ways than one. Until then, wars had been a series of battles with days, even months, in between. These lulls enabled soldiers to rest, calm jangled nerves, and share their feelings with comrades. Not at Petersburg. There, as in the twentieth century, warfare became a steady, grinding process. Danger lurked everywhere, and no one felt safe for an instant. There was constant skirmishing, artillery duels, and night raids. Although enemies still met to talk and trade, these meetings were few and far between. At Petersburg, both sides played for keeps.

Discomfort was added to danger. The booming of artillery and calls to arms at all hours made it impossible to get a night's sleep. By day, the temperature rose to 110° Fahrenheit in the shade. Sunstroke became a serious problem, and each day scores of men had to be carried to the rear on stretchers. Virginia was also in the midst of a three-month drought, which turned the soil into a fine dust that got into everything. "One's mouth will be so full of dust that you do not want your teeth to touch one another," a Yankee reported.[30] Rain only made matters worse, as a soldier wrote his father in Massachusetts: "Pleasant life we lead here, I can assure you. Yesterday we had our first rain [in] six weeks. . . . The trenches were half full of mud and water, as [were] the officers' quarters. I slept last night in a perfect mud-hole, half drenched myself. Today we have a regular hot day. Hot and sultry, a day that makes one feel dirty and sticky all over."[31]

A person can only escape so many near misses, take so much discomfort, without feeling the effects. As the siege continued, doctors noted an unusual illness. They called it "nostalgia"; today it is known as shell shock or combat fatigue. Nostalgia was a nervous breakdown brought on by stress. Victims stared blankly into space with glazed eyes, drooling, their bodies trembling. Many cried uncontrollably and could not eat; some went crazy. Nostalgia could happen to anyone, coward or hero, and so carried no shame for the victim; it was another type of wound, one without bleeding. The only treatment was plenty of rest and quiet, away from the horrors of the trenches.

The Yankees tried to end the siege as best they could. Some of their ideas were pure idiocy. An engineer wanted to build a wall around Petersburg and divert the James River into it to drown the Rebels. Another officer advised firing snuff-filled artillery shells so that the Rebels would be too busy sneezing to defend themselves. Other plans called for fire hoses to wash away earthworks, squirting flaming oil into enemy trenches, and using extralong bayonets to jab the Rebels at a safe distance.

There was nothing idiotic about Lieutenant Colonel Henry Pleasants's plan. Pleasants commanded the 48th Pennsylvania infantry, a unit made up of mainly coal miners. The 48th was posted opposite a Confederate fort. One day he overheard a soldier say that "we could blow that damned fort out of existence if we could run a mine shaft under it." He liked the idea and his corps commander, General Ambrose Burnside, was persuaded to let him try. Digging began on June 25; by July 23, his miners had dug a 511-foot tunnel under the fort. A room was then hollowed out and filled with 320 kegs of gunpowder weighing twenty-five pounds each. The Rebels were sitting on top of a four-ton bomb!

Behind the Confederate trenches was an undefended ridge that overlooked Petersburg. Capturing that ridge was the key to capturing the town and Richmond beyond. The plan was secretly to mass four divisions and 141 cannon opposite the fort. The instant the mine exploded, the artillery would cut loose while the infantry charged through the gap to take the ridge. If all went well, Grant would be in Richmond the next day.

Of the four divisions, three had seen hard fighting since the Wilderness and one, the 4th Division, a black outfit, had hardly seen any combat at all. The blacks were chosen to lead the assault and given special training. They welcomed the mission for two reasons. For one thing, it made them feel proud. As they trained (or "studied"), they sang:

> *We looks like men a-marchin on;*
> *We looks like men o'war.*[32]

Equally important, they had a score to settle. On April 12, Nathan Bedford Forrest overran Fort Pillow near Memphis, Tennessee. Half the fort's 550-man garrison were black soldiers. After the surrender, a number of blacks—how many is unclear—were murdered. If the killers expected this to terrorize other blacks, they were mistaken. If anything, it had the opposite effect. Blacks fought more desperately, fearing the same would happen to them if they surrendered. And they fought for revenge. At certain times they raised a black flag, an ancient sign that they would take no prisoners and ask no mercy for themselves. Confederates dreaded capture by blacks, while at the same time their hatred of blacks grew. As a Yankee wrote from Petersburg, "they hate a nigger worse than they hate a copperhead Snake."[33]

The 4th was ready to lead the assault, but at the last moment the white divisions were ordered to go in first. Grant had changed the plan for political, not military, reasons. As the attack drew near, he began to have second thoughts. If the attack failed, people might accuse him of using blacks as bullet-stoppers because he considered the lives of white soldiers more valuable. However untrue, Lincoln's opponents might make heavy black losses an election issue. Rather than hurt the president's re-election chances, Grant decided to use the whites, even though they had not been trained for the mission.

On July 30, at 4:44 A.M., Colonel Pleasants lit the mine's fuse and ran out of the tunnel. Moments later, a huge dome of earth rose into the air and burst open, gushing fire and smoke. It hung there for a few seconds, then came crashing down amid showers of dirt, stones, and timbers. The mine blew three hundred Rebels into the air and blasted a crater 170 feet long, 60 feet wide, and 30 feet deep. One fellow was still going up while comrades were on the way down; "Straggler!" they shouted as they passed him. The crater itself was full of bodies and pieces of bodies; some men were buried up to their necks, others to their waists, and some headfirst, with only their legs sticking out of the earth. The explosion was so unexpected that Rebels in trenches for hundreds of yards on either side of the crater fled to the rear. Once again, the road to Petersburg was open.

At this point, the Yankee effort began to fall apart. Unprepared for their mission, the assault divisions came forward in a disorganized mass; in fact, one division commander, Brigadier General James H. Ledlie, was so scared that he hid in a bomb shelter while calming his nerves with whiskey. Rather than bypass the crater, troops climbed *into* it to see the sights, collect souvenirs, and aid wounded Rebels. More troops were sent up from the rear, and these, too, went into the crater—without ladders. Meantime, the Rebels recovered from their shock and counterattacked.

By the time the 4th Division went into action, it was too late. To get at the enemy, the blacks had to push their way through hordes of disorganized whites. The sight of black soldiers whipped the Rebels into a killing frenzy. "Take the white men and kill the niggers!" they shouted as they charged. Blacks were shown no mercy. A Rebel officer named John S. Wise had the scene burned into his memory. He wrote thirty-five years later: "Our men . . . disregarded the rules of warfare which had restrained them in battle with their own race, and brained and butchered the blacks until the slaughter was sickening."[34]

Finishing with the blacks, the Rebels swept to the edge of the crater. It was like shooting fish in a barrel. Volley after volley was poured into the tightly packed mob. The ground was littered with bayoneted muskets left by the fleeing Yankees. These, too, were fired into the crater; and when they were empty, Rebels hurled them "like pitchforks" into the huddled mass below.

The "Battle of the Crater" was a fiasco. It cost Grant 3,798 men—a third of them blacks—to the Confederates' 1,500. "It was the saddest affair I have witnessed in the war," he wired Old Brains Halleck. "Such an opportunity for carrying fortifications I have never seen and do not expect again to have."[35] Tourists can still see the remains of the crater, where Grant's hopes for a quick victory were buried on a hot July day.

The siege continued.

Meantime, the war spread to Virginia's Shenandoah Valley. Lying between the Allegheny and Blue Ridge mountains, the Shenandoah was home to Quakers and other pacifists, people whose religion forbade them to own slaves or participate in war. Devout and hardworking, they had turned the valley into one of the most prosperous farming areas on earth. Throughout the Civil War, it was the breadbasket of the Confederacy, providing food for its armies and fodder for its horses. Running from southwest to northeast, it also formed a natural highway leading to Washington. In the past, whenever Richmond was threatened, Lee had sent troops into the valley to menace the Yankee capital, forcing them to divert forces from Virginia.

Shortly after the armies dug in at Petersburg, Lee sent General Jubal A. Early into the valley with fifteen thousand men. Tall, thin, and hot-tempered, "Old Jube" was a daring cavalry leader. During the first week in July, he burst out of the valley and made a beeline for Washington. News of his coming set the capital humming. Anyone who could carry a musket was mobilized for the city's defense. Government clerks stood in the battle lines next to wounded soldiers from the local hospitals. Grant, however, refused to loosen his grip on Petersburg. Rather than go to the capital in person, he sent heavy reinforcements.

By the time Early appeared on July 11, the Yankees were ready and waiting. After some skirmishing, Early retreated without knowing how close he had come to harming the Union cause. Abraham Lincoln had watched the fighting from Fort Stevens on the city's outskirts. He stood atop the wall, towering above everyone, a perfect target for Rebel sharpshooters. He had never been under fire, and found it fascinating. Polite requests to take cover were ignored. Finally, when a man fell dead beside the president, a captain used stronger language: "Get down, you damn fool, or you'll be killed!"

Lincoln got down. "Well, captain," he said, smiling. "I see you have already learned how to address a civilian."[36] The captain was Oliver Wendell Holmes, Jr., a future justice of the U. S. Supreme Court.

Determined to clean out the Shenandoah once and for all, Grant called in the Army of the Potomac's new cavalry commander,

Philip Sheridan. The son of Irish immigrants, Sheridan stood five feet five inches tall, had short black hair, a thick black mustache, and a face the color of raw hamburger. He had a heavyset body, with long arms and short legs. Lincoln described him in his own humorous way: "I will tell you what kind of chap he is. He is one of those long-armed fellows with short legs that can scratch his shins without having to stoop over."[37]

There was nothing funny about Sheridan the soldier. "Little Phil" was Grant's best cavalryman. He was utterly fearless and a born leader. As at Missionary Ridge, he led from the front, and soldiers knew that he would never send them anywhere he was not willing to go himself. Sheridan was no sportsman when it came to war. He did not believe that winning isn't everything; it was the *only* thing. He once told a brother officer, "I have never in my life taken a command into battle and had the slightest desire to come out alive unless I won."[38] His men loved him and would follow him anywhere.

In August, Grant ordered Sheridan into the Shenandoah Valley with forty-five thousand infantry and cavalry. He was to latch onto Jubal Early and "follow him to the death." And since the valley was one of the enemy's main food sources, its crops were to be destroyed. Sheridan must turn it into "a desert," ruining it so completely that "crows flying over it for the balance of the season will have to carry their provender with them."[39] Thus, three months before Sherman began his march to the sea, his friend was waging total war in Virginia.

On September 19, Sheridan stormed the Rebel defenses at Winchester. Shouting "come on, boys, come on," he led his troopers in a reckless charge. A shell burst directly overhead, but Little Phil kept going, laughing at the near miss. Early retreated to Fisher's Hill, where Sheridan beat him again three days later. It was a stunning defeat, Yankees thought, one that should get him out of the way permanently.

The garden of the Shenandoah became a wasteland. From Winchester in the north to Staunton in the south, a distance of ninety-

General Philip H. Sheridan. The son of Irish immigrants, "Little Phil" commanded the cavalry corps of the Army of the Potomac. After the war, he directed the campaign that broke the power of the Indian tribes on the Great Plains.

two miles, columns of smoke hid the sun at midday. Sheridan burned crops in the fields and silos filled with grain. Farmhouses, flour mills, corncribs, wagons, plows, reapers: all went up in flames. Over two thousand barns loaded with wheat were torched and seven thousand farm animals slaughtered or driven away in less than six weeks.

The valley people were made homeless and forced aboard trains to the North. One of Early's officers told what it was like for these peaceful folk: "I saw mothers and maidens tearing their hair and shrieking to Heaven in their fright and despair, and little children, voiceless and tearless in their pitiable terror."[40] This was not Rebel propaganda, nor was it an exaggeration. Yankees told the same story in diaries and letters home. Wherever they went, people begged them to spare their homes. Ironically, many of these were not only pacifists, but supporters of the Union.

Sheridan was sorry for the people, but not for what he had done. Years later, he told a friend how he felt about burning the Shenandoah Valley. He didn't do it for the sake of being nasty. Like Grant and Sherman, he destroyed property in order to shorten the war. Whatever shortened the war automatically saved lives and was merciful, he believed. "If I had a barn full of wheat and a son, I would much rather lose the barn than my son. . . . The question was, must we destroy their supplies or kill their young men? We chose the former."[41] His victims, however, were not so calculating. For generations thereafter, whenever valley people got angry, really angry, their worst insult was "May the curse of Sheridan be upon you!"

Meanwhile, Early refused to accept defeat. After fleeing the valley, he regrouped his army and quietly returned. The Yankees were camped at Cedar Creek, fourteen miles southeast of Winchester. Sheridan himself was at Winchester, just back from meetings in Washington. As far as he and his staff were concerned, everything had gone splendidly. The Confederates were beaten and the valley swept clean of provisions. In a few days, the strike force would return to regular duty at Petersburg. Everyone was relaxed, as they had been at Shiloh.

At dawn, October 19, Early attacked the sleeping camps. In a replay of Shiloh, he overran the camps and sent the Yankees into a panicky retreat.

And, as at Shiloh, the Yankee commander was sitting down to breakfast when he heard the distant rumble of artillery. Like Grant, Sheridan decided to see what was happening. But instead of boarding a steamboat, he mounted a jet-black stallion called Rienzi. Then, with a small cavalry escort, he set out in the direction of the firing. It was the start of "Sheridan's ride," one of the most dramatic episodes of the Civil War.

Signs of disaster soon came into view. There were the walking wounded, hundreds of them, hobbling along on their own or assisted by comrades. Wagons sped by, going God knows where. Unwounded infantrymen shouted that the battle was lost and the army defeated.

Defeated? Not Phil Sheridan! "About face, boys!" he cried. "We are going to lick them out of their boots. Sock it to them. Give them the devil. I am going to sleep in that camp tonight or in hell." Then he dug his spurs into Rienzi's side and galloped off in a swirl of dust.

Each time he came to a group of men, he pointed to the front and told them to get moving. The effect was magical. The instant they saw him, they cheered, grabbed their muskets, and started back. With Little Phil leading them, there was nothing to fear, and nothing they couldn't do. "We were safe," a soldier recalled, "perfectly and unconditionally safe, and every man knew it."[42]

The cheers grew louder as Little Phil neared the battlefield. "Sheridan! Sheridan!" men chanted, calling to comrades up ahead.

Sheridan, however, was out for blood, not cheers. "God *damn* you, don't cheer me!" he shouted. "If you love your country, come up to the front! God *damn* you, don't cheer me! There's lots of fight in you men yet! Come up, God damn you! Come up!"[43] They kept cheering, but they also "came up." And they destroyed Old Jube's army as a fighting force. At last the Shenandoah Valley was quiet.

Eighteen sixty-four had been a bad year for the Confederacy. Grant, Sherman, and Sheridan had given it a terrific pounding. Although the siege of Petersburg continued, the Civil War had entered its final stage.

VIII ✦ AN AFTERNOON AT APPOMATTOX

HEADQUARTERS

APPOMATTOX C.H., VA.

April 9th, 1865, 4:30 P.M.

HON. E. M. STANTON,

Secretary of War,

Washington.

General Lee surrendered the Army of Northern Virginia this afternoon upon terms proposed by myself.

U. S. GRANT,

Lieut.-General

Although Lee continued to hold the line at Petersburg, powerful forces were working against him during the winter of 1864–1865. Those forces had nothing to do with fighting skill or military organization. They were economic forces and, in the end, they destroyed the Confederacy as surely as Grant's two-front strategy.

The North was steadily growing stronger. Since the war began, it had become a major industrial power, rivaling England, the "workshop of the world." Practically overnight, towns that had never seen a smokestack or heard a factory whistle became bustling manufacturing centers. Much of their production was of poor quality, but it was good enough for the front; there was never a shortage of anything needed by the Union armies. These, too, were expanding, thanks to European immigration and the draft, which went into effect in 1863.

You only had to stroll through the camps at Petersburg to see how war and industry worked together. To supply Grant's forces, army engineers took over City Point, Virginia. Once a sleepy harbor where the Appomattox River flows into the James, it became one of the world's busiest seaports. The harbor swarmed with steamers, sailing ships, barges, tugs, and troop transports. There was so much traffic that vessels might have to wait for days to tie up at one of the docks that lined the shore. Perishable cargo was

160

stored in huge warehouses; wagons and artillery were kept in vast open-air "parks." A ten-mile-long railroad connected the supply depots with the trenches. Each day the telegraph office sent and received hundreds of messages.

The Army of the Potomac spent a comfortable winter. Of course, frontline troops lived in constant danger, but they never went hungry or barefoot. Rear-area camps were safe, snug, and warm. The people of the North went all out to give their men a merry Christmas. Each soldier received a boxed dinner containing turkey, stuffing, cranberry sauce, and mince pie. Soldiers rang in the New Year with band concerts and sing-alongs; some lucky fellows, mostly officers, were visited by their wives. The Grants lived in a small house, while their children attended a private school in New Jersey.

It was different across the way, where the main problem was finding enough to eat. Farm families still had the basics: bacon, sweet potatoes, corn bread, vegetables. But as the blockade tightened, even they felt the pinch. Tea was brewed from holly or blackberry leaves. Coffee was made from sweet potatoes, peanuts, and ground acorns; or, said one joker, from "anything that turned water brown in a dirty pot."

Scarcity caused prices to skyrocket. By 1865, prices were ninety-two times higher than at the start of the war, while wages only tripled. This meant that a Southerner had to work weeks, or

A view of Grant's supply base at City Point, Virginia, in 1864. Thanks to the efficient Union supply system, Grant could keep up the pressure on Lee's Confederates, who ran short of everything except courage.

A Union "artillery park" at City Point, Virginia. The cannonballs in the foreground are filled with gunpowder and set to explode when they reach their targets. Behind them are mortars, short-barreled cannons that throw heavy iron balls at high angles. In the background are regular cannons, which fire exploding shells.

months, for any bit of clothing or food. Shoes cost $125 (Confederate) a pair, beef $15 a pound, and flour $275 a barrel; in Richmond, flour went for as much as $1,200 a barrel. Soldiers' pay was nearly worthless. Johnny Reb earned $18 a month, a $7 increase since the start of the war, but this only equaled the cost of one $15 watermelon and a $3 quart of milk. To make matters worse, the government paid its bills by printing millions of dollars in paper money. Things became so bad that money was not worth the paper it was printed on.

High prices and low incomes made life a daily struggle for the average person. "My God!" exclaimed a Richmond woman, "how can I pay such prices? I have seven children; what shall I do?" "I don't know, madam," the shopkeeper replied, "unless you eat your children."[1]

Desperation triggered food riots in several cities. Rather than see their children starve, women raided bakeries and food shops; in Richmond, Jefferson Davis threatened to have looters shot if they did not go home at once. Meantime, blockade runners, swift vessels able to slip through the Union blockade, carried cotton overseas and returned with scarce supplies. Profits were so high that ship owners could afford to light cigars with $5 Confederate bills and eat imported delicacies.

For the men at Petersburg, the winter was as harsh as the one Washington's army had spent at Valley Forge in 1777. There was never enough to eat. By February 1865, Confederate soldiers were living on a daily ration of a pint of cornmeal and two spoonfuls of sugar; now and then, if they were lucky, they received a scrap of fatty bacon. Men became too weak to work for any length of time. They would start to dig a trench, but gasp for breath and feel faint after half an hour. Private John Casler knew how far hunger could force a person to go. Assigned to bury dead Yankees, he searched their pockets for food before rolling them into the grave. "I have been so hungry," he said, "that I have cut the blood off from [hardtack] crackers and eaten them."[2] Casler's comrades were only sorry that he had gotten to the crackers ahead of them.

Nakedness went along with hunger. Thousands went barefoot, leaving bloody footprints in the snow. What uniforms there were had become threadbare rags that let in the cold. Lookouts at Fort Hell, a Union outpost, had a clear view of Confederate work details. They were a sorry sight, a Yankee wrote: "I could not help comparing them with so many women with cloaks, shawls, double-bustles and hoops, as they had thrown over their shoulders blankets and tents which flapped in the wind."[3]

Whenever Lee rode through the camps, soldiers called out: "General Lee, I am hungry."[4] There was no anger in their voices, much less disrespect; they knew he was doing the best he could for them. But even Marse Robert was helpless, given the attitude of the Confederate government. It was hardly a government anymore, but a bunch of do-nothings paralyzed by defeat. His trips to Richmond became so frustrating that he burst out, "I have been up to see Congress and they don't seem to be able to do anything except eat peanuts and chew tobacco while my army is starving."[5]

By February 1865 the armies of the Confederacy had an official strength of 400,000. Of these, 198,494 were absent, with over 100,000 listed as deserters. Even the Army of Northern Virginia was losing an average of a hundred men a day through desertion. Johnny Reb had not run out of courage. He still fought as hard as ever until the moment of desertion. Yet, for growing numbers, it was clear that no amount of sacrifice would change the outcome. The war was lost, the Confederacy collapsing. By deserting, therefore, they were refusing to sacrifice themselves in a lost cause. Those who remained did so not because they expected to win, but out of a sense of duty to their comrades and their flag.

Sherman's march through Georgia and the Carolinas also had an effect. Southern women, once so patriotic, lost faith in the war. During the winter of 1864–1865, they flooded governors' offices with protests. For example, Governor Zebulon B. Vance of North Carolina received a letter signed "A Poor Woman and Children." Her words reflected the feelings of her Confederate sisters. She said: "You know as well as you have a head that it is impossible to whip the Yankees, there for I beg you for God's sake to try and make peace on some terms. . . . I believe slavery is doomed to dy out that god is agoing to liberate the niggers and fighting any longer is fighting *against* God." Another woman said families were starving and demanded that husbands be sent home before it was too late. She warned the governor: "If you dont provide some way for us to live we will be compell to take our little children and [go] to our Husband or they must Come to us."[6]

The men at Petersburg followed Sherman's march closely. Newspapers told of his movements in great detail, paying special attention to the bummers. Each mail brought letters filled with stories of hardship and despair. Mothers, wives, and sisters told of the difficulty of feeding children and caring for elderly parents. They begged soldiers to return to harvest crops and cut a fresh supply of firewood. The letter Private Edward Cooper received from his wife in North Carolina was typical:

> My dear Edward—I have always been proud of you, and since your connection with the Confederate army, I have been prouder of you than ever before. I would not have you do anything wrong for the world, but before God, Edward, unless you come home we must die. Last night I was aroused by little Eddie's crying. I called and said, 'What is the matter, Eddie?' and he said 'O Mamma, I am so hungry.' And Lucy, Edward, your darling Lucy, she never complains, but she is getting thinner and thinner every day. And before God, Edward, unless you come home, we must die.[7]

Small wonder that Cooper and others like him "voted with their feet." Unable to bear the sufferings of loved ones, they deserted in growing numbers during that last winter of the war. Hundreds

were caught and executed by firing squad. The majority, however, returned home to pick up the pieces of their lives.

Grant knew about Lee's problems and how to take advantage of them. Using his four-to-one superiority in manpower, he kept pushing, probing, and pounding the Petersburg defenses. In the spring, as the snow melted and the ground began to dry, he extended his lines further west, threatening Lee's right flank. Lee had to meet the challenge, or wake up one morning to find the Yankees in his rear. But the more he stretched his line, the thinner it became, until his men stood fifteen feet apart in certain places. Time was running out. Unless he acted soon, one of two things would happen: Sherman's army would come up from North Carolina or Grant would break through and take Richmond.

Lee decided to take a last, desperate, gamble. He planned to leave Petersburg secretly, put his army aboard trains, and join forces with Joe Johnston in North Carolina. That would mean abandoning Richmond to Grant, but, he felt, Sherman had to be stopped before he invaded Virginia. If Lee succeeded against Sherman, his combined forces might then turn on Grant, defeat him, and regain the lost territory. It was the Confederacy's only hope, Lee believed. Even if he failed to destroy his opponents, a serious setback might persuade Northerners to recognize Southern independence.

Before Lee could leave, however, he had to get around the

"Dictator," a super-mortar used by Grant to bombard Confederate positions during the siege of Petersburg. Lee, however, was the first general to mount artillery on railroad flatcars, an important innovation in the art of war.

Army of the Potomac's left flank. That was tricky. If Grant learned of the move, he would try to block it with all the forces at his command. Worse, if he caught the Rebels in the open, he would roll right over them.

Lee had to create a diversion to clear a path for his escape. Late in March 1865, he ordered John Gordon to mass troops on the east side of Petersburg. Gordon was to launch a surprise attack to break through the center of the Union line. This would force Grant to draw troops from his left flank to mend the break, thereby shortening his line. In the meantime, Lee would load his trains and race down to North Carolina.

Gordon attacked at 4:00 A.M. on March 25. His objective was Fort Stedman near the south bank of the Appomattox River. At first, everything went smoothly. Advancing under cover of darkness, his men seized the fort and fanned out to take a mile of Yankee trenches on either side of it. But Grant would not take the bait. Rather than weaken his left flank, he called in his artillery. The guns roared, smothering the fort with shells. The Confederates retreated with losses of forty-eight hundred men; the Yankees lost about two thousand.

Lincoln had arrived at City Point the day before. Thin and drawn, wearing a black suit and a tall silk hat, he did not seem very presidential. "The President is, I think, the ugliest man I ever put my eyes on," an officer remarked with a snicker; another said he "looked like a boss undertaker."[8]

After retaking Fort Stedman, Grant invited the president to tour the area. Lincoln had seen Jubal Early driven from Washington, but had never been on a battlefield. Now he saw all there was to see. He saw puddles of blood, burial details gathering the dead, and surgeons tending the wounded. Confederate prisoners—hundreds of them—were being rounded up and herded toward holding pens in the rear. Dirty and ragged, they staggered along, drunk with fatigue. Although elated at the victory, Lincoln was saddened by its aftermath.

The president stayed with the Army of the Potomac for nearly two weeks. He slept aboard the steamer *River Queen,* but spent most of his time in the camps. He walked among the troops, visited the wounded in the hospitals, and hung around the telegraph office, hungry for news of the fighting. On one of his walks, he noticed men splitting logs to build a cabin. This brought back memories, and the men cheered as "Old Abe" grabbed an ax and sent the chips flying. In the evenings, he sat by the fire at Grant's

headquarters, chatting with the officers and telling funny stories. On one of these evenings, however, he grew serious. Grant had asked him, "Mr. President, did you at any time doubt the final success of the cause?" Lincoln raised his right hand as if swearing an oath and replied, "Never for a moment!"[9]

Lincoln had come to City Point to meet with his top commanders. On March 28, Grant, Sherman, and Admiral David Dixon Porter, now commander of the North Atlantic Blockading Squadron, joined him aboard the *River Queen*. Clearly, they said, the war was drawing to a close. As they spoke, Lincoln kept asking the same questions: "Must more blood be shed? Cannot this last bloody battle be avoided?" Grant explained that Lee was "a real general," and that he would fight even if there was only a slim chance of success.[10] The president then described the kind of peace he had in mind. A harsh peace, he explained, meant that harshness and hatred, would poison the future. There must be no revenge, no punishment for misguided people. All he wanted was for the Rebels to be disarmed and to go home. Grant agreed that this was the only way to rebuild the nation.

Lincoln had a dream that night. He dreamed he was awakened by the sound of crying from somewhere in the White House. Leaving his bed, he went from room to room, but found nobody until he entered the East Room. There he saw a platform on which lay a corpse wrapped in a black shroud. It was guarded by soldiers, and there was a crowd of mourners surrounding the platform. "Who is dead in the White House?" he asked a soldier. "The President," was the answer; "he was killed by an assassin." At that moment, the crowd moaned and Lincoln awoke.[11]

On March 28, 1865, President Lincoln met with his commanders aboard the River Queen *anchored off City Point. General Grant is to the right of the president, with General Sherman at the far right. Admiral Porter is at the far left. The meeting was commemorated in a painting,* The Peacemakers, *by George P. A. Healy. It is a fitting title, for the president insisted that the South be readmitted to the Union on the most generous terms possible.*

When Lincoln described the dream to his wife, she was terrified. "Well, it is only a dream," he said, apologizing for frightening her. The dream did, indeed, seem like a fantasy. People dismissed the very idea of assassination in the United States. Secretary of State William H. Seward insisted that "assassination is not an American practice or habit, and one so vicious and desperate cannot be engrafted into our political system."[12] No American leader had ever been assassinated, and there was no reason to believe this would change even during a bitter civil war. The president himself was careless about security. Once, when a cavalry guard was put around the White House, he sent it away; at other times, he walked between government buildings without an escort.[13] In any case, the dream was forgotten in the days that followed.

Those were some of the most exciting days in the history of the republic. Grant realized that Lee had struck Fort Stedman out of weakness, not strength. That was all he needed to know! On March 29, he sent Phil Sheridan on a wide sweep to the southwest. The cavalryman was to cut the Southside Railway, Lee's last supply line and his only remaining link to the outside world.

Sheridan commanded ten thousand cavalry and seventeen thousand infantry, veterans of the Shenandoah campaign. Opposing him were ten thousand men under General George E. Pickett, leader of the disastrous charge at Gettysburg. Pickett was posted at a crossroads called Five Forks, the key to the Confederate right flank. Lee underlined its importance in a brief telegram: "Hold Five Forks at all hazards."[14]

On April 1, Sheridan lined up his men for a pep talk. There was fire in his eyes as he trotted back and forth on Rienzi. Stopping, he held up his fist and cried, "I want you men to understand we have a record to make . . . that will make hell tremble!" He then turned to General George Armstrong Custer, commander of the 3d Cavalry. "I want you to *give* it to them!" he snapped. Custer, known as "Old Curly" because of his long blond hair, cried: "Yes, yes. I'll give it to them!"[15]

Yet it was Little Phil who did most of the "giving" that day. As always, he led from the front. He seemed to be everywhere at once, galloping to and fro, waving his battle flag, and shouting encouragement.

A man at his side staggered, blood spurting from a bullet hole in his neck. "I'm killed," he screamed and dropped to his knees. "You're not hurt a bit," Sheridan roared. "Pick up your gun, man, and move right on to the front." Those words had the effect of a whiplash. The man rose, ran a few feet, and dropped dead.[16]

Sheridan led the final charge in person. Eyewitnesses described him as a "god of war" dressed in blue. Digging his spurs into Rienzi, he jumped a barricade, followed by a swarm of troopers with blazing six-shooters. The Yankees took about fifty-two hundred prisoners and killed hundreds of others. "Go right over there," Sheridan called to the captives. "Drop your guns; you'll never need them any more. . . . We want every one of you fellows."[17]

Sheridan sent word of the victory to headquarters. His chief was sitting with his aides when the report arrived. At first, the aides laughed, thinking it an April Fool's joke. But when they realized the news was true, they went wild, whooping for joy and slapping each other on the back. Grant sat quietly, his eyes half-closed, beneath a cloud of cigar smoke. "All right," he said, and began to write an order. It was the death warrant for the Army of Northern Virginia.[18]

Dawn, Sunday, April 2, found Grant's artillery lined up in rows, wheel to wheel. Slowly at first, then building in fury, the guns roared as if it was doomsday. After an hour of this, they fell silent. Grant's infantry charged. The Confederates put up a good fight, but not good enough. Waves of blue-clad men struck their line and tore it to shreds. As the sun rose in the east, Lee began to evacuate Petersburg. He still meant to reach North Carolina, but from now on his men would have to walk.

At 10:40 A.M., Jefferson Davis was attending church in the Confederate capital. He had just sat down when a messenger handed him a telegram from Lee. The general said that his lines were broken in three places and that Richmond must be evacuated by evening. Davis rose and walked out, his face pale, his lips tightly pressed together. There was no need to ask his reason for leaving. Instantly, the congregation sensed that Grant was coming. Word spread quickly, and the city began to shut down.

Thousands rushed to the railroad depot, hoping to buy a ticket to anywhere. People crowded into the shabby passenger cars, standing packed together or sitting on one another's laps. Anything with wheels—wagons, carts, carriages—was pressed into service. By noon, the roads were jammed with vehicles piled high with baggage. Most of the city's poor, however, had no choice but to stay behind.

To prevent rioting, the government ordered liquor supplies destroyed. Hundreds of barrels of whiskey were rolled into the streets, their tops bashed in, and their contents spilled. Streams of whiskey flowed in the gutters, forming puddles in the low places. The poor collected it in pots, pans, and cups. Some sopped it up in pieces of cloth, then sucked them dry; others lay on their bellies and lapped it up. These people were hungry, and the whiskey went into their empty stomachs. Almost immediately, the streets became filled with rowdy, foul-mouthed drunks staggering about and looking for trouble.

Drunken townspeople, joined by retreating soldiers, broke into shops and private homes, taking whatever they could carry. Women ran from shop to shop, filling their aprons with stolen goods. People fought over stolen property with fists, teeth, and guns. Those too drunk to stand fell into the gutter, to be crushed under wagon wheels or drowned in whiskey puddles. The police having joined the retreat, everyone did as they pleased.

Another American city began to go up in flames. Although the rioters were partially responsible, the Confederate government was the worst offender. The government had several warehouses filled with supplies that it was saving "in case of emergency," as if Lee's men had been on a ten-month picnic at Petersburg. In addition, there were nine gunboats anchored in the James, plus an arsenal filled with ammunition and gunpowder. These were to be burned to keep them out of Yankee hands.

As soon as the fires were lit, they raced out of control. Exploding artillery shells from the arsenal and cinders from the warehouses drifted down to start more fires, turning Richmond into an inferno. "The explosions began just as we got across the river," recalled Private Robert Stiles. "When the [arsenal] . . . went off, the solid earth shuddered convulsively; but as the ironclads—one after another—exploded, it seemed as if the very dome of heaven would be shattered down upon us. Earth and air and the black sky glared in the lurid light. Columns and towers and pinnacles of flame shot upward to an amazing height, from which, on all sides, the ignited shells flew in arcs of fire and burst as if bombarding heaven."[19]

The Yankees came early next morning, April 3. A black cavalry unit was first to arrive. The troopers galloped through the smoke-filled streets, waving swords and singing "John Brown's Body." Before long, a stream of Yankee cavalry and infantry was pouring into the center of town. The Confederate flag that had flown over the Capitol since 1861 came down and the Stars and Stripes rose in its place. Onlookers were horrified. That flag, more than anything else, brought home the reality of defeat. "We covered our

faces and cried aloud," a woman recalled. "All through the house was the sound of sobbing. It was the house of mourning, the house of death."[20]

Others, however, were glad that the Yankees had come in time. Fires were still burning out of control when they rode into town. The moment they arrived, they began to restore order. Military police guarded shops and cleared the streets of rioters. Soldiers manned fire engines to save entire blocks of buildings. Had it not been for them, Richmond might have vanished in a sea of flame. As it was, about one-third of the city lay in ruins.

Lincoln wanted to see things for himself. On April 3, Grant gave him a tour of Petersburg. The following day, while Grant attended to his duties, Admiral Porter took him to Richmond aboard the *River Queen*. The presidential party consisted of Lincoln, his twelve-year-old son, Tad, Porter, and William H. Crook, Lincoln's personal bodyguard. Apart from Crook and twelve sailors armed with muskets, they had no protection whatsoever. Still, no one worried. It made no difference that they were entering the enemy capital. Richmond was an American city, and they assumed that Americans would act properly. "Our people," Porter wrote, "were not given to assassination, and if anyone had told me that the President stood in danger of his life, I would have laughed at him."[21]

A group of laborers, former slaves, saw Lincoln land at Rockett's Wharf. Within minutes, every black person in the area knew of his arrival and ran to greet him. The sailors tried to keep them at a safe distance, but it was no use. Cheering and weeping, the blacks crowded around "Father Abraham." An old man threw him-

Richmond arsenal in ruins, April 1865. Rather than leave behind anything of value, retreating Confederates blew up this and other government buildings. Unfortunately, exploding shells from the arsenal set fire to the rest of the city.

self at the president's feet, crying, "Bless the Lord! The great Messiah! Glory, hallelujah!" This was the way a king or a saint was welcomed, and Lincoln knew he was neither. "Don't kneel to me," he said, embarrassed. "That's not right. You must kneel to God only, and thank Him for liberty. . . . My poor friends, you are free—free as air. You can cast off the name of slave and trample upon it; it will come to you no more. . . . There, now. Let me pass on. I have but little time to spare. I want to see the capital."[22] He spent the rest of the day touring Richmond and relaxing in the Confederate White House. It was a happy day, one of the best in his life.

U. S. Grant was too busy for sightseeing. After leaving the president at Petersburg, he set out to trap Lee's army, which was fleeing westward along the northern bank of the Appomattox River. Grant divided his own army into two parts. The first part, the largest, was led by George Meade. It followed close behind the Rebels, nipping at their heels and forcing them to fight rear-guard actions. The second part, under Phil Sheridan, kept to a parallel course, along the river's southern bank. His job was to cut Lee's line of retreat, allowing the main force to close in and finish the job.

Time seemed to stand still for the Army of Northern Virginia. Day and night, night and day, were the same—a continuous battle to stay alive. A regiment from the rear guard would have to drive off one of Meade's forward elements. Or a wagon train caught by enemy cavalry had to be rescued. Or a roadblock had to be cleared. In each case there was a short, sharp fight costing dozens of lives. John Gordon told of the survivor of one of these little battles. He was a mere boy, and he ran as if the devil himself were after him. Asked why he was running so fast, he shouted, "Golly, I'm running 'cause I can't fly!"[23]

Lee's first objective was Amelia Court House, thirty-five miles west of Petersburg. A supply of food, ordered a few days before, was supposed to be waiting at the rail depot. But due to some mix-up, he found only ammunition when he arrived on April 5. An entire day was lost in collecting food and forage from the countryside. Very little was found, and his men had to get along as best they could. Corn on the cob, meant for the horses, was heated and mixed with salt; chewing it made men's jaws ache and gums bleed. Boiled cow hoofs mixed with flour and fried in fat were considered a delicacy.

Dizzy with fatigue, soldiers marched asleep, waking when they bumped into the man in front or tripped over something. The way was littered with the debris of war. They passed abandoned guns and overturned wagons, many of them in flames. Personal items—canteens, knapsacks, blankets, shaving kits, books—were scattered about, tossed away by men too weary to carry anything but the clothes on their backs. Countless muskets were stuck in the ground by the bayonets, their owners having given up the fight. Now and then, they sang a Negro song borrowed from the Yankees:

> *Ole Massa run away,*
> *De darky stay at home;*
> *I b'lieve in my soul dat the Kingdom am a comin';*
> *And de year ob Jubilo!*[24]

Just as Lincoln had freed the slave, the war's end would free Johnny Reb from his ordeal.

Guided by scouts, Sheridan's cavalry allowed the retreating army no rest. Scouts were volunteers who daily risked their lives behind enemy lines. Dressed as Virginia farmers, even as Confederate soldiers, they moved ahead of Little Phil's force in groups of from two to six. Always alert, they followed every trail and back road, learning where it began and where it went. To gather information, they visited Rebel outposts, rode alongside Rebel wagon trains, and mingled with the troops. There was no room for error; if a scout was captured, the Rebels hanged him from the nearest tree as a warning to others.

The scouts' work paid off in a stunning victory. On April 6, three Confederate divisions were trapped along Sayler's Creek, a branch of the Appomattox River. Sheridan's cavalry hit them as they were crossing, while his infantry and artillery opened fire from a hilltop. Taken by surprise, the Rebels panicked, sometimes with tragic consequences. Many wore captured Yankee overcoats and, in the confusion, could not identify their own men. An officer wrote that "I saw a young fellow of one of my companies jam the muzzle of his musket against the back of the head of his most intimate friend, clad in a Yankee overcoat, and blow his brains out."[25]

The battle of Sayler's Creek cost the Rebels eight thousand men, about a third of the force that had left Amelia Court House the previous day. Seven Confederate generals were among the prisoners, including Richard Ewell, Grant's West Point classmate, and Custis Lee, Marse Robert's eldest son.

The Southerners were amazed at finding their captors in such fine shape. "Oh my, oh my! you look like you wuz sich a happy man!" a soldier called to a Yankee cavalryman. "You got on sich a nice new uniform, you got sich nice boots on, you ridin' sich a nice hoss, an' you look like yer bowels wuz so reglar."[26] Diarrhea, apparently, had become more a problem for Rebels than for Yankees toward the end of the war.

It was close to midnight when Sheridan sent Grant a report from his camp at Sayler's Creek. The Rebels, he knew, were on their last legs. After describing the battle, he wrote, "If the thing is pressed, I think Lee will surrender." Grant immediately wired the message to Lincoln at City Point. The president sent Grant a reply: "Let the *thing* be pressed."[27]

Grant, however, did not want another battle unless absolutely necessary. On April 7, he sent Lee a personal note. In it he said that the last week's fighting should have convinced him (Lee) of "the hopelessness of further resistance." Grant went on to say that he wanted to shift from himself the responsibility for any further bloodshed by asking Lee to surrender the Army of Northern Virginia. Although Lee's commanders knew nothing of the message, many had reached that conclusion on their own. Still, Lee would not hear of surrender. So long as there was a shred of hope, he vowed to keep fighting.

One officer thought this foolish, and said so to Lee's face. General Henry A. Wise had been governor of Virginia at the time of John Brown's raid. An ardent secessionist, he played a leading role in forcing Virginia into the war. Now that the war was obviously lost, he believed its continuation would be a cruel farce.

When Lee asked his opinion of the situation they faced, Wise exploded, "Situation! There is no situation! Nothing remains, General Lee, but to put your poor men on your poor mules and send them home in time for spring planting. This army is hopelessly whipped, and is fast becoming demoralized. These men have already endured more than I believed flesh and blood could stand, and I say to you, sir . . . that to prolong the struggle is murder, and the blood of every man who is killed from this time forth is on your head, General Lee."

"Oh, General, do not talk so wildly," Lee replied. "What would the country think of me, if I did what you suggest?"

"Country be damned!" Wise snapped. "There is no country. There has been no country, general, for a year or more. You are the country to these men. They have fought for you. They have shivered through a long winter for you. Without pay or clothes, or care of any sort, their devotion to you and faith in you have been the only things which have held this army together. If you demand the sacrifice, there are still thousands of us who will die for you. You know the game is desperate beyond redemption, and that, if you so announce, no man or government or people will [dispute] your decision. That is why I repeat that the blood of any man killed hereafter is upon your head."[28]

Lee wanted to go on a little longer; honor demanded that he try everything before admitting defeat. His destination was Appomattox Station, a hundred miles west of Petersburg and a mile from the village of Appomattox Court House. Four supply trains were waiting for him at the depot. If he could reach them in time, and break free of his pursuers, he might still get to North Carolina.

It was not to be. Next day, April 8, Sheridan's scouts found the supply trains. Once again, he sent Custer on one of those slashing raids for which he was becoming famous. The Rebels were loading food into their wagons when Old Curly charged at the head of his cavalry. While some troopers tore up tracks to prevent the trains from escaping, their comrades captured the trains themselves.

By early evening, Sheridan reached Appomattox Station with more cavalry. In the distance, to the east, he could see the glare of Confederate campfires. *To the east!* He was in front of the enemy, blocking his path!

Sheridan ordered his troopers to dig shallow trenches and prepare for battle by morning. Yet cavalry alone could not fight off a determined assault. They needed infantry support, and plenty of it. Little Phil's own infantry units were still thirty miles to the southeast. Hurry-up orders were tapped out; the infantry was to come as quickly as possible. Grant, with the main force bearing down on Lee from the rear, was also notified. All that remained was to finish the job.

The Union infantry marched throughout the night. Soldiers marched double-time, resting for only a few minutes every half hour. This was not something they wanted to do, or did without protest. "We marched on as best we could, tired, hungry, and mad," recalled Private Theodore Gerrish. "If the artillery horses came too near, we would hammer them over their heads with our guns."[29] Their officers drove them mercilessly, while encouraging them with promises of victory at the end of the road.

Lee, meantime, held his last war council in the woods near

Appomattox Court House. His headquarters wagons had been lost, so they sat around the fire on blankets. Pete Longstreet was there, having recovered from his Wilderness wounds; also present were generals John B. Gordon, William N. Pendleton, and Fitzhugh Lee, the commander's nephew. Never had the situation been so grim. They were boxed in on the west, south, and east; it was no use going north, since no food was to be had in that direction. There was only one chance, and a slim one at that. If the Yankees up ahead were only cavalry, they might break through. But if infantry were there, too, they were finished. It was decided to test the Yankee line at daybreak.

Before turning in for the night, Lee shared his feelings with Longstreet. He had been thinking about Grant, and his voice was harsh. "I tell you, General Longstreet," he said, "I will strike that man a blow in the morning!"[30] Were it not for "that man," the Confederacy might have had a real chance at survival.

April 9, 1865.

It was Palm Sunday, the Sunday before Easter, the oldest feast of the Christian calendar. The day dawned bright and mild, ideal for celebrating the Prince of Peace. After a brief artillery bombardment, Lee's infantry and cavalry charged. Then, for the last time in battle, they gave the Rebel yell: *"Yip-yip-yip-e-e-e-e-e-e-e! Yah-ah-ah-yah-e-e-e-e-e-e-e!"*

At first, they seemed unstoppable. Pausing only to load and fire, they overran the Yankee positions, taking several cannons, which were hauled to the rear and added to the Confederate batteries. Cheering wildly, they pushed on, driving the dismounted cavalrymen before them. It was just like in the old days—at least for a few minutes.

And then it happened. Suddenly, the Rebels halted in their tracks, stunned by what they saw ahead of the fleeing Yankees. There stood a wall of blue two miles wide. The Union infantry had arrived in the nick of time. On their right, off to a side, was Sheridan with the entire cavalry corps of the Army of the Potomac. Except for the whinnying of horses, they stood silent and still, battleflags fluttering in the breeze.

Sheridan turned to Major General Joshua Lawrence Chamberlain, a former college professor who had won the Medal of Honor for heroism at Gettysburg. Little Phil did not waste words. Pointing to the enemy, he snapped a command: "Now smash 'em, I tell you; smash 'em!"[31]

The Union line advanced to within range of the waiting Rebels.

God, how they dreaded that first blast of musketry! They were bracing for the shock when a lone horseman rode out from the Confederate lines. He was waving a white towel as a flag of truce. At that moment, everyone realized that he would live to see Easter.

Minutes earlier, Lee had received a message from General Gordon, the assault leader: "My command has been fought to a frazzle and . . . I cannot long go forward." The Army of Northern Virginia was caught, pinned, trapped. Its twenty-three thousand troops were hemmed in, front and rear, by eighty thousand Yankees, with more on the way.

Several of Lee's officers refused to admit the game was up. A general suggested that the army "scatter like rabbits" and carry on as guerrillas. Marse Robert rejected this idea. His troops had fought honorably, "as Christian men," and must not disgrace themselves by living like outlaws. Then he declared, somberly, "There is nothing left me but to go and see General Grant, and I would rather die a thousand deaths."[32]

Grant was at field headquarters when a courier brought a letter from Lee. He had been suffering with a pounding headache since the previous day; not even Julia's recipe of foot baths and mustard plasters brought relief. But the moment he read the letter, he was cured. Several staff officers cried when he had it read aloud.

He arrived at Appomattox Court House at 1:00 P.M., after a thirty-five-mile ride over muddy roads. Little Phil was waiting for him at the edge of the village.

"How are you, Sheridan?"

"First-rate, thank you; how are you?"

"Is Lee over there?"

"Yes, he is in that brick house, waiting to surrender to you."

"Well, then, let's go over."[33]

The house belonged to Wilmer McLean. By coincidence, Mr. McLean had owned a house at Bull Run, where the first big battle of the war had been fought in 1861. Deciding that the fighting was too close for comfort, he moved his family to this peaceful village. Thus the Civil War began and ended on his property.

The rival commanders met in Mr. McLean's parlor. Eyewitnesses were struck by the contrast between them. Lee was dressed magnificently. When his baggage was abandoned the day before, he kept his best uniform for such an occasion. This he wore with a silk sash, fine gloves, high boots, gold spurs, and a sword whose hilt was studded with jewels; he expected to be arrested and wanted to look his best.

There was nothing fancy about Grant. He had come directly from the field, and his clothes were with the wagon trains somewhere in the rear. He wore a private's uniform, only the three stars on the shoulder straps showing his rank. He had no sword, and his pants were tucked inside muddy boots without spurs. Yet he radiated self-confidence and authority. Joshua Chamberlain remembered that "he seemed greater than I had ever seen him— a look as of another world about him."[34]

Grant found Lee in the McLean parlor. They greeted each other, shook hands, and sat down. Grant did not feel like a conquering hero. "What General Lee's feelings were I do not know," he recalled twenty years later. "But my own feelings, which had been quite jubilant at the receipt of his letter, were sad and depressed. I felt like anything rather than rejoicing at the downfall of a foe who had fought so long and valiantly, and had suffered so much for a cause, though that cause was, I believe, one of the worst for which a people ever fought. . . ."[35]

They began to talk about the old days in Mexico. Grant mentioned that he had met Lee there, and that he had left such a deep impression that he could have recognized him anywhere. Lee said he remembered the meeting but, try as he might, could not recall Grant's face. After some more talk about Mexico, Lee reminded Grant of the purpose of their meeting.

Grant's surrender terms were in line with President Lincoln's wishes. The defeated enemy was not to be punished or humiliated in any way. Lee's men were to be sent home after pledging not to renew the war—that was all. Lee's officers would be allowed to keep their pistols, swords, and horses; everything else was to be handed over at a formal surrender ceremony. Lee accepted the terms, but noted that common soldiers in his army—cavalrymen and gunners—owned their own horses. Grant knew that most Rebel soldiers had small farms and could not get along without a horse. Without waiting to be asked for a favor, he said they could take their animals home "to put in a crop." In addition, he allowed the starving Confederates to take supplies from the trains at Appomattox Station. Lee then signed the surrender papers and the meeting ended.

As Grant and Lee left, Union officers ransacked the house for souvenirs. Sheridan tossed two ten-dollar gold pieces at Mr. McLean for the table on which the surrender terms had been written. His companions offered money for other items, or simply took whatever they could grab. Chairs, candlesticks, an inkstand,

even Lulu McLean's doll, vanished in the blinking of an eye. Sofas were cut up and strips of upholstery taken away. Ordinary Billy Yanks, barred from the house, tore up the garden and pressed the flowers between pieces of paper.

Union troops went wild when they learned of the surrender. Artillerymen fired salutes. Cavalrymen dashed about, waving swords and firing pistols into the air. Infantrymen sang, danced, and shouted. Bearded veterans fell into each other's arms to "embrace and kiss like schoolgirls."[36] Grant had gotten over his sadness, but the shooting was in bad taste, he felt. He sent officers to stop it, saying: "The war is over; the Rebels are our countrymen again."[37]

That night, a Yankee bugler sounded taps. Buglers throughout the Army of the Potomac took up the notes, as if passing them from one to another. When they finished, a hush fell over the encampments. At that moment, one of Sheridan's bands struck up an army favorite: "Home, Sweet Home."

News of Appomattox spread quickly. By evening, Washington was celebrating as never before. Fireworks exploded over the Potomac and church bells rang. Everything with a whistle—ships, locomotives, fire engines—let go at once. Flags sprouted from thousands of windows, and the Capitol was illuminated with colored lights. On April 11, a rider galloped into Sherman's camp near Raleigh, North Carolina. "Lee has surrendered!" he cried, going from unit to unit. "You're the man we've been waiting for these three years!" soldiers shouted in return.[38]

A woman was standing at her gate with her children when she heard the shouting. The little ones looked up at her, puzzled at the outcry. But she knew. She looked down at them, tears stream-

Wilmer McLean's front parlor, Appomattox Court House, Virginia, April 9, 1865. Generals Lee and Grant sit, surrounded by their aides, as a Union officer transcribes Grant's terms on the official surrender document.

ing down her cheeks, and said, "Now father will come home."[39]

The Confederates gave up their weapons the following day, April 12, at Appomattox Court House. The commanding generals were gone by then, Lee to his home in Richmond, Grant to Washington for high-level meetings.

Joshua Lawrence Chamberlain supervised the ceremony. In his book, *The Passing of the Armies,* he describes one of the most dramatic scenes in American history. He had assembled the Union troops before dawn, forming them into lines of battle along both sides of a road. At sunrise, the Army of Northern Virginia set out on its last march. Its artillery was towed to an open field and left for the Yankees. John B. Gordon then appeared at the head of a seemingly endless column of men. Chamberlain was deeply moved by the Southerners' dignity. They carried themselves as proud men who had fought bravely. Such courage deserved to be recognized even in defeat.

The Union troops were standing at "shoulder arms," muskets over the right shoulder. As Gordon passed, Chamberlain ordered them to shift to "carry arms," the salute position. Gordon rode with his head bowed, but he looked up when he heard the sound of the shifting muskets. Instantly, he touched his spurs to his horse's side. As the animal reared, he touched the point of his sword to the tip of his boot and told his men to hold their muskets at carry arms. Chamberlain knew what that meant; it was "honor answering honor."

Let Chamberlain describe what happened next: "On our part not a sound of trumpet . . . , nor roll of drum; not a cheer . . . but an awed stillness . . . as if it were the passing of the dead! As each . . . division halts, the men face inwards toward the road, twelve feet away; then carefully dress their line . . . worn and half-starved as they were. They fix bayonets, stack arms; then, hesitatingly, remove cartridge boxes and lay them down. Lastly . . . they tenderly fold the flags, battle-worn and torn, blood-stained, heart-holding colors, and lay them down; some frenziedly rushing from the ranks, kneeling over them, clinging to them, pressing them to their lips with burning tears."

Chamberlain watched the gray divisions pass. Their passing called up memories of places where he had met them before: Antietam, Gettysburg, Wilderness, Spotsylvania, Cold Harbor. "How," he wrote, "could we help falling on our knees, all of us together, and praying God to pity and forgive us all!"[40]

The Civil War was over.[41]

IX ✦ IN THE END

Washington was in a holiday mood, decked out with pictures of the nation's leaders. Grant's picture seemed to be everywhere. "U. S. Army, U. S. Navy, U. S. Grant," signs read, "Glory to God Who to US GRANTED the victory." He was the man of the hour; already people were talking about him as the next president of the United States.

While her husband tended to army business, Julia visited with the wives of generals and politicians. The one wife she did not visit—*would not* visit—was Mary Lincoln. The president's wife was an emotionally unstable person who imagined insults where none were intended. During her stay at City Point, she had accused Julia of disrespect for daring to sit down in her presence. Julia said she meant no disrespect, but she never forgot the incident.

On April 14, Lincoln invited the Grants out for an evening at Ford's Theater. A new play had opened, an English comedy called *Our American Cousin,* and he thought that seeing it would be a nice way to relax. Knowing how Julia felt about Mrs. Lincoln, the general begged off as politely as he could; he said they had to see their children at school in Burlington, New Jersey. They did, but most people would have postponed the visit to spend an evening with the First Family.

Later that afternoon, Julia told her husband of a strange

incident. She was having lunch in the dining room of Willard's Hotel, where they were staying, when she noticed a man at a nearby table. A thin man with a mustache, he began to stare at her, a crazy look in his eyes. He made her so uncomfortable that she left without finishing her meal. Ulysses told her to forget about it; the fellow was probably on the lookout for celebrities to tell the folks about back home.

Toward evening, they took a carriage to Union Station. They had no bodyguards or military escort. As they rode along Pennsylvania Avenue, a horseman suddenly came up from behind. He galloped past the carriage, circled around, and stared at them through the window before riding off. "That is the same man who sat down at the lunch-table near me," said Julia. "I don't like his looks."[1] A few days later, Grant recognized the stranger from a newspaper picture. He was John Wilkes Booth, an actor who blamed the nation's troubles on Lincoln and his advisers.

The Grants reached Philadelphia about midnight and checked into a hotel. Julia had just taken off her hat when a knock came at the door. A clerk appeared with a telegram, soon returning with another. Grant read them and sat down without saying a word.

The actor John Wilkes Booth stalked General Grant only hours before shooting President Lincoln at Ford's Theater, April 14, 1865. Even staunch Confederates denounced Booth as a coward and a lunatic.

"Ulyss, what do the telegrams say?" she asked, seeing the sad expression on his face. "Do they bring any bad news?"[2] He replied that they were from the War Department and contained the worst news an American could receive. Abraham Lincoln had been shot at Ford's Theater "and cannot live."

Grant returned to Washington, where he learned the assassin's identity: John Wilkes Booth. Only then did he realize that Booth had been stalking him during his stay in the capital. Had he gone to Ford's, he, too, would have been a target. By refusing the president's invitation, he probably gained another twenty years of life.

A funeral service for Lincoln was held on April 19. It was almost an exact replay of the president's dream two weeks earlier. The casket lay on a platform in the East Room of the White House. It was guarded by soldiers and surrounded by mourners. There was only one difference: U. S. Grant stood alone on the plat-

The Grant family in about 1866. By then, Grant was the most popular man in the country, seen by many as the next president of the United States.

form, a black mourning band on his arm, tears rolling down his face. He had loved Lincoln who, above all others, had trusted him and given him a chance to prove himself. Trying to sum up his feelings toward the president, he could only say: "He was incontestably the greatest man I have ever known."[3]

Lincoln had guided the Union through a dreadful war; now it was up to others to win the peace. One of the first tasks was to disband the army, which was costing $4 million a day, an enormous sum back then. The new president, Andrew Johnson of Tennessee, gave the assignment to the nation's leading general. Grant did it so well that in July 1866 he was promoted to General of the Army and given a fourth star, the first to be so honored. He even outranked George Washington. In 1867–1868, he served for five months as secretary of war.

The nation was lucky to have Grant in that position. Angry voices were calling for vengeance against those who had plunged the nation into civil war. Rebels, they insisted, had been let off

Ulysses S. Grant *by Henry Ulke. This portrait of the eighteenth president of the United States hangs in the White House.*

too easily; they must be tried for treason and punished. In Washington, politicians called for the arrest of former Confederate officers, starting with Robert E. Lee. The General of the Army disagreed. He had given his word of honor at Appomattox: the Rebels could live in peace so long as they obeyed the laws of the United States. He would not break his promise. If politicians wanted it otherwise, they must find someone else; he would resign the command of the army. The matter was quickly dropped.

Goodwill was answered by goodwill. Lee, too, was a man of his word. In the five years until his death in 1870, he wrote hundreds of letters advising former Confederates to become law-abiding citizens. To one woman, bitter at the South's defeat, he wrote: "Madam, don't bring up your sons to detest the United States Government. Recollect that we form one country now. Abandon all these local animosities and make your sons Americans."[4] Words like these, coming from Marse Robert, carried weight in the South. Without saying whether the "lost cause"— Southern independence—had been right or wrong, he was telling people to admit that the war was over and go on with their lives from there.

Meantime, Grant became the most popular man in the country. Banquets, receptions, and parades were held in his honor. Colleges gave him honorary degrees. Grateful citizens showered him with gifts. Wealthy Philadelphians gave him a mansion complete with everything from fine linen for the beds to expensive china for the dining room table. New York businessmen handed him a check for a hundred thousand dollars. It was said that more babies were named Ulysses in 1866 than in the entire history of the nation.

The nation could deny Grant nothing. Nominated by the Republican party, he easily won the presidential election of 1868. That victory was not a good thing for him or the country. Though a brilliant soldier, Grant was ill equipped for the highest office in the land. He saw the presidency as "a gift of the people," another reward for winning the war. Running the country, however, was another matter entirely. The job was too complicated for him, he said, and he could not be bothered with the details of government.[5]

President Grant was little more than a glorified general-in-chief. One reason was that he had grown too used to army ways. As a general, he had come to rely upon staff officers to work out the details of his plans. He continued this practice as president, leaving things to Cabinet members and government officials. That was a mistake. Good as he was at managing soldiers, he was naive when it came to politicians. Although honest himself, he trusted corrupt men who cared nothing for him or the welfare of their country. William Tecumseh Sherman, always a true friend, warned him about such men, but he would not listen.

Grant served two terms in the White House. During that time, he pushed for adoption of the Fifteenth Amendment guaranteeing that no state shall prevent a citizen from voting on account of "race, color, or previous condition of servitude." He also encouraged completion of the transcontinental railroad and the creation of Yellowstone National Park.

Julia Dent Grant never lost faith in her husband, even in the bleakest times.

These accomplishments were tarnished by "Grantism," the corruption that flourished during the Grant administrations. Many of those he appointed to high office grew rich at the expense of their fellow Americans. Among the worst offenders was a member of the president's official family. His personal secretary, General Orville E. Babcock, was involved with the Whiskey Ring, a plot by whiskey producers and corrupt tax officials to defraud the government of millions of dollars in taxes. Cabinet members like Secretary of the Navy George Robeson made fortunes in a very short time. Robeson entered office with $20,000 in savings and a salary of $8,000; he left with $800,000 in bank deposits.

On leaving office in March 1877, Ulysses and Julia set out on a world tour lasting two years. Wherever the general went, he was hailed as the greatest warrior of the age. In London, he dined with Queen Victoria, a special honor since Her Majesty was not very comfortable with "commoners." In Berlin, he met Prince Otto von Bismarck, the warrior-statesman who had created modern Germany. After reviewing the German troops, he told Bismarck: "I am more of a farmer than a soldier. I take little or no interest in military affairs, and, although I...have fought in two wars...I never went into the army without regret and never retired without pleasure."[6] From Berlin, he traveled southward and eastward meeting nearly every emperor, king, queen, president, and prime minister in Europe and Asia.

Grant's Republican friends tried to nominate him for a third term in 1880 but failed. Early the next year, he moved to New York City and bought a mansion on Sixty-sixth Street off Fifth Avenue. There he hobnobbed with bankers, stockbrokers, and railroad tycoons. They "adopted" him, inviting him to their clubs and suggesting profitable investments. Army friends found him a changed man. Sheridan said he never mentioned the army or the war, but talked only of business and money. Sherman thought it undignified of him to spend time with millionaires, "who would have given their all to have won any of his battles."[7]

At the urging of Ulysses, Jr., he went into business with a stockbroker named Ferdinand Ward. This proved to be the biggest mistake of his life. Ward was a swindler who used the general's name to get people to invest in their business. On May 4, 1884, he ran off with the firm's money, as well as his partner's personal fortune.[8] Grant was stunned. He had left home that morning a rich man; by noon he was broke. Once again, he could not provide for his family. The future looked as grim as it ever did during the hardscrabble days in Missouri.

In the end, he returned to the Civil War. In the 1880s, as today, Americans were fascinated by their greatest conflict. Most of the war's leading figures had already told their stories in print; most, that is, except Lee, who had wanted to forget, and Grant, who had been too busy to remember.

To help pay his bills, Grant wrote an article on the battle of Shiloh for *The Century* magazine. The money was good—five hundred dollars—and he needed as much work as he could get. Mark Twain, the creator of Tom Sawyer and Huckleberry Finn, was his friend as well as a publisher. When he suggested that Grant write his memoirs, he decided to go ahead. It was a big project, but he was desperate. In the summer of 1884, he was diagnosed as having throat cancer. Since retired presidents did not receive pensions in those days, he hoped that sales of his book would give Julia an income after he was gone.

The Personal Memoirs of U. S. Grant is probably the best first-hand account of the Civil War. The book is dedicated to "the American soldier and sailor," the real saviors of their country.

Beautifully written, it is also an accurate history of the war as seen through the eyes of the Union's supreme commander. Knowing he was in a race with death, Grant threw himself into the task with every ounce of his energy. For five hours each day, he dictated to a secretary. As the cancer attacked his vocal cords, he was forced to write by hand. Each page was agony, but he wrote with the same determination as he had faced the enemy on the battlefield.

He kept up this pace for a full year. By the summer of 1885, he was nearly done. It was a hot, humid summer, and to escape the city he accepted the loan of a cottage at Mount McGregor in the Adirondack Mountains of upstate New York.

Tormented by cancer, Ulysses S. Grant put the final touches to his Memoirs *at Mount McGregor, New York, in the summer of 1885.*

Grant's train headed north alongside the Hudson River. As it passed West Point, he asked to be lifted up for a last look at the gray buildings across the river. Later, the train stopped briefly at a signal light. A flagman stood on the tracks below Grant's window. Glancing upward, he noticed a familiar face peering down at him. The flagman lifted his arm—an arm without a hand. "Thank God I see you alive, General Grant," he cried. "I lost that with you at The Wilderness, and I'd give the other one to see you well!"[9] Grant bit his lip and took off his hat to the flagman. Julia wept.

In the weeks after Grant's arrival on June 16, people from all walks of life came to Mount McGregor to pay their respects. Most were strangers; they simply walked past the cottage, paused for a moment, and went on their way. Old soldiers came to say goodbye. None was more welcome than Simon Bolivar Buckner. They had always been friends, despite the fact that he had made the "unconditional surrender" at Fort Donelson. Buckner spoke of the past; Grant answered with written notes. When he grew weary, his visitor rose to leave. "Grant," he said, touching his friend's arm, choking back the tears. "Buckner," Grant whispered back.[10]

Grant finished his *Memoirs* on July 16, not knowing that it would be an all-time best-seller in America and bring his widow $450,000. He died a week later, Thursday, July 23, 1885, at the age of sixty-three.

His body was taken back to New York City and buried temporarily in Riverside Park. The funeral service was a reunion of Civil War veterans. Sherman, Sheridan, and Buckner served as honorary pallbearers; Joe Johnston, Fitzhugh Lee, and John B. Gordon prayed for the soul of the man they would have gladly shot twenty years earlier. Yet it was no accident that they came. By giving such generous terms at Appomattox, Grant had taken the first step toward reconciling the Rebels and building a truly united country.

In 1897, Grant's body was moved to a marble tomb in Riverside Park. The tomb is on a bluff overlooking the Hudson River. A motto, taken from his speech accepting the Republican nomination in 1868, is carved in stone over the entrance:

LET US HAVE PEACE

Peace. Yes, let that be the legacy of Unconditional Surrender Grant, the soldier who hated war.

NOTES

Prologue

1. Quoted in Bruce Catton, *Grant Takes Command* (Boston: Little, Brown, 1969), 124.
2. Quoted in Stephen B. Oates, *With Malice Toward None: The Life of Abraham Lincoln* (New York: Harper & Row, 1977), 347.
3. Quoted in J. F. C. Fuller, *Grant and Lee: A Study in Personality and Generalship* (Bloomington, Ind.: University of Indiana Press, 1982), 83.
4. Sam R. Watkins, *"Co. Aytch," Maury Grays, First Tennessee Regiment: or, A Side Show of the Big Show* (Jackson, Tenn.: Mowat-Mercer Press, 1952), 202.

Chapter 1

1. Ulysses S. Grant, *Personal Memoirs of Ulysses S. Grant and Selected Letters, 1839–1865* (New York: The Library of America, 1990), 17.
2. In all, Hannah bore three sons and three daughters.
3. Quoted in Lloyd Lewis, *Captain Sam Grant* (Boston: Little, Brown, 1950), 43.
4. Quoted in W. E. Woodward, *Meet General Grant* (New York: Liveright, 1928), 33.
5. Grant, *Memoirs*, 28.
6. Quoted in Bruce Catton, *U. S. Grant and the American Military Tradition* (Boston: Little, Brown, 1954), 106.
7. Quoted in Mary Scott and Dwight Anderson, *The Generals: Ulysses S. Grant and Robert E. Lee* (New York: Knopf, 1988), 57.
8. Quoted in Ulysses S. Grant, III, *Ulysses S. Grant: Soldier and Statesman* (New York: Morrow, 1969), 14–15.
9. Grant, *Memoirs*, 31.
10. *Ibid.,* 34–35.
11. Mr. Dent had never served in the army but, like other prosperous Southerners, liked to be called "colonel" as a sign of respect.
12. Quoted in Robert Leckie, *None Died in Vain: The Saga of the American Civil War* (New York: Harper Collins, 1950), 224.
13. Quoted in Woodward, *Meet General Grant*, 59–60.
14. Quoted in Lewis, *Captain Sam Grant*, 164.
15. *Ibid.,* 126.
16. *Ibid.,* 145.
17. *Ibid.,* 303.
18. *Ibid.*
19. *Ibid.,* 313, 314.
20. Grant, *Memoirs*, 953–954.
21. Quoted in Gene Smith, *Lee and Grant: A Dual Biography* (New York: McGraw-Hill, 1984), 66.

22. Quoted in Lewis, *Captain Sam Grant,* 346.
23. *Ibid.,* 376.

Chapter 2

1. These words were constantly used in nineteenth-century America. Though they are distasteful, I have included them for the sake of accuracy in quotations given in this book.
2. Quoted in James Mellon, ed., *Bullwhip Days: The Slaves Remember* (New York: Weidenfeld & Nicolson, 1988), 421.
3. Quoted in James M. McPherson, *Ordeal by Fire: The Civil War and Reconstruction* (New York: Knopf, 1982), 35.
4. Quoted in Woodward, *Meet General Grant*, 127.
5. *The Collected Works of Abraham Lincoln*, ed. Roy P. Baker, vol. 3 (New Brunswick, N.J.: Rutgers University Press, 1953), 145–146.
6. Quoted in George Sinkler, *The Racial Attitudes of American Presidents: From Abraham Lincoln to Theodore Roosevelt* (Garden City, N.Y.: Doubleday, 1971), 49.
7. Quoted in James M. McPherson, *Marching Toward Freedom: The Negro in the Civil War, 1861–1865* (New York: Knopf, 1967), 166.
8. Quoted in Belle Irvin Wiley, *The Life of Billy Yank: The Common Soldier of the Union* (Baton Rouge, La.: Louisiana State University Press, 1978), 39.
9. Lincoln to Horace Greeley, August 22, 1862, in Archer H. Shaw, ed., *The Lincoln Encyclopedia* (New York: Macmillan, 1950), 370.
10. Watkins, *"Co. Aytch,"* 150–151.
11. Quoted in Sinkler, *The Racial Attitudes of American Presidents,* 119.
12. Quoted in Lewis, *Captain Sam Grant,* 368.
13. *Ibid.,* 393.
14. *Ibid.,* 394–395.
15. Quoted in Smith, *Lee and Grant,* 91.
16. Quoted in Wiley, *Billy Yank,* 54.
17. *Ibid.,* 64.
18. Grant, *Memoirs*, 67.
19. Quoted in James I. Robertson, *Soldiers Blue and Gray* (Columbia, S.C.: University of South Carolina), 149.
20. Quoted in Belle Irvin Wiley, *The Life of Johnny Reb: The Common Soldier of the Confederacy* (Baton Rouge, La.: Louisiana State University Press, 1978), 248.
21. Quoted in Robertson, *Soldiers Blue and Gray,* 152.
22. Quoted in Belle Irvin Wiley, *The Plain People of the Confederacy* (Baton Rouge, La.: Louisiana State University Press, 1943), 11.
23. Quoted in Wiley, *Billy Yank,* 240.
24. Quoted in Robertson, *Soldiers Blue and Gray,* 67.
25. Grant, *Memoirs*, 160–161.

26. *Ibid.,* 164–165.
27. Quoted in Smith, *Lee and Grant,* 111.
28. Quoted in Bruce Catton, *Grant Moves South* (Boston: Little, Brown, 1960), 123.
29. Quoted in Leckie, *None Died in Vain,* 242.
30. Quoted in Samuel Carter, *The Final Fortress: The Campaign for Vicksburg, 1862–1863* (New York: St. Martin's Press, 1980), 45.
31. Quoted in Catton, *Grant Moves South,* 167.
32. *Ibid.,* 173.
33. Grant, *Memoirs,* 208.
34. Quoted in Catton, *Grant Moves South,* 179.

Chapter 3

1. Quoted in Wiley Sword, *Shiloh: Bloody April* (New York: Morrow, 1974), 108.
2. *Ibid.,* 127.
3. Grant, *Memoirs,* 998.
4. Quoted in Sword, *Shiloh: Bloody April,* 109.
5. *Ibid.,* 148.
6. Quoted in Otto Eisenschiml and Ralph Newman, *The Civil War: The American Iliad as Told by Those Who Lived It* (New York: Grosset & Dunlap), 200.
7. Quoted in Catton, *Grant Moves South,* 236.
8. Quoted in James Lee McDonough, *Shiloh: In Hell Before Night* (Knoxville, Tenn.: University of Tennessee Press, 1977), 92.
9. Quoted in Sword, *Shiloh: Bloody April,* 175.
10. Quoted in Catton, *Grant Moves South,* 223.
11. Quoted in McDonough, *Shiloh: In Hell Before Night,* 28.
12. Watkins, *"Co. Aytch,"* 65.
13. Quoted in Wiley, *Billy Yank,* 77.
14. Quoted in Robertson, *Soldiers Blue and Gray,* 217; Wiley, *Johnny Reb,* 29.
15. Grant, *Memoirs,* 1005.
16. Watkins, *"Co. Aytch,"* 64.
17. Quoted in Earl Schenck Miers, *The General Who Marched to Hell: William Tecumseh Sherman and His March to Fame and Infamy* (New York: Knopf, 1951), 22.
18. Quoted in McDonough, *Shiloh: In Hell Before Night,* 108.
19. Quoted in Gerald F. Linderman, *Embattled Courage: The Experience of Combat in the American Civil War* (New York: Free Press, 1987), 124.
20. Quoted in Wiley, *Billy Yank,* 72.
21. Quoted in Sword, *Shiloh: Bloody April,* 277.
22. Joseph Allan Frank and George A. Reaves, *"Seeing the Elephant": Raw Recruits at the Battle of Shiloh* (Westport, Conn.: Greenwood Press, 1989), 120.
23. Quoted in Sword, *Shiloh: Bloody April,* 261–262.
24. *Ibid.,* 287.
25. Quoted in Catton, *Grant Moves South,* 240.
26. Quoted in Sword, *Shiloh: Bloody April,* 351.
27. *Ibid.,* 360.
28. Quoted in Catton, *Grant Moves South,* 242.

29. Quoted in Lloyd Lewis, *Sherman: Fighting Prophet* (New York: Harcourt, Brace, 1958), 230.
30. Quoted in Allan Nevins, "The Glorious and the Terrible," *Saturday Review,* September 2, 1961.
31. Quoted in Victor Davis Hanson, *The Western Way of War: Infantry Battle in Classical Greece* (New York: Knopf, 1989), 197.
32. Quoted in Frank and Reaves, *"Seeing the Elephant,"* 107.
33. Quoted in Reid Mitchell, *Civil War Soldiers* (New York: Viking, 1988), 6, 62.
34. Quoted in Robertson, *Soldiers Blue and Gray,* 160–161.
35. Quoted in Phillip Shaw Paludan, *"A People's Contest": The Union and the Civil War* (New York: Harper & Row, 1988), 326.
36. Quoted in Richard Wheeler, ed., *Voices of the Civil War* (New York: Meridan, 1990), 103.
37. *Ibid.,* 101.
38. Quoted in Sword, *Shiloh: Bloody April,* 427.
39. Quoted in Lewis, *Sherman,* 233.
40. Watkins, *"Co. Aytch,"* 48.
41. War dead: American Revolution, 10,623; War of 1812, 6,675; Mexican War 5,885—a total of 23,273 compared to Shiloh's 23,741.
42. Grant, *Memoirs,* 246.

Chapter 4

1. William Tecumseh Sherman, *Memoirs of General W. T. Sherman* (New York: The Library of America, 1990), 276.
2. The Mississippi has changed course many times over the centuries. Today, it follows a completely different channel at Vicksburg than during the Civil War.
3. Quoted in U. S. Department of the Interior, *Vicksburg and the Opening of the Mississippi River, 1862–63* (Washington, D.C., 1986), 17.
4. Quoted in Earl Schenck Miers, *The Web of Victory: Grant at Vicksburg* (New York: Knopf, 1955), 115.
5. Quoted in Richard Wheeler, ed., *The Siege of Vicksburg* (New York: Thomas Y. Crowell, 1978), 111.
6. Quoted in Catton, *Grant Moves South,* 424–425.
7. Quoted in Wiley, *Billy Yank,* 101.
8. Quoted in Robertson, *Soldiers Blue and Gray,* 112.
9. Quoted in Wheeler, *Siege of Vicksburg,* 158.
10. *Ibid.,* 27.
11. Quoted in U. S. Department of the Interior, *Vicksburg,* 49.
12. Quoted in Miers, *Web of Victory,* 247.
13. Quoted in U. S. Department of the Interior, *Vicksburg,* 52.
14. Quoted in Linderman, *Embattled Courage,* 148.
15. Quoted in Fuller, *Grant and Lee,* 60.
16. Quoted in Wiley, *Billy Yank,* 350, and Linderman, *Embattled Courage,* 67.
17. Quoted in Lewis, *Sherman,* 287.
18. Quoted in Mitchell, *Civil War Soldiers,* 37.

19. Quoted in Peter F. Walker, *Vicksburg: A People at War, 1860–1865* (Chapel Hill, N.C.: University of North Carolina Press, 1960), 174.
20. *Ibid.,* 167.
21. *Ibid.,* 176.
22. Grant, *Memoirs,* 368.
23. Quoted in Wheeler, *Siege of Vicksburg,* 223.
24. Quoted in Catton, *Grant Moves South,* 141.
25. Quoted in McPherson, *Marching Toward Freedom,* 9.
26. Quoted in James McPherson, *The Negro's Civil War: How Black Americans Felt and Acted During the War for the Union* (New York: Ballantine Books, 1991), 303.
27. Quoted in McPherson, *Marching Toward Freedom,* 40.
28. *Ibid.,* 84–85.
29. Quoted in McPherson, *Ordeal by Fire,* 355.
30. Quoted in Carter, *Final Fortress,* 250.
31. Quoted in McPherson, *Negro's Civil War,* 287.
32. Quoted in Wheeler, *Voices of the Civil War,* 398.
33. Quoted in Eisenschiml and Newman, *The Civil War,* 449.
34. Quoted in Carter, *Final Fortress,* 290.
35. Quoted in Wheeler, *Voices of the Civil War,* 349.
36. *Ibid.,* 349.
37. Quoted in Grant, *Memoirs,* 379.
38. Quoted in Carter, *Final Fortress,* 302.
39. Quoted in McPherson, *Ordeal by Fire,* 333.

Chapter 5

1. Grant, *Memoirs,* 390.
2. Quoted in Fairfax Downey, *Storming the Gateway: Chattanooga, 1863* (New York: David McKay, 1960), 137–138.
3. Watkins, *"Co. Aytch,"* 121–122.
4. *Ibid.,* 108–109.
5. General Horace Porter, *Campaigning with Grant* (New York: The Century Co., 1897), 7.
6. Quoted in Eisenschiml and Newman, *The Civil War,* 531–532.
7. Grant, *Memoirs,* 421.
8. Quoted in Richard Wheeler, ed., *We Knew William Tecumseh Sherman* (New York: Thomas Y. Crowell, 1977), 58–59.
9. Watkins, *"Co. Aytch,"* 71.
10. Quoted in Lewis, *Sherman,* 323.
11. Quoted in Eisenschiml and Newman, *The Civil War,* 543.
12. Quoted in Lewis, *Sherman,* 322–323.
13. *Ibid.,* 323.
14. *Ibid.,* 323.
15. Watkins, *"Co. Aytch,"* 125–126.
16. Quoted in Eisenschiml and Newman, *The Civil War,* 547.
17. Grant, *Memoirs,* 473.
18. *Ibid.,* 481–482.
19. *Ibid.,* 481.
20. Quoted in Carl Sandburg, *Abraham Lincoln: The Prairie Years and the War Years* (New York: Harcourt, Brace & Co., 1954), 672.

Chapter 6

1. Quoted in Woodward, *Meet General Grant,* 181.
2. Quoted in T. Harry Williams, *McClellan, Sherman and Grant* (New Brunswick, N.J.: Rutgers University Press, 1962), 63.
3. Quoted in Woodward, *Meet General Grant,* 181.
4. Quoted in Lewis, *Sherman,* 138.
5. Quoted in Burke Davis, *Sherman's March* (New York: Random House, 1980), 130.
6. Quoted in Allan Nevins, *The War for the Union: The Organized War to Victory, 1864–1865* (New York: Scribner's, 1971), 26.
7. Quoted in Joseph T. Glatthaar, *Forged in Battle: The Civil War Alliance of Black Soldiers and White Officers* (New York: Free Press, 1990), 17.
8. Quoted in Lewis, *Sherman,* 315.
9. Quoted in Miers, *The General Who Marched to Hell,* 45.
10. Quoted in John F. Marszalek, *Sherman's Other War: The General and the Civil War Press* (Memphis, Tenn.: Memphis State University Press, 1981), 145.
11. Watkins, *"Co. Atych,"* 132, 135.
12. Quoted in Lewis, *Sherman,* 360.
13. Quoted in Wheeler, *We Knew William Tecumseh Sherman,* 69.
14. Watkins, *"Co. Atych,"* 159.
15. Quoted in Wiley, *Billy Yank,* 356.
16. Quoted in Richard Wheeler, ed., *Sherman's March* (New York: Thomas Y. Crowell, 1978), 26.
17. Watkins, *"Co. Atych,"* 174.
18. Quoted in McPherson, *Ordeal by Fire,* 449.
19. *Ibid.,* 601–602.
20. Quoted in Glatthaar, *Forged in Battle,* 135.
21. Quoted in Wheeler, *We Knew William Tecumseh Sherman,* 44–45.
22. Quoted in Lewis, *Sherman,* 429.
23. Quoted in Davis, *Sherman's March,* 6.
24. Dolly Sumner Lunt, *A Woman's Wartime Journal* (New York: The Century Co., 1918), 25–42.
25. Quoted in Edgar L. MacCormick, Edward G. McGelee, and Mary Strahl, eds., *Sherman in Georgia* (Boston: D. C. Heath, 1967), 100.
26. Quoted in Eisenschiml and Newman, *The Civil War,* 651.
27. Quoted in Wiley, *Billy Yank,* 234.
28. *Ibid.,* 350.
29. Quoted in Lewis, *Sherman,* 450.
30. Quoted in Davis, *Sherman's March,* 94–95.
31. Quoted in MacCormick, McGelee, and Strahl, *Sherman in Georgia,* 38.
32. Quoted in J. G. Randall and D. H. Donald, *The Civil War and Reconstruction* (Lexington, Mass: D. C. Heath, 1969), 431.
33. Quoted in Marszalek, *Sherman's Other War,* 168–169.
34. Quoted in Davis, *Sherman's March,* 44.
35. Quoted in Lewis, *Sherman,* 438, and Davis, *Sherman's March,* 32.

36. Quoted in Lewis, *Sherman,* 439.
37. Quoted in Wheeler, *Sherman's March,* 107–108.
38. Quoted in Wiley, *Johnny Reb,* 343.
39. Quoted in Lewis, *Sherman,* 489.
40. Quoted in Davis, *Sherman's March,* 141.
41. Quoted in Miers, *The General Who Marched to Hell,* 292.
42. Quoted in Wheeler, *Sherman's March,* 190.
43. Quoted in Miers, *The General Who Marched to Hell,* 310–311.
44. Quoted in Davis, *Sherman's March,* 168.
45. Quoted in Wheeler, *Sherman's March,* 207.

Chapter 7

1. Quoted in Bruce Catton, *A Stillness at Appomattox* (Garden City, N.Y.: Doubleday, 1953), 39.
2. *Ibid.,* 46.
3. Grant, *Memoirs,* 598.
4. Quoted in Smith, *Lee and Grant,* 53.
5. Quoted in Gamaliel Bradford, *Lee the American* (Boston: Houghton Mifflin, 1912), 41–42.
6. *Ibid.,* 35.
7. *Ibid.,* 36.
8. *Ibid.,* 156.
9. *Ibid.,* 126.
10. Quoted in Smith, *Lee and Grant,* 303.
11. Quoted in Bradford, *Lee the American,* 215.
12. Quoted in Richard Wheeler, ed., *On Fields of Fury. From the Wilderness to the Crater: An Eyewitness History* (New York: Harper Collins, 1991), 82–83.
13. Quoted in Eisenschiml and Newman, *The Civil War,* 561–562.
14. Porter, *Campaigning with Grant,* 64.
15. Quoted in Smith, *Lee and Grant,* 194–195; Anderson, *The Generals,* 372–374.
16. Porter, *Campaigning with Grant,* 69–70.
17. Quoted in Smith, *Lee and Grant,* 198.
18. Quoted in Clarence E. Macartney, *Grant and His Generals* (New York: McBride, 1953), 320–321.
19. Quoted in Wheeler, *On Fields of Fury,* 202.
20. *Ibid.,* 204.
21. *Ibid.,* 211.
22. Quoted in Shelby Foote, *The Civil War, A Narrative: From Red River to Appomattox* (New York: Random House, 1986), 290.
23. Quoted in Wheeler, *On Fields of Fury,* 259.
24. Quoted in Burke Davis, *Gray Fox: Robert E. Lee and the Civil War* (New York: The Fairfax Press, 1981), 321.
25. Quoted in Wheeler, *On Fields of Fury,* 261–262.
26. Porter, *Campaigning with Grant,* 179.
27. Lewis, *Sherman,* 382.
28. Quoted in U. S. Department of the Interior, *Campaign for Petersburg* (Washington, D.C., 1985), unpaged.
29. Quoted in Catton, *A Stillness at Appomattox,* 191.
30. *Ibid.,* 201–202.
31. Quoted in Linderman, *Embattled Courage,* 146.

32. Quoted in Wheeler, *On Fields of Fury,* 279.
33. Quoted in Mitchell, *Civil War Soldiers,* 175.
34. John S. Wise, *The End of an Era* (Boston: Houghton Mifflin, 1899), 366.
35. Quoted in Catton, *A Stillness at Appomattox,* 252.
36. Quoted in Burke Davis, *The Civil War: Strange and Fascinating Facts* (New York: The Fairfax Press, 1982), 73.
37. Quoted in Richard O'Connor, *Sheridan the Incredible* (Indianapolis: Bobbs Merrill, 1953), 150.
38. Porter, *Campaigning with Grant,* 441.
39. Quoted in Catton, *A Stillness at Appomattox,* 275.
40. *Ibid.,* 305.
41. Quoted in O'Connor, *Sheridan,* 16–17.
42. Quoted in Thomas A. Lewis, *The Guns of Cedar Creek* (New York: Harper Collins, 1988), 256.
43. Quoted in Bruce Catton, *Never Call Retreat* (Garden City, N.Y.: Doubleday, 1965), 393.

Chapter 8

1. Quoted in McPherson, *Ordeal by Fire,* 377.
2. Quoted in Wheeler, *Voices of the Civil War,* 390.
3. Quoted in Catton, *A Stillness at Appomattox,* 329–330.
4. Quoted in Smith, *Lee and Grant,* 232.
5. Quoted in Anderson, *The Generals,* 421.
6. Quoted in Wiley, *Plain People of the Confederacy,* 67, 47.
7. Quoted in Robertson, *Soldiers Blue and Gray,* 136.
8. Quoted in Burke Davis, *To Appomattox: Nine April Days, April 1865* (New York: Rinehart and Co., 1959), 26; Woodward, *Meet General Grant,* 345.
9. Porter, *Campaigning with Grant,* 408.
10. Quoted in Philip Van Doren Stern, *An End to Valor: The Last Days of the Civil War* (Boston: Houghton Mifflin, 1958), 101.
11. Quoted in Oates, *With Malice Toward None,* 225–226.
12. *Ibid.,* 416.
13. *Ibid.,* 248.
14. Quoted in Smith, *Lee and Grant,* 246.
15. *Ibid.,* 245.
16. Quoted in O'Connor, *Sheridan,* 253.
17. *Ibid.,* 253.
18. Quoted in Anderson, *The Generals,* 427.
19. Quoted in Richard Wheeler, ed., *Witness to Appomattox* (New York: Harper & Row, 1989), 99.
20. Quoted in A. A. and Mary Hoehling, *The Last Days of the Confederacy* (New York: Crown, 1981), 200.
21. Quoted in Wheeler, *Witness to Appomattox,* 125.
22. Quoted in Davis, *To Appomattox,* 184–185.
23. Quoted in Eisenschiml and Newman, *The Civil War,* 671.
24. Quoted in Rembert W. Patrick, *The Fall of Richmond* (Baton Rouge, La.: Louisiana State University Press, 1960), 14.
25. Quoted in Wheeler, *Witness to Appomattox,* 178.
26. Quoted in Wiley, *Johnny Reb,* 252.
27. Quoted in Sandburg, *Abraham Lincoln,* 686.

28. Wise, *The End of an Era,* 434–435.
29. Quoted in Wheeler, *Witness to Appomattox,* 209.
30. Quoted in Smith, *Lee and Grant,* 263.
31. Joshua Lawrence Chamberlain, *The Passing of the Armies* (New York: G. P. Putnam's Sons, 1915), 236–237.
32. Quoted in Davis, *Gray Fox,* 403; Wheeler, *Witness to Appomattox,* 217.
33. Porter, *Campaigning with Grant,* 469.
34. Quoted in Chamberlain, *The Passing of the Armies,* 246.
35. Grant, *Memoirs,* 735.
36. Quoted in McPherson, *Ordeal by Fire,* 482.
37. Porter, *Campaigning with Grant,* 486.
38. Quoted in Wheeler, *Sherman's March,* 219–220.
39. *Ibid.,* 220.
40. Chamberlain, *The Passing of the Armies,* 261–265.
41. Joe Johnston's army was still intact, but in no condition for a major campaign. Johnston surrendered on April 26.

Chapter 9

1. Porter, *Campaigning with Grant,* 498–499.
2. *Ibid.,* 499.
3. Quoted in Catton, *Grant Takes Command,* 479.
4. Quoted in Bradford, *Lee the American,* 98–99.
5. Quoted in Anderson, *The Generals,* 464.
6. Quoted in Woodward, *Meet General Grant,* 76.
7. Quoted in Macartney, *Grant and His Generals,* 302.
8. Ward was later captured and sent to prison for ten years, but the stolen money was never recovered.
9. Quoted in Smith, *Lee and Grant,* 359.
10. *Ibid.,* 361.

Some More Books

The number of books on the Civil War is enormous and has been growing for more than a century. Here are a few of the ones I found most helpful.

Anderson, Nancy Scott, and Dwight Anderson. *The Generals: Ulysses S. Grant and Robert E. Lee.* New York: Knopf, 1988.

Barrett, John G. *Sherman's March Through the Carolinas.* Chapel Hill, N.C.: University of North Carolina Press, 1956.

Carter, Samuel. *The Final Fortress: The Campaign for Vicksburg, 1862–1863.* New York: St. Martin's Press, 1980.

Catton, Bruce. *Grant Moves South.* Boston: Little, Brown, 1960.

———. *Grant Takes Command.* Boston: Little, Brown, 1969.

———. *Mr. Lincoln's Army.* Garden City, N.Y.: Doubleday, 1962.

———. *Never Call Retreat.* Garden City, N.Y.: Doubleday, 1965.

———. *A Stillness at Appomattox.* Garden City, N.Y.: Doubleday, 1953.

———. *U. S. Grant and the American Military Tradition.* Boston: Little, Brown, 1954.

Chamberlain, Joshua Lawrence. *The Passing of the Armies.* New York: G. P. Putnam's Sons, 1915.

Coggins, Jack. *Arms and Equipment of the Civil War.* New York: The Fairfax Press, 1983.

Davis, Burke. *Gray Fox: Robert E. Lee and the Civil War.* New York: The Fairfax Press, 1981.

———. *Sherman's March.* New York: Random House, 1980.

Downey, Fairfax. *Storming the Gateway: Chattanooga, 1863.* New York: David McKay, 1960.

Eisenschiml, Otto, and Ralph Newman. *The Civil War: The American Iliad as Told by Those Who Lived It.* New York: Grosset & Dunlap, 1956.

Foote, Shelby. *The Civil War: A Narrative.* 3 vols. New York: Vintage Books, 1986.

Frank, Joseph Allan, and George A. Reaves. *"Seeing the Elephant": Raw Recruits at the Battle of Shiloh.* Westport, Conn.: Greenwood Press, 1989.

Fuller, J. F. C. *Grant and Lee: A Study in Personality and Generalship.* Bloomington, Ind.: University of Indiana Press, 1982. Reprint of a 1932 edition.

Glatthaar, Joseph T. *Forged in Battle: The Civil War Alliance of Black Soldiers and White Officers.* New York: Free Press, 1990.

———. *The March to the Sea and Beyond: Sherman's Troops in the Savannah and Carolinas Campaigns.* New York: New York University Press, 1986.

Grant, Ulysses S. *Personal Memoirs of Ulysses S. Grant and Selected Letters, 1839–1865.* New York: The Library of America, 1990.

Grant, Ulysses S., III. *Ulysses S. Grant: Soldier and Statesman.* New York: Morrow, 1969.

Hamilton, James J. *The Battle of Fort Donelson*. New York: Thomas Youseloff, 1968.

Hoehling, A. A. *Vicksburg: 47 Days of Siege*. New York: Harper, 1969.

Hoehling, A. A., and Mary Hoehling. *The Last Days of the Confederacy*. New York: The Fairfax Press, 1981.

Hughes, Nathaniel, Jr. *The Battle of Belmont: Grant Strikes South*. Chapel Hill, N.C.: University of North Carolina Press, 1992.

Leckie, Robert. *None Died in Vain: The Saga of the American Civil War*. New York: Harper Collins, 1990.

Lewis, Lloyd. *Captain Sam Grant*. Boston: Little, Brown, 1950.

———. *Sherman: Fighting Prophet*. New York: Harcourt, Brace, 1958.

Linderman, Gerald F. *Embattled Courage: The Experience of Combat in the American Civil War*. New York: Free Press, 1987.

Macartney, Clarence E. *Grant and His Generals*. New York: McBride, 1953.

McDonough, James Lee. *Shiloh: In Hell Before Night*. Knoxville, Tenn.: University of Tennessee Press, 1977.

McDonough, James Lee, and James Pickett Jones. *War So Terrible: Sherman and Atlanta*. New York: W. W. Norton, 1987.

McFeely, William S. *Grant: A Biography*. New York: W. W. Norton, 1981.

McPherson, James M. *Battle Cry of Freedom: The Civil War Era*. New York: Oxford University Press, 1988.

———. *Marching Toward Freedom: The Negro in the Civil War, 1861–1865*. New York: Knopf, 1967.

———. *The Negro's Civil War. How Black Americans Felt and Acted During the War for the Union*. New York: Ballantine Books, 1991.

———. *Ordeal by Fire: The Civil War and Reconstruction*. New York: Knopf, 1982.

Marszalek, John F. *Sherman's Other War: The General and the Civil War Press*. Memphis: Memphis State University Press, 1981.

Mellon, James, ed. *Bullwhip Days: The Slaves Remember*. New York: Weidenfeld & Nicolson, 1988.

Miers, Earl Schenck. *The General Who Marched to Hell: William Tecumseh Sherman and His March to Fame and Infamy*. New York: Knopf, 1951.

———. *The Last Campaign: Grant Saves the Union*. Philadelphia: Lippincott, 1972.

———. *The Web of Victory: Grant at Vicksburg*. New York: Knopf, 1955.

Mitchell, Reid. *Civil War Soldiers*. New York: Viking, 1988.

Morris, Roy, Jr. *Sheridan: The Life and Wars of General Phil Sheridan*. New York: Crown, 1992.

Nevins, Allan. *The War for the Union: The Organized War to Victory, 1864–1865*. New York: Scribner's, 1971.

Oates, Stephen B. *With Malice Toward None: The Life of Abraham Lincoln*. New York: Harper & Row, 1977.

O'Connor, Richard. *Sheridan the Incredible*. Indianapolis: Bobbs-Merrill, 1953.

Paludan, Phillip Shaw. *"A People's Contest": The Union and the Civil War, 1861–1865*. New York: Harper & Row, 1988.

Patrick, Rembert W. *The Fall of Richmond.* Baton Rouge, La.: Louisiana State University Press, 1960.

Porter, General Horace. *Campaigning with Grant.* New York: The Century Company, 1897. Reprinted by Time-Life Books, 1981.

Robertson, James I., Jr. *Soldiers Blue and Gray.* Columbia, S.C.: University of South Carolina Press, 1988.

Ross, Ishbel. *The General's Wife: The Life of Mrs. Ulysses S. Grant.* New York: Dodd, Mead, 1959.

Royster, Charles. *The Destructive War: William Tecumseh Sherman, Stonewall Jackson, and the Americans.* New York: Knopf, 1991.

Sherman, William Tecumseh. *Memoirs of General W. T. Sherman.* New York: The Library of America, 1990.

Sinkler, George. *The Racial Attitudes of American Presidents: From Abraham Lincoln to Theodore Roosevelt.* Garden City, N.Y.: Doubleday, 1971.

Smith, Gene. *Lee and Grant: A Dual Biography.* New York: McGraw-Hill, 1984.

Stern, Philip Van Doren. *An End to Valor: The Last Days of the Civil War.* Boston: Houghton Mifflin, 1958.

Sword, Wiley. *Shiloh: Bloody April.* New York: Morrow, 1974.

Symonds, Craig E. *Joseph E. Johnston: A Civil War Biography.* New York: W. W. Norton: 1992.

Walker, Peter F. *Vicksburg: A People at War, 1860–1865.* Chapel Hill, N.C.: University of North Carolina Press, 1960.

Watkins, Sam R. *"Co. Aytch," Maury Grays, First Tennessee Regiment: or, A Side Show of the Big Show.* Jackson, Tenn.: Mowat-Mercer Press, 1952.

Wheeler, Richard, ed. *On Fields of Fury. From the Wilderness to the Crater: An Eyewitness History.* New York: Harper Collins, 1991. This and the following books edited by Wheeler are invaluable collections of eyewitness accounts of the Civil War.

——. *Sherman's March.* New York: Thomas Y. Crowell, 1978.

——. *The Siege of Vicksburg.* New York: Thomas Y. Crowell, 1978.

——. *Voices of the Civil War.* New York: Meridian, 1990.

——. *We Knew William Tecumseh Sherman.* New York: Thomas Y. Crowell, 1977.

——. *Witness to Appomattox.* New York: Harper & Row, 1989.

Wiley, Belle Irvin. *The Life of Billy Yank: The Common Soldier of the Union.* Baton Rouge, La.: Louisiana State University Press, 1978.

——. *The Life of Johnny Reb: The Common Soldier of the Confederacy.* Baton Rouge, La.: Louisiana State University Press, 1978.

——. *The Plain People of the Confederacy.* Baton Rouge, La.: Louisiana State University Press, 1943.

Williams, T. Harry. *Lincoln and His Generals.* New York: Knopf, 1952.

——. *McClellan, Sherman and Grant.* New Brunswick, N.J.: Rutgers University Press, 1962.

Wise, John S. *The End of an Era.* Boston: Houghton Mifflin, 1899.

Woodward, W. E. *Meet General Grant.* New York: Liveright, 1928.

INDEX